HALF MOON EMBER

HALF MOON

Ember

HALF MOON EMBER

Half Moon Bay
Book 6

ERIN BROCKUS

GREEN SAGE
PRESS

Chapter One

MAY...

THE CHEVY MALIBU COUGHED, then lurched disconcertingly, causing Heather Galen to return both hands to the steering wheel. She had been driving with her knees while hastily twirling her long, copper-colored hair into a bun. The car returned to its usual purr, and she relaxed, speeding up a little more as she drove north toward Half Moon Bay on the western side of St. Croix.

Heather glanced at her watch and winced, stomping harder on the gas pedal. It was 11:45 and the burning sun was nearly overhead. She'd gotten out the door later than she'd hoped because of her less-than-ideal living situation. "I need to set my alarm a few minutes ear—"

The Malibu gave another wheezing, chugging cough and she gasped. Heather gripped the wheel, knuckles white, as she stared in stunned disbelief at the gas gauge. The needle pointed at *Empty*, and its ominous amber light flashed. The faltering cough became continuous as she murmured, "No, no, no..."

Then... silence.

The sound of birds singing in the bush around her amplified as the car slowly decelerated. With the wheel now heavy and sluggish under her hands, Heather eased the Malibu to the side of the narrow highway. Her heart hammered as she slammed a fist into the wheel. "I can't be late! I just can't! How could I be so stupid?"

Pressing her lips into a grim line, she studied her watch before glancing at her surroundings. "Ok, I'm less than a mile from the resort. If I hurry, I can still make it on time. Get a move on, girl."

Heather grabbed her purse from the passenger seat and exited. Shimmering waves of air rose from the black asphalt as she locked the car and hurried along the left shoulder. *It's still so weird, driving on the left side of the road.*

She wore her work uniform of a light blue polo shirt with Half Moon Bay Resort's logo on the left breast and black capris, which didn't make her any cooler.

She turned left off the highway and rushed down a paved access road as trickles of sweat raced down her back. The jungle vegetation arched overhead, making a tunnel over the road and holding in the stifling humidity.

Can't be late, can't be late.

All Heather could think as she trotted down the road was that she'd been fired from *two* jobs in the last three months. She'd moved to the island from California to make a new start, yet failure trailed behind her like a black, sulfurous cloud.

Before long, the road ended in a circle in front of a cheery, yellow one-story cottage—the lobby. But Heather hurried around the bright building, following the brick path to her destination. Soft calypso music filled the air as she breathed a relieved sigh and swiped a hand over her sweaty forehead. A long, rectangular infinity pool opened before her, with a thatch-roof bar attached at one end. One side of the bar held a row of bar stools, with tables placed along the tile floor or out in the sand. The opposite side was next to the pool, where patrons could sit on submerged stools.

A tall, thin man of about thirty with ebony skin stood behind the bar, polishing wine glasses as Heather rushed behind the warm, polished-wood structure. She glanced at her watch and smiled triumphantly—it was exactly noon. "I'm here, Clark! And on time, too." Her shirt stuck to her torso, and sweat dripped down her face and arms.

Clark's brows rose to the sky as he looked her up and down. "What happened to you? Did you run here?"

"Almost. My car ran out of gas, and I had to hurry." She plucked her shirt away, waving it to dry off.

He laughed, his silver tooth glimmering. "You could have called, you know. I wouldn't have minded."

"Nope. I refuse to be late."

Heat rose to her face, no doubt even redder now. She was pretty sure everyone at the resort knew why she'd been fired from her previous position as bartender at the upscale apartment complex Serenity. The official version anyway, which was euphemistically listed as *Excessive Tardiness* on her termination paperwork. But *Refusing to Sleep with the Boss* would hardly work, would it?

Clark stopped polishing and gave her a long look, tilting his head to one side as he spoke with a lilting Caribbean accent. "You can be late once in a while. We understand, and none of us believe Wayne Timmons's side of things, anyway. We all met him, remember?" He laughed again, then hung the glass upside-down from a rack in the ceiling.

She had only worked at Half Moon Bay for a week and was determined to make a good impression. Despite her life being turned upside down yet again. "Thanks, but I'm usually very dependable. I can't believe I let my car run out of gas."

He waved absently at her. "Don't worry about it. We're pretty laid back. Here at the resort, anyway. You don't want to show up late down at the dive shop. Alex is a different story."

Clark broke into musical laughter again, and she couldn't help joining in. Heather had met the undisputed alpha male of the resort her first day. Tall, bronzed, and excessively handsome, with a natural authoritative air, Heather had expected to hate Alex Monroe at first sight. But he'd pleasantly surprised her by not exhibiting the typical alpha male personality, being friendly and affable. As they had been talking, his wife, resort owner Hope Monroe, had joined them, and Heather had further warmed to both after seeing how devoted they were. If nothing else, the experience had been a pointed reminder not to make hasty judgements about people. And if anyone should know not to do that, it was Heather.

She turned to Clark with a laugh. "Alex has been pretty nice every time I've met him."

"He is nice. As long as you don't make him mad. Then it's a whole different story."

"Duly noted. I'll try not to do that. Which shouldn't be too hard, since our paths don't cross that often."

She could believe he had a harder side. An article displayed in the lobby described his history as a Navy SEAL and an altercation where he'd been shot protecting Hope. Friendly or not, Alex wasn't someone to be trifled with.

The dive staff worked from a long wooden pier that jutted into the Caribbean Sea, using the resort dive boat *Surface Interval* for scheduled dive trips several times each day. But Heather wouldn't have minded if her path crossed with one particular member of the dive staff a little more often.

When she had interviewed for the job, she'd run into a

couple who had lived at Serenity, Hope's sister Sara Collins and divemaster Jack Powell. With them had been another divemaster, Robert Davis. When the resort manager, Patti Thomas, had introduced them, Heather had been captivated, hardly able to believe her reaction.

Robert was a local and looked in his early thirties, slightly older than her twenty-eight. His shaved head emphasized his rich brown skin, but his eyes had positively entranced her. A much lighter brown than his dark complexion, they had held a warm expression, and his dazzling smile made her heart pound. But a casual question to Clark had revealed that Robert was only an occasional worker at the resort, instead spending much of his time as a professional photographer.

Now, Heather bent down and rummaged under the counter, finally locating the spare staff shirt she kept handy. Being a bartender ensured that wardrobe changes were not infrequent. She held it up. "I should probably go change."

Clark grinned. "Good idea. You look like you just ran a marathon."

Behind him, Clark had pinned a family photo of himself and his wife Kamila with their two children into the wall. The main reason she'd been hired was to give Clark some much-needed backup and time off. "How's Eli?" she asked.

"He's hangin' in there, poor little guy." Clark's wife had delivered Elijah a few months previously, but he had suffered a succession of stomach maladies, eventually needing surgery. "We've got the operation scheduled in St. Thomas next week. We were hopin' to get it done here, but they decided he needed a more complicated procedure, which isn't available on St. Croix."

"Oh! I'm sorry. Poor baby."

"Thanks. But the doctor said this should cure his problems, so it'll be worth it. Kamila has family there, so we'll probably stay there for a month or so. I'm thinkin' about takin' off two months total. Hope said it should be fine. And you're pickin' the job up fast, so the resort will survive. Probably."

Grinning, Heather shook out the shirt to air it out. "Thanks. I really like it here." Clark was a dream to work with, funny and self-deprecating despite winning an island-wide bartending contest the previous year.

Hope appeared and sat down on a stool, accompanied by her yellow dog Cruz, who circled and lay down at her feet. A beautiful woman, Hope's rich chestnut hair fell to her shoulders, and she wore a colorful pink sundress. She gave them a sunny smile, which faded when she took in Heather's sweaty, disheveled appearance. "Are you ok?"

Heather laughed and held up the polo shirt. "Yeah. My car ran out of gas, and I had to rush here on foot. I keep a spare shirt under the bar, so I'll head to the restroom to clean up."

Inside the deserted ladies' room, she quickly changed out of her sodden shirt, and a quick wipe-down with wet paper towels washed the worst of the sweat away. She wet her hair to tame the flyaways, and returned, looking—and feeling—more professional.

When Heather walked behind the bar again, Hope pointed at her. "Clark just told me about you not wanting to be late. Don't worry about it. I have extensive experience with what a jerk Wayne Timmons is, and you're doing a great job here."

"Thanks, but I do my best to be on time. I hope you have enough work for me after Clark gets back from his leave." Heather was under no delusions who the primary bartender was, which she worried about.

Hope's eyes became round. "That's actually why I came down here! To check if Clark has any last-minute instructions for either of us, since I help out too. And we're getting busier by the day, with six new bungalows being built. I'm planning on adding a permanent bar to the restaurant, so the waitstaff won't have to trudge back and forth from here. So, we'll need both of them staffed."

"That's music to my ears," Heather said with a big smile.

Clark hung up the final wine glass and stood somberly with his hands clasped in front of him. "Well, I guess it's official then. Since I only have a couple of days left, it's time to pass on my secrets."

Hope drummed her feet on the ring at the base of her stool, a wide grin forming. "Oh! You're finally going to spill the beans?"

Clark lifted his chin, his serious expression remaining as he turned to Heather, though his cheek was twitching a bit. "Heather, this is a great responsibility. I'm goin' to teach you how to make my secret drinks, Half Moon Hope and Half Moon Dream. Especially the second one." That was the drink that had won the competition. Heather had tasted both and they were spectacular, particularly Half Moon Dream.

Hope was still grinning broadly, but Heather stilled her face, trying to match the mock seriousness of the occasion. "I'm honored that you're passing on your knowledge, Clark."

"You should be," Hope said. "He only gave me the recipe because I've been filling in for him. Otherwise, I'd still be in the dark."

Finally, Clark's serious expression morphed back into his typical smile. "Ah, it's not too complicated. But there's a special ingredient in Dream that's unusual." The drink was based on a mudslide, and he'd added orange liqueur to it. There was a subtle flavor underneath that anchored the whole drink, and she hadn't been able to figure it out.

"I can't wait to learn your secret ingredient."

Clark glanced around the bar, but the dive boat was still out, so it was empty. He leaned close and spoke *sotto voce*. "I'm swearin' you to secrecy, ok? It's cloves. A pinch of ground cloves."

Heather opened her eyes wide. "Cloves? You put that in a drink? Seriously?"

"I had the same reaction," Hope added.

Clark busied himself with the blender, making a double batch. "I'm makin' the base drink now, without the cloves." He quieted while the blender whirred, then poured a full glass before setting the container back onto the blender. Reaching under the counter, he withdrew a small, unlabeled glass jar. Taking a pinch of dark-brown powder between two fingers, he sprinkled it in before running the blender again. "Not too much, or you'll overpower it." After pouring the second drink, he topped each with his signature—a cut banana with its stem split and a cherry wedged between, so it looked like a dolphin carrying a ball in its mouth.

He pushed the first drink toward her. "Here. Taste."

Heather took a healthy sip, swishing the icy drink around before swallowing. It was delicious, and she said so.

Then he handed her the glass of Half Moon Dream. "Now taste it with the cloves."

She repeated the exercise, and the flavors exploded in her mouth. The chocolate and orange were more vibrant, and the myriad flavors combined as if they were meant to be together. Her face must have betrayed her thoughts because Hope laughed, lightly slapping her hand on the counter. "Amazing, isn't it? What just one ingredient can do?"

"It really is. Don't worry, Clark. I promise I'll guard the recipe with my life."

He grinned. "Good, because people ask me for it almost daily. But I always say no."

"It's hard to believe," Heather said, staring at her hurricane glass. "The drink tastes amazing without the cloves. You don't realize there's something missing until it appears and changes everything."

Hope smiled at her. "That's a rather profound statement."

Heather laughed. "Guess that did sound kind of deep, huh?"

And strangest of all, Robert's face had flashed into her mind when she said it...

Chapter Two

ROBERT CAREFULLY BALANCED a platter of rice and beans on one forearm and dinner rolls on the other as he made his way to the dining table. No matter how many times he told his mother there were only four people in the family, she made enough to feed an army. His father, Bennett, sat at the table. He had removed his customary battered Davis Fishing baseball hat for the meal, leaving a crease in his more salt than pepper hair.

As Robert moved sideways to place the rice and beans on the table, there was a "Watch it!" from his younger brother Eddie behind him. Eddie whirled in a circle, deftly hanging on to the large salad bowl he carried despite his large frame.

"Don't follow so close, then," Robert replied mildly as their mother came out of the kitchen carrying a large roast chicken.

"Don't fight, boys," she said. "We don't do this nearly often enough, so I won't have the occasion ruined by you two fightin'." Placing the chicken at the center of the table, she straightened and removed her faded white apron to reveal a light-green dress which was nearly fluorescent against her stout ebony figure. Robert and Eddie exchanged a sardonic glance, but remained quiet as they took their seats across from one another.

She sat down and held out a hand expectantly to each of them, raising her brows at her husband at the head of the table. The two men took one of her hands and automatically held the other out to their father, who sighed and reached for a nearby jumbo-sized bottle of antacid tablets, crunching three. "Now if the good Lord would just cure my heartburn. You want me to say grace, Althea?"

"That would be wonderful, dear," she said, smiling around the table at her family.

All inclined their head as Bennett intoned in his deep baritone, "Thank you Heavenly Father for this bounty, both the food on this table and the fish in the sea, which put it there. Amen." Quiet Amens echoed around the table as they unclasped hands.

The somewhat somber mood was broken when Eddie rubbed his hands together, mouth spreading into a gleeful smile, and said, "All right, then! Let's get to it." He helped himself to a heaping serving of jerk chicken as Robert placed a more moderate portion on his own plate. Three years younger than Robert's thirty-two, Eddie took after their mother in form while Robert more resembled their thin, wiry father. Despite Althea's proclamation, family dinner was a regular occasion, held at least twice a month.

"How's business goin'?" Althea said with practiced casualness to Robert.

"Good. I'm gettin' regular photography gigs and I still work occasionally at Half Moon Bay. One of their guests bought two large glass prints from me." He didn't mention they had paid $1000 each for them. Hope had come up with the arrangement some time ago, splitting the profits from regular sales with him.

"Still photographin' sunburned tourists too?" Eddie asked with a grin.

Robert smiled. "It's part of the job. A lot of us depend on tourists, sunburned or not."

"You can make your livin' in other ways, but you're well aware of that," his father said.

"Pop, you can't deny I'm a lot better diver than I am a fisherman," Robert said.

Bennett gave an uncomfortable roll of his shoulders. "Nothin' more experience wouldn't cure."

They were venturing into dangerous and very tired territory now. "Besides, Eddie's better at it than I ever will be."

"And that's the truth," Eddie said, pointing a fork at Robert.

"Edward! Manners," Althea said.

"Sorry, Mother."

"That's all right." She was too happy with both sons at the table to make a fuss.

Their father owned two fishing boats which had been a staple of the local St. Croix fishing industry for decades. Bennett had hoped his prosperous business would escalate further under the leadership of both his sons.

Except that Robert had no inclination for the family business.

"Face it, Pop. I'm better at photographin' fish than catching them. You're lucky to have Eddie workin' for you."

Bennett gave his younger son a fond smile. "You're doin' fine, son. Learned most jobs on the boat now."

Robert sat back in his chair, surprised. "That mean you're ready to let him captain a boat?"

Eddie and Althea stilled as all eyes turned toward Bennett. "Not quite yet," he said after a hesitation. "He needs to work with me more."

Eddie turned back to his plate, spearing a piece of chicken and ramming it into his mouth. Althea opened her mouth, then shut it again and scooped a spoonful of rice and beans instead.

Robert stifled a sigh and returned to his own dinner. *It comes down to that. Pop wants me to captain, not Eddie. Even though he's better at it in every way.*

It was a familiar argument, one that had worn thin over the years. Robert was surprised Eddie didn't bring up that their father had owned his own boat when he was only twenty-five, several years younger than Eddie. That was usually the next level of the discussion. The Davises were a traditional family, steeped in traditional values. Such as the first-born son taking over the family business, while the younger one played a supporting role.

"Oh!" Mom said, turning to Robert with a smile. His gratitude at the obvious subject change disappeared with her next sentence. "I ran into Leticia at the craft market a few days ago!"

Robert winced and almost dropped his fork at his ex-wife's name, staring straight at his mother. "Is that supposed to make me happy?"

"Oh—well, I thought you'd be interested to know."

"Althea," Bennett said wearily, "How could that possibly interest him? The woman went off and left him. Last I heard, she was shackin' up with a guy in St. Thomas."

"It's no matter anyway," Althea said. "She was just visitin' family. She's likely back in St. Thomas now."

Heat rose up Robert's neck as Eddie gave him a sly smile, enjoying his discomfort. "Nope, Mother," Robert said. "Leticia is in the past. Permanently."

Her ears perked up. "Does that mean there's someone in the present?"

Robert couldn't resist a grin. "No, it doesn't. But if I get involved with someone, I'll be sure to let you know."

. . .

A soft band of lavender streaked across the horizon as Robert sat on the front porch of his childhood home. Quiet sounds of a baseball game on TV came from the room behind him, his parents settling in to watch the Tampa Bay Rays. The front door opened with a squeak as Eddie came out to join him and handed him a Leatherback beer.

"Thanks, man," Robert said as they clinked them together.

"So, you're not gonna run out and beg Leticia to come back, I take it?" Eddie asked with a laugh.

Robert swiped a hand over his forehead. "I can't believe Mom brought that up."

"That's how desperate she was to change the subject. Your cheatin' ex-wife is a safer topic than the family business."

"And that's a shame."

Robert shook his head, staring at the horizon as the lavender faded to black. He'd been positive he and Leticia would last forever. But things changed after they got married. She wanted more from life and became increasingly blunt in her desires. Until they'd had an awful argument and she left him. The wound had stung for a long time, but he was much happier without her. "You're perfect to take over the business. Pop's lucky to have you."

"They're both old-school. Down to their bones."

"Yeah. Except the world is changin'."

"It is. Pop will come around eventually."

"He's not gettin' any younger. You need the experience of bein' a captain while he's still around."

"We've been workin' on it. You happy with how your photography business is doin'?"

Robert smiled. "I am. Makin' my livin' by takin' photos and divin' is pretty much my dream life. Even if it's not Pop's."

"You're not seein' anyone?"

"No," Robert answered after a slight pause.

Eddie picked up the hesitation immediately. "What's that mean?"

"It's nothin'. A new bartender started at Half Moon Bay. She's pretty gorgeous. I've only seen her a couple of times. Hardly even talked to her."

Eddie's grin could have split his face. "Doesn't sound like nothin' to me. Get to know her! What's stoppin' you?"

Robert shrugged. *That is an excellent question. I've never been afraid to break with tradition, have I?* "Just not workin' at the resort that much, I guess."

"Don't believe you. Spill, Robert. I know you too well."

He sighed as he looked at Eddie. "She's from California. And white."

Eddie stared at him for a long moment, then broke out into quiet laughter, mindful of the television behind them. "Oh, man! You do make me look like the good son, don't you?"

"Pop won't care."

"About her bein' white? No—he won't. But as far as he's concerned, California is Mars. Besides, he's not the one you need to worry about."

Robert snorted. "Yeah, I know. But I already married myself a nice, local girl. Look how that turned out."

"Not sure Mom will see it that way."

Robert drained the rest of his beer. "I've hardly even had a conversation with this woman. No use gettin' worried about somethin' that might never happen."

But as Robert drove back to his house, his mind was full of Heather's flowing red hair and her ivory skin. She'd knocked him speechless when he'd met her, and he'd only glimpsed her from afar since she started at Half Moon Bay. But he couldn't stop thinking about her, and he'd felt a connection between them when they shook hands. She might be trouble, but he couldn't wait to find out.

Chapter Three

HEATHER POURED two beers into plastic cups and handed them to the guests sitting on submerged stools, laughing at their big smiles. "Enjoy!" She was glad the resort had a strict no-glass-in-the-pool policy since glass and pools never mixed well together, even without alcohol added into the mix. The bar afforded a magnificent view of the setting sun, which was still over an hour from the horizon. When she went to the other side, Sara was sitting on a stool in front of the bar. "Well, hello there. Here to wet your whistle?"

Sara smiled at her. Her long brown hair was curled and, as usual, she was dressed sharply in a colorful blouse and flowing black skirt. "Yes. A glass of white wine would be lovely."

"I've already got a Chardonnay open, and I recall you ordering it at Serenity. Will that work?"

"Perfect." Sara took a sip and gave Heather an appreciative nod. "So, tell me. How are things going here? You doing ok on your own?"

Clark's last shift had been several days prior, and the Bailey family was on their way to St. Thomas for baby Eli's surgery.

"Piece of cake. And I've discovered I love working at a dive resort. Last call is at 9 p.m. since the divers are all beat at the end of the day. It's great!"

Sara joined in her laughter. "Hope likes to keep it low key. And I agree, the place has a wonderful vibe."

"Not low key for long. They're already starting construction on the new bungalows. Your sister moves fast."

"Oh yes. When she knows what she wants, nothing gets in her way."

"I saw some heavy machinery at the north end of the beach. What's that about?"

Sara's eyes became round, and she leaned forward. "They're clearing land for my new spa! It will be the best on this side of the island. I can't wait."

"Sounds incredible. Things are going to be hectic around here."

Sara waved a hand carelessly. "Hope has a plan for that. When she renovated after the hurricane, she did it slowly so the noise wouldn't disturb guests. But this time, she's ripping the Band-Aid off to get it done as quickly as possible. They're doing the three northern bungalows first, then they'll construct the southern ones when those are finished. She's also got big plans for the beach bungalows."

Heather smiled, happy to be working at a place that was investing in the future. "She mentioned building a second bar and said that there should be plenty of work for me and Clark."

"How long have you been a bartender?"

Oh boy. And there's a loaded question if ever there was one... "You could say I've rediscovered it. I worked at a bar a long time ago and when I moved to St. Croix, I tried it again. I'm a people person, so it's a good fit for me."

"Maybe here more than Serenity."

"No doubt there. So, you and Jack moved in together?"

A dreamy smile lit up Sara's face, and she took another

drink. "Yes, we're renting a great little beach house north of here. The whole thing worked out great. Jack had his own furniture, and Hope picked out mine before I arrived. So, I just gave it back to her and we're using Jack's now. She's been wanting to update their house forever, so everyone's happy."

Beats the hell out of my living situation. I need to do something about it soon.

"What part of California are you from?"

"The Bay Area. I got tired of the big city and the cold, dreary weather." Her statement was true, but a very long way from the whole truth.

"Well, there is some dreary weather here, but you don't have to worry about the cold, at least." Sara finished her drink and stood. "Well, I'd better get going. Jack's off work today and he's probably rewired the kitchen by now."

Heather broke into laughter. "What?"

"I'm kidding. Our cottage is a bit... rustic. Showing its age a little, though I think that only adds to the charm. But Jack has a background in construction and is a bit more critical than me. I have a feeling he's going to barter a reduction in rent at some point. It's my job to keep him suitably distracted."

Heather's mind turned over the possibilities of who might work if Jack was off that day. She hadn't seen Robert, but they worked in different parts of the resort. She turned her mind from his light-brown eyes and focused on Sara. "Living on your own private beach, I can't imagine that's too difficult."

Sara gave her a sly smile. "Oh no. The possibilities are endless." She cocked her head. "Several of us get together for a girls' night out, including Selena and Hope. You want to join us?" Selena was a massage therapist at Hibiscus, Half Moon Bay's spa, and Heather had met her a time or two. Making friends hadn't been on the top of her list since moving. Surviving had. But it was time for that to change.

Heather's heart thumped in her chest. "I'd love to. I'm still finding my way here, so let me know the next time you guys get together. Thanks, Sara."

A group of thirsty divers arrived, and the stylist waved goodbye as Heather filled a bucket of beers for them. They clustered around one of the tables in the sand, watching the approaching sunset. The sky was especially pretty that evening, with long, wispy clouds becoming bright fuchsia as the sun eased toward the sea.

The next time Heather glanced up, Robert stood outside the bar, facing the sunset and wearing a backward-turned baseball hat. An SLR camera with long lens was held up to one eye. After a moment, he lowered the camera, a satisfied smile rising to his handsome face. He wore a Half Moon Bay Resort shirt, answering her question about whether he had filled in for Jack.

Robert turned his head and caught her staring straight at him. A hot flush spread across her face as he broke into a brilliant smile and approached the bar.

"Good night to photograph the sunset," she said.

"Yeah, I couldn't resist it."

"Do you always bring your camera to work?"

Robert shrugged. "Most of the time. That way I'm prepared when beautiful sights turn up." He raised a brow, staring evenly at her and she couldn't resist a smile in return.

"How was the diving today? That group over there looks happy."

"They should be. We saw a big pod of dolphins."

The fuchsia sky was now transitioning to crimson, and Robert stared at it, his expression a mixture of yearning and regret. "I'd better get back to it. That color's not goin' to last much longer." Then he turned back, and their eyes locked as he smiled faintly. "See you around, Heather."

As he walked out of the bar, Heather took several deep

breaths to quell her racing heart, her palms sweating. She swallowed, wetting her dry throat.

Ok, I am definitely not imagining the sparks there. Damn, he is smoking hot!

HEATHER PARKED her car in the lot and let herself into Tina's apartment, which was a tiny one-bedroom. She glanced around, confirming it was empty, and breathed out a long sigh. Tina was also a bartender at Serenity, and would work until 1 a.m. Unlike Heather, she had been treated well and enjoyed her job. Tina had lived in the cramped apartment for two years, though it wasn't so cramped with just one tenant.

When Heather had gotten the position at the luxury apartment resort, she'd been thrilled that a furnished studio apartment had been available at an employee rate. When Heather had been fired, her apartment lease had also been terminated, and she was given forty-eight hours to vacate it.

Tina had come to her rescue and offered Heather her couch until she could find a new place to live. But after nearly a month, she hadn't found anything suitable. And Tina's recent hints about their cramped quarters indicated Heather's time was running out. She needed to find new digs, even if it meant finding a roommate.

I made the choice to move here, so I need to accept any complications. I can make this work.

Heather picked up her blanket and pillow from the corner of the living room and spread them on the couch before changing and brushing her teeth. After flopping onto the cushions, she pulled the blanket over herself and clicked on the television. Her mind wandered, uninterested in the latest reality show, but not motivated enough to find something else to watch.

She was off the following day, which should have filled her

with excitement. Hope and head server Charlotte were covering her days off until Clark returned. She had an entire tropical island to explore, but she didn't know where to start. Sara was friendly, but she worked during the day, and Tina would sleep until noon.

I need to find something to fill my time. Maybe volunteer at the hospital or something?

She had been staring absently at the TV when a commercial came on for dog food. A happy family had just picked out a puppy from the pet shelter, and were ecstatically loading the fuzzball into their car. Heather bolted upright and grabbed her phone, inspired now. A quick Google search turned up a pet shelter just outside Frederiksted and she grinned. "Perfect! I'll head down tomorrow and see if they need help. Maybe walk the dogs or something."

Lying back on the couch, Heather turned off the program and stared at the ceiling, her happiness evaporating. Desperate to leave San Francisco, she'd simply jumped on a plane to St. Croix with no plan. But crashing on a friend's couch after getting fired was not how she had imagined things working out.

She snorted. "The weather might be nicer here, but am I any less miserable? Should I tuck my tail between my legs and run home to Mom and Dad?"

No. Running was the absolute last-ditch option. Not because she didn't love them—in fact, they were surprisingly supportive of her unconventional choices. But she had spent most of her life trying to escape the shadow of the Galen name. Here in St. Croix, no one knew who she was.

She was just Heather, which was an incredible change of pace.

At ten the next morning, Heather parked in front of a one-story bright purple building on the outskirts of Frederiksted. Next to it was a large meadow, with an immense banyan tree sprawling in the middle. A chain-link fence surrounded part of the grassy area. She opened the front door of Pet Paradise and entered to the distant sound of barking dogs. An overweight woman with frizzy gray-blonde hair and tanned skin sat behind a battered wooden desk, reading glasses perched on her nose. The obligatory chain attached to each earpiece hung around her neck. She took off the glasses and looked up with a warm smile. "Good morning, dear. How may I help you?"

"Hi, I'm Heather Galen. I was wondering if you needed any help. I've got some extra time, and I'd like to volunteer."

The woman's mouth dropped open before spreading into a wide smile. She vaulted to her feet, holding her hand out for Heather to shake. "Oh, my goodness, yes! I'm Donna Nelson, and Pet Paradise is a one-woman show. I'll take all the help I can get. You want a quick tour?"

"That sounds great. I can get started right away."

With her reading glasses resting against her ample bosom, Donna led Heather through a metal door with a reinforced-glass panel, and the sound of barking increased by orders of magnitude. A large red dog jumped against the chain-link door of its kennel, tongue lolling. Donna waved at it, but continued down the cement aisle. "That's Bentley. He's a sweetheart. I've got a family interested in him, so hopefully he'll have his home soon. I run a no-kill shelter, so all the animals stay until they get adopted. This is the Dog House, as you can probably tell."

On the other side of the room, they traveled through a matching door into a large storeroom, which was stuffed with bags and cans of pet food, kitty litter, leashes, and other miscellaneous pet paraphernalia. Another metal door led into a smaller room, also lined with wire cages, but these were smaller, and the sounds of meowing filled the surrounding air. Heather looked to her left at three orange tabby kittens reaching through the door with their paws and couldn't resist stroking one soft leg. "Hi there, sweetie."

About half the cages were filled, and they went through another door, entering a third room. But this one was silent and dimly lit. "This is where we keep the exotics. Fortunately, we don't get many. A few iguanas, an occasional guinea pig, and there was a chinchilla craze a few years ago."

They crossed the room, and Donna ushered her through a door back into the reception area.

"Wow, this is quite the operation."

"It is. And I'm not getting any younger." Donna patted her broad abdomen and smiled. "Or thinner, either! Where would you like to start?"

Heather worked her bottom lip between her teeth, then nodded at the far door. "Let's start with the dogs."

Within minutes, the two women stood in front of a kennel containing a short-coated brown and black dog. It sat behind the door, quiet but paying attention raptly, one ear floppy and the other fully cocked. "How about walking this guy?"

"Perfect! This is Lucky, and he's older." Donna tapped on the chain link door and Lucky thumped his tail. "His owner passed away a few months ago, and we're hoping to re-home him. He's an absolute sweetheart, but hasn't been around children, which makes him harder to place."

"Well, I'd be happy to lavish some attention until he finds his home."

Donna beamed, giving Heather an all-encompassing hug, even though she only came up to Heather's shoulders. "He'll love that. I'll show you where the leashes are kept, and you can get to work. I'm so excited to have you!"

Five minutes later, Heather and Lucky were walking

through the grassy meadow next to the shelter. He snuffled at the enticing scents, tail wagging, but was happy to stay by her side and showed no signs of running off. "Ok, Lucky. Looks like we're getting off to a good start here. We'll try to get you adopted soon."

He looked at her and sneezed, hopefully in agreement.

Chapter Four

ROBERT EASILY CAUGHT the vest-like buoyancy compensation device Jack Powell tossed him and grinned. "That all you got? Weak, man."

Jack stroked his dark-brown beard with his middle finger, then laughed when Robert's smile widened. "Next time I'll throw a tank at you, then."

"Don't make me separate you two boys," Alex said mildly as he climbed down from *Surface Interval's* elevated wheelhouse, a captain's logbook tucked under one arm. Several inches taller than either Robert or Jack, Alex's light hair was hidden under a Half Moon Bay baseball hat.

Robert looped the BCD over his right shoulder as he threw another over his left. The two divemasters had each led a group of six divers, and they'd just finished a picture-perfect morning. Only one group would go out on the afternoon trip, so Robert deferred to Jack, wanting to spend the rest of the day processing the photos from a recent family reunion he'd shot.

The three men loaded themselves up with scuba equipment and were heading toward the rinse tanks when Hope stepped out of the dive shop. Her cell phone was pressed to her ear as she walked toward them. "I'm working on it right now, Rachel. I'll call you right back, ok?"

They stopped as Hope ended the call and looked at Robert. "I've got a bit of a problem on my hands. A couple staying here just got engaged yesterday, and the groom-to-be arranged a photo shoot before coming here. He surprised her with it after proposing. But now the photographer has flaked out and canceled, and they leave tomorrow. Rachel is just about in tears and asking me for help." Hope pressed her hands together, phone tucked between, and raised them to her mouth. "Can you do a last-minute photo shoot this afternoon? Pretty please?"

"Jeez, baby," Alex said with a grin. "At least let the poor man empty his arms before you put the thumbscrews to him." She narrowed her eyes at him, which only made his smile broaden.

Robert laughed. "It's ok. I don't want to start a marital spat between you two. I don't have anythin' goin' on this afternoon that I can't reschedule. Sure, I'll do their shoot."

Tension fled from Hope's shoulders as they dropped. "Thank you! Robert, you're my hero."

"Ouch," Alex said. "I guess the honeymoon's over."

Hope arched a brow. "You started it. Don't blame me."

"What did I just say about the marital spat?" Robert tried to hold his laughter inside.

Jack came up and took Robert's BCDs from him. "I'll take over. Sounds like an emergency, so it's time to call Camera Man. Maybe we can get you a searchlight signal, like Batman."

They all laughed as Alex tossed his BCD into the fresh-water tank and pulled Hope against the front of his body, wrapping his arms around her waist. She tilted her face up for a kiss, then said, "There's room in my heart for two heroes."

Jack turned back after dumping his BCDs in the tank.

"Besides, how can the honeymoon be over? It hasn't even started."

"You guys are finally gettin' away for a while?"

Hope smiled, leaning her head back against Alex's chest. "Yes. We've got some business in Miami next week, then we're going to travel down The Keys."

"I could only talk Boss Lady into a week away, though," Alex said. "We'll do a little diving while we're there. Hit some wrecks, then relax in Key West for a while."

"Sounds like a great trip," Robert said. "But back to your couple. Where do they want their photo shoot?"

Hope disengaged herself to dial her phone and asked Robert's question. After listening, she gave Robert a shaky smile. "She doesn't know."

"Ok, no problem," Robert said. "Would they prefer beach or waterfall?"

"Waterfall," Hope answered after Rachel passed along their preference.

He looked at the sun, evaluating the daylight. "We're in business, then. Tell them to meet me at Silver Veil Falls in two hours. Any local cabbie will know it. I'll meet them there."

Hope passed on the information, then hung up. "You're a lifesaver. Seriously."

"Don't mention it. It's a beautiful setting. They'll love it."

Hope bit her lip. "I'm sure they will. Just one other thing, Robert. They're... um... an interesting-looking couple, but maybe not the most photogenic people."

He threw his head back and laughed. "So, you're sayin' I've got my work cut out for me?"

"Well, maybe. But I'm sure you're used to that kind of thing."

A COUPLE OF HOURS LATER, Robert drove down the twisty road to Silver Veil Falls. As he reached the parking lot, the only other vehicle there was a battered old brown sedan. He grinned, recognizing it. Parking nearby, he got out as the elderly cab driver stood from his car, a wide smile creasing his lined face. "Well, if it isn't Robert Davis."

Robert shook hands. "How you doin', Malcolm? Been a while."

"Doin' just fine. Had a beer with your dad last week." He jerked his head toward the taxi. "When do you want me to pick these folks up?"

"An hour should be plenty."

Malcolm leaned over and peered into the back seat through the open window. "I'll return here in an hour. You folks are in expert hands—I've known Robert his whole life." He opened the door, and the couple exited the car, thanking the cabbie.

Robert's heart sank as he evaluated the couple, fixing a happy, expectant smile on his lips. *Oh, Hope. You're always diplomatic, aren't you?* The man was probably 6'4", and his fiancée was over a foot shorter. He held his hand out to Robert. "Thank you so much. I'm Josh and my fiancée is Rachel."

Josh had pale, sallow skin with big fleshy lips and wide-spaced, protuberant eyes. He turned to Rachel and burst into laughter. "Did you hear that? I just introduced you as my fiancée! Awesome."

She beamed up at him, her mousy, stringy, dishwater-blonde hair hanging to her shoulders. Robert was surprised she could even see Josh through her thick, coke-bottle glasses. "Right? It'll never get old."

Malcolm shot Robert a wry smile as he climbed back into his sedan and trundled down the road, and the photographer turned back to the couple. "Ok, then. Let me grab my cameras and we'll head to the falls."

. . .

An hour later, Robert wore a wide smile—genuine this time —as he pressed the shutter of his Nikon SLR, taking a long series of shots. In front of the serene waterfall, Josh sat on a boulder while Rachel stood next to him. That way, Robert could get them both in the same shot. Both wore enormous, elated smiles. Their love for each other was palpable, and despite their physical difference, Robert had taken plenty of great photos. "I think this should do it. Good thing there are plenty of rocks here, so I could even up your heights."

Josh stood and shook hands with Robert. "We can't thank you enough. I set this up months ago, and Rach was so excited when I told her about it last night. We were crushed when that guy canceled on us this morning."

After Josh gave Robert the man's name, he wasn't surprised. The photographer wasn't well regarded by other professionals on the island. After Josh completed payment on Robert's phone with their contact information, the small group headed away from the waterfall down a crushed-gravel path. When they reached the parking lot, Malcolm was already waiting.

Josh smiled at Robert. "You don't make it easy to find the tip section on your payment screen."

"Nah. I charge a fair rate, and don't want to look greedy. You don't need to tip me."

Josh held up a finger. "Didn't make it easy, I said. But I found it and gave you a little extra. I mean it—you saved our trip."

Robert laughed. "Well, thanks. But I wouldn't go that far."

"Really," Rachel said. "I can't wait to see them!"

As they drove away in Malcolm's old sedan, Robert was still smiling. No matter what he had scheduled, he would have figured out how to make this shoot work. He never refused a request from Hope. She was the main reason his business was doing so well. But there had been an unexpected silver lining to this gig.

When he'd seen Rachel and Josh, he'd despaired of getting any decent photos. But true love transcended physical differences, as the pair had just shown. Robert had completed many photo shoots with couples where finding winning pictures had been challenging because they didn't *look* good together. He had a sixth sense about photography and was confident he'd find plenty of great shots of Rachel and Josh. Smiling, Robert placed his cameras in the back of his SUV and got in the driver's seat, shaking his head. "Just goes to show—true love can't be faked, and there's someone out there for everyone."

LATER THAT NIGHT, Robert poured himself a glass of red wine and sat down on his patio, listening to the chorus of crickets filling the air. He lived in a three-bedroom house in the hills above town. His home wasn't fancy, but it was clean and in good repair. Taking a sip, he opened his phone to check his payment app and nearly dropped his glass.

Josh had given him a $1000 tip.

Laughing, he gripped his glass more firmly and held it up in a toast. "How 'bout that. I spent my morning divin' in clear, warm water and the afternoon getting paid to take photographs. And in the process, I got to help a friend." His smile softened.

I made a real difference to that couple. This is how I want to live. Not haulin' fish out of the sea.

Yet fishing was what Eddie wanted with all his heart. But getting their father to understand that was a different story...

Chapter Five

A WEEK LATER, Heather was enjoying a busy afternoon at the bar. The infinity pool was filled with guests and several more sat at tables. According to the enthusiastic divers around her, the morning dive had been a great success.

Laughter caused her to look up as Sara, Hope, and Alex approached. Following just behind them were Robert and a dark-skinned young man with delicate features, and Heather's heart gave an excited flutter when she saw Robert. He was saying something to Zach Turner, a high-school senior who worked at the dive shop. As the others sat around a large table in the sand, Alex branched off and headed toward her, slapping a hand on the wooden counter. "A bucket of beers, please, plus one Coke. We're celebrating."

"I can see that. What's the occasion?"

"Three newly certified Nitrox divers," he said, waving an arm in a broad stroke toward the table.

"Excellent. Have a seat and I'll bring them right over."

After filling a steel bucket with six Leatherbacks and one soft drink, she headed over. Robert turned his smile to her, making her heart flip-flop even more.

"Congratulations, guys," Heather said. "But I'm confused. Alex said three Nitrox divers, and he's the instructor. So, who's the extra?"

Their heads all turned to Robert, who sat back with a shrug. "That would be me. I'm already certified, but wasn't about to say no to free beer." Then he grinned and their gazes held for a long moment.

"A sensible choice," she said, smiling back.

Hope passed the beers around. "We might be celebrating prematurely. The class is only the first part of our advanced certification. Sara, Zach, and I still have a way to go."

"You guys will all do great," Robert said.

Alex raised his brows at Heather. "I teach open water too. You want to get certified?"

She propped an arm on her hip, smiling. "Who says I'm not?"

His eyes grew wide as he held a hand against his chest. "A thousand pardons! What about advanced? You want to join in with these guys?"

"No, but thanks for the offer. I've got my open water and Nitrox. I dove a fair amount in California, but it's been a couple of years since the last time."

"Kelp beds and Garibaldis, not to mention cold water," Alex said with a nod.

"You've dived there?"

"A time or two."

Heather recalled the article about him that hung in the lobby. "That's right! You were a SEAL. Were you stationed at Coronado?"

"No, mainly on the East Coast. But I helped with some teaching at Coronado."

Heather laughed. "Ok, if you taught SEALs, I definitely don't want to take a class from you!"

"Hope, Zach, and I survived our open water classes," Sara said. "Of course, now we're taking the advanced course. We're probably all in trouble."

Alex just grinned but didn't reply as two guests came up to the bar.

"I'd better get back to work," Heather said. "Let me know if you want another round."

She got the guests refilled and was wiping the counters down when Sara approached. "Something else?"

Sara sat on a stool. "Just a glass of water. I need to drive home. Do you like working at night?"

"This place wraps up by 9:30 usually. For a bartender, that's a dream."

"Where do you live?"

Sara knew about her exodus from Serenity, but not all the details. "They kicked me out of my apartment when I got fired. So, I've just been crashing with a friend. I need to get a roommate, but I haven't had much luck so far."

Sara nodded. "Yeah, answering an ad is kind of scary. I'm sure you'll find someone soon. You want to come diving? I'm going on the boat in a couple of days and could use a dive buddy."

Heather paused. "That sounds great, but I don't have another day off for a while. I might be late for my shift."

"Tell you what. Bring over a pitcher of water and we'll see what we can do. I happen to know the owners rather well."

When Heather brought over the pitcher and a tray of glasses, Sara's and Hope's heads were together, then Hope turned to the bartender with a smile. "Of course you can join the morning trip! Someone can cover for an hour or so."

Heather hesitated. She didn't want to inconvenience anyone so she could spend the morning playing. "Thank you. I haven't dived in a while and could use a refresher. But I don't have time for it today or tomorrow, and I don't want to be a bother."

"That's no problem," Alex said. "Robert and Jack are both working that morning, and I'm driving for Tommy. Any of us can give you a quick tune-up. Just show up at the boat at 8 a.m." Tommy Williams was Half Moon Bay's primary boat captain. A St. Croix native and long-time employee, he was getting additional much-needed days off with more staff working. Alex was the only other licensed boat captain, but additional divemasters freed him up to help Tommy.

Heather turned back to Hope. "You're sure no one would mind?"

"I promise. Most of our workers have been here a long time," Hope said. "And that's because we make sure the job stays fun. This is a resort in paradise, after all."

"Besides," Sara said with a smirk. "She owes me. While they're gallivanting all over Florida, Jack and I are watching her newly neutered dog. I'm sure he'll be a peach."

Alex winced, taking another drink. "I'm afraid Cruz got the short end of the stick on this one."

Hope pressed her lips together. "I'm a responsible pet owner. I won't have a bunch of little Cruzes running around, however cute they might be." She turned back to Heather. "Go diving. Please."

As a pet shelter volunteer, Heather couldn't help but approve. "Thank you. I'd love to come along."

Sara cocked her head. "We haven't had a girls' night out in a while. We can arrange one for your next day off. You want to come?"

"That's a great idea!" Hope said.

Heather blinked, surprised that she'd gotten two invitations in the last five minutes. "Fantastic! Let me know the details and I'll be there."

She returned to the bar, looking forward to getting in the water again. And much warmer water than California! Since he was the instructor, no doubt Alex would teach her refresher. But Heather couldn't help hoping it might be Robert instead...

Two mornings later, Heather strolled down the pier, dressed in a sporty black two-piece swimsuit covered with board shorts and a loose tank top. It was just before 8 a.m. and the sound of clanging scuba tanks echoed in the morning air. Her stomach was fluttering at the prospect of diving again after a long layoff, but the sunny weather eased her mind. The water was a bit choppy, making the boat bob up and down. As she neared *Surface Interval*, Robert was loading tanks at the stern while Alex kneeled over an open panel in the fiberglass deck.

She addressed the boss, shading her eyes with a hand. "Good morning. Anyone got time for a refresher?"

Alex turned with a smile. "Absolutely. Jack isn't here yet, and I need to work on the boat before we go." He glanced at Robert. "You want to do the honors?"

Robert turned to her with a slight smile. "Of course. We can kit up here and just jump off the dock. Come on board." He held a hand out and steadied her as she climbed aboard. A jolt ran through her as their hands touched.

He dropped the contact, and pointed to a tank, complete with BCD and regulator attached to the valve. "That's your tank. We already set it up for you to save some time. Don't worry about a wetsuit—this shouldn't take too long. I'll get ready and help you in a minute."

"Thanks, Robert." As he turned away, she slid carefully around Alex, who was bent over the open hole with a wrench in one hand. "The problem isn't serious, is it?"

He glanced up with a laugh. "No, just preventative mainte-nance. Believe me, Tommy and I both take care of boat problems before they become serious. We learned that lesson the hard way."

She nodded at this reassuring yet cryptic answer and removed her tank top and board shorts, storing them in the expansive dry storage area. When she returned to the stern, Robert was already wearing his tank over a rash guard, and she felt slightly self-conscious in her swimsuit. But he was a profes-sional, putting her at ease, and soon they stood on the edge of the dock. The tank was heavy on her back as she peered into the clear water, colorful tropical fish darting about.

"It's about twenty feet deep here," Robert said. "We'll kneel on the sand, and you can practice floodin' your mask and do a regulator retrieval. Then we'll swim around a little and make sure you're weighted ok for the dive. Sound good?"

She nodded. "I'm a little more nervous than I thought I'd be."

He gave her a warm smile. "That's normal. After a few minutes, it will come back to you."

Heather placed the regulator in her mouth, and Robert counted down from three. They jumped in unison, landing with a splash, and were soon descending. She experienced some initial fumbles trying to decipher the unfamiliar equipment, but Robert was there to help. She settled quickly and completed the required skills with no issues.

They went on a quick tour, and she tried to mimic his relaxed, horizontal position in the water. There wasn't much to see in the white sandy area, but coral was growing on the pilings beneath the pier, with a multitude of fish darting in and out. Fifteen minutes later, they climbed back onto the pier to a completely different scene.

Alex had replaced the large fiberglass panel and most of the divers were on board. Jack walked around, doing a head count. Heather dripped saltwater as she sat down in the stern section, sliding her tank into its holder behind her.

Sara approached, wearing a long gray cover-up. "How did it go?"

"Great," Heather said. "I'm glad I did it. Got all the nerves worked out."

Robert and Jack untied them as Alex eased the large boat away from the dock. Though excited about diving with Sara, Heather was drawn to Robert.

Too bad I'm in Jack's group instead of his.

***

Robert's group consisted of six experienced divers. Which was good, because he spent most of the morning fighting to keep his mind on his job. He'd been delighted when Alex had asked him to give Heather the refresher, eager to spend a little time with her. *And that swimsuit!* She was a tall woman, nearly equal to his 5'10", and her red hair was contained in a long braid. Nervous at the start, streams of bubbles had risen from her regulator with each rapid breath. But she'd quickly settled, clearly enjoying the refresher, and examined the fish around the pilings closely. Too bad she was in Jack's group.

Both dives passed in a blur, and the ocean's surface swells picked up noticeably over the morning. By the time they surfaced after the second dive, the stern ladders were rocking in the swell. Alex had thrown out two trailing lines so the divers could hold on while they removed their fins.

Jack's group was already on board, and Robert swam near the ladder and faced his group. "Ok, hand me your fins and watch the ladder. Carefully! Climb up quick, and Alex will help you. Do not approach the ladder when a wave is movin' under it, or you'll get clobbered in the head."

Everyone made it safely back on board. The only mishap was an older woman who saw a perfect opportunity to grab the ladder and let go of her fins, forcing Robert to retrieve them. But he'd do that all day if it prevented an injury. Last on board, he quickly shrugged out of his tank.

A large wave rolled under the boat and an excited "Oooh," came out of several mouths as people lurched. Alex frowned from the wheelhouse, waiting for Jack and Robert to raise the ladders so they could get moving.

Sara and Heather stood in front of Robert, laughing as they steadied themselves. He was moving toward the ladder when a much bigger wave came at them nearly broadside, causing the tanks to rattle in their holders. The boat lurched sideways, dipping several feet toward starboard, and several *whoops* sounded from the divers as they were thrown off balance.

The next thing Robert knew, Heather was falling into his arms with a laughing screech. He caught her, steadying her in his arms and matching her grin as their eyes met. Her skin was warm and smooth, and he couldn't resist running his thumb over her back, just above the strap of her swimsuit.

Sara tumbled onto the side bench next to them, but he hardly noticed, lost in Heather's soft green eyes. He had an almost irresistible urge to kiss her. Sara prevented that when she hollered, "Jeez, Alex! Did you get your captain's license inside a cereal box?"

That broke the spell, and several people started laughing. He and Heather blinked rapidly—she looked as stunned as he was, and he quickly stood her upright.

"Sorry, guys!" Alex called down. "That was a weird one. Everyone all right?"

Reluctantly, Robert stepped back, his hands tingling, and

glanced around as divers righted themselves. Everyone was laughing though, except Sara, who glowered at the wheelhouse. He turned back to Heather. "You all right?"

She stared at him, her chest rising and falling deeply. "Yes, I'm fine. Thanks for catching me."

That made him grin. "You can fall into my arms anytime. You want me to ask Alex to do it again?"

A strong blush crept up her neck, and he bit his cheek, not wanting to embarrass her further. "No, I think once was enough. But I'm lucky you were here."

"I don't know. Maybe I'm the lucky one—"

"*Robert!*" Alex boomed in a voice that clearly indicated he'd already called out several times, and the divemaster looked up. Alex's face was tight, and his eyes bored into Robert's. "If it's not too much trouble, would you kindly raise the ladder so we can get underway before any more waves swamp us?"

"Aye aye, captain!" Robert said, but refrained from saluting, worried that might get him punched. He felt giddy, nearly laughing, which could be dangerous in Alex's present mood. He turned to Heather. "I'd better get back to work before I get fired."

She broke into a grin. "Yes, good idea."

When they returned to the dock, Robert was disappointed when Heather had to hurry to start her shift. But she made up for it by smiling shyly at him. "Thanks for your help today. All of it."

He bowed gallantly. "At your service, fair lady."

With another smile, she turned and walked gracefully up the pier. Robert was slightly dizzy as he stared at her back.

"What the *hell* is wrong with you?"

He turned around and Alex stood before him, both hands

propped on his hips, his sunglasses on his head, and a very perplexed look on his face.

Fumbling for an acceptable response, Robert was saved by Jack's laughter. "Pretty sure he's got the hots for your new bartender, boss."

Alex's face went slack. "Really?"

Robert tried to play it cool. "She's an attractive woman, and I wasn't going to just let her fall. I was only being helpful."

The former SEAL arched a brow, trying to hide a smile. "Uh-huh. Helpful. Or maybe you're so horny you can't keep your mind on your job?"

Robert burst into guffaws, bending at the waist as he clutched his stomach. "Seriously? That sentence just came out of *your* mouth?"

Alex waved a hand at him, and the smile finally escaped as he turned away. "Yeah, yeah. Get back to work, lazy ass."

Chapter Six

HEATHER FOLLOWED in her car as Sara turned north onto the highway, driving to a place called Marimba. Fellow spa employee Selena sat in Sara's passenger seat, and she and the stylist were having an animated conversation from the way their heads kept turning toward each other. Heather was touched they had scheduled their next night out to coincide with her day off. Working evenings had some distinct disadvantages.

Sara turned left and slowly bounced over a rutted dirt track. Vegetation closed in on both sides, the narrow track twisting and turning. Heather craned her head, looking up through the windshield. "What are you getting me into, Sara?"

But after several hundred yards, the road ended in a gravel parking lot, a thatch-roofed bar just behind. An expansive ocean vista opened up when Heather got out of her car, and she turned toward Selena, a wide smile cracking her face. "After all that jungle, I can't believe this!"

The massage therapist grinned. "Yeah, it's a hidden gem. We alternate between this place and Charlie's, which isn't quite as picturesque."

Under the roof, several tables were placed over the white

sand floor. But Sara and Selena headed straight toward the uncovered beach section and a tanned blonde woman who sat alone at a table for six. The woman smiled as they approached, her dark blue eyes crinkling.

"This is April," Sara said. "She's a divemaster and works at Half Moon Bay part-time."

April, who looked in her mid-thirties, held out her hand. "Nice to meet you, Heather. Glad you could join us." Then she glanced at the other two. "I already ordered beers."

Heather sat next to Sara, enjoying the sound of waves rushing onto the shore. The setting was beautiful, with several palm trees sighing in the steady breeze. Two other tables were being used, also by locals enjoying the evening. "I can't believe this place isn't more crowded."

"Depends on when you come in," Selena said, tucking her straightened hair behind one ear. "At times, it is hoppin'! But they don't advertise, so it's mostly a local hangout." A middle-aged man with a frizzy halo of salt-and-pepper hair and a white apron arrived with two buckets of beer. He deposited one at each end of the table.

The women were just passing around the bottles when Hope arrived, accompanied by a tall, fit woman with ebony skin and incredible cheekbones. Her long hair was separated into thin braids, several framing her face dyed bright pink.

Hope sat on Heather's other side. "I'm glad the beer is already here. Today Cindy got her physical therapist assistant license!" There was a round of applause while Hope introduced Heather. The setting sun made the diamonds in Hope's wedding ring sparkle. It was a lovely set, with a large Princess-cut solitaire accented by smaller stones. "Cindy and I have been friends since I moved here."

"Thanks, ladies," Cindy said. "It's taken a while, but I finally did it. And got a nice raise too, thank goodness. I just bit the bullet and re-signed the lease on my house. My landlord raised the rate, so I'm probably goin' to need a roommate."

Sara slammed her bottle down. "Oh, my God! I love when things work out like that." She wrapped an arm around Heather's shoulders and leaned in to smile at Cindy. "Guess who needs a place to live?"

Cindy cocked her head, staring at Heather. "Really?"

"Yeah," Heather said. "I've been crashing on a friend's couch for a month. I really need to find a place."

Cindy shrugged. "Well, I can at least offer you a bedroom. The house isn't anythin' fancy, a two bedroom, two bath in Frederiksted. And it's set up as two master suites on opposite sides of the house, so it's got plenty of privacy."

Heather couldn't believe her luck. "Sounds perfect. Can I come take a look?"

"Of course."

"I can vouch for both of you," Hope said. "What a great idea. Cheers!" Six beers clinked together across the table.

"So, you're new to the island?" April, whose long hair was a sun-streaked golden blonde, asked Heather.

"I've been here almost six months."

"What made you decide to move here, anyway?" Sara asked.

Heather took another sip, giving herself time to formulate an answer. "To make a new start. On my own." She didn't want to keep anything from her new friends, and glanced around the table. "My last name is Galen."

Five pairs of eyes stared blankly at her.

"I'm sorry," Hope said. "Other than your employee paperwork, I'm not familiar with the name."

Heather burst into laughter, holding up her beer. "And that, ladies, is exactly why I'm here." She took a quick drink, then held out a hand, ready to explain. "Have you heard of Galendo?" Of course, they all nodded. The video sharing and entertainment app was a worldwide staple, and nearly a media empire. "My father is Tim Galen."

"Oooh, that Galen," April said, her eyes wide.

"You don't get along with your parents?" Selena asked, her tone sympathetic.

"No, that's not it at all. They've both been supportive of me, but I have absolutely no talent or interest in programming or app technology. I just want to be known as myself, not as Tim and Laura Galen's daughter. And I'm not a poor little rich girl, either—I *like* being a bartender." With Hope there, she didn't want to mention that it wasn't exactly her ideal job.

"St. Croix must be quite a change for you," Cindy said.

"Definitely. And things didn't start out well, but I'm turning the corner." She smiled at Hope and Sara. "Thanks to these two ladies."

AN HOUR LATER, they were on their second round, and Heather was grateful to be part of such a diverse group. Not just racially, but also life experience. She fit right in. Sara was telling the group about the dive Heather had come along on. Warmth spread through her chest as Robert's face popped into her mind. He had been charming and modest, and she swore her skin still tingled where he had touched her after she stumbled. Unfortunately, she hadn't seen him since.

"So, there are two absolute truths we can draw from the experience," Sara said. "One—only dive when Tommy is working. Hope's husband is a terrible boat driver and should have his license revoked."

A round of laughter went around the table as Hope firmly shook her head. "It was one wave, Sara. It happens. If you don't think he's qualified, you're more than welcome to tell him yourself."

Sara grinned. "I might just do that. Now I have something to hold over him again."

April cocked her head. "You said there were two truths. What's the other one?"

Sara opened her eyes wide, placing both hands on the table. "Oh, this one is juicy! The other truth is the definite sparks which are flying between a certain divemaster and a certain bartender!"

Heather's stomach flopped over, and she ducked her head.

Cindy stared at Sara, wrinkling her brow. "Jack?"

"Oh, please. Jack and I are as happy as two little clams. Living in a love shack on our own beach. What more could a girl want? No, I'm talking about Robert and our own Heather here."

Heather had blushed as soon as Sara mentioned *sparks*. Now she probably resembled a pomegranate, as Sara stared gleefully at her. Hope wrapped an arm around Heather's shoulders sympathetically, shaking her head. "Her nickname is Hurricane Sara, by the way. I apologize."

"I did *not* approve of that nickname! Who came up with that, anyway?"

Hope's face was carefully blank as she swept her hair off her forehead. "Oh, I might have let it slip out."

Sara stared at her, narrowing her eyes. "Yeah? Sounds more like Alex than you."

"Oh, who cares about that?" Selena said, leaning forward and staring at Heather. "You and Robert are together? He's such a great guy! He helped me move a new massage table into the spa—I didn't even have to ask him."

Panic was twisting Heather's stomach now. "No, no! Nothing's going on. We hardly know each other."

Sara was willing to be diverted from her nickname, giving Heather a sly smile. "You forget I was standing right next to you. Even as I fought for my life after Alex tried to capsize the boat

—" Sara paused while everyone laughed at Hope's eye roll. "—I saw you fall into Robert's arms, his face inches above yours. The two of you, just staring into each other's eyes. I tell you, it was the stuff romance novels are made of!"

They were all laughing, but Hope came to Heather's rescue. "Knock it off, Sara! You're embarrassing her. Of course, that's never stopped you before." She turned to Heather, who swore the sandy beach was twenty degrees warmer than when she had arrived. "Robert is one of my favorite people."

"I think you guys are making *way* too much of this!" she squeaked.

"All right, all right," Cindy said. "We'll change the subject and let you off the hot seat. Hope and Alex are goin' on a belated honeymoon soon." She pointed at Sara. "Which means you should be safe to go divin', since Tommy will be the captain."

"Thank God," Sara said, and held up her beer. "Let's drink to that!"

As she raised her bottle, Heather's thoughts turned to whether Alex's absence might result in Robert filling in more. Not to mention more opportunities to talk to him.

Chapter Seven

JUNE...

A BEAUTIFUL CARIBBEAN morning bloomed as Robert climbed aboard *Surface Interval*, with thin, lacy clouds diminishing the sun's heat. Tommy and Jack scurried back and forth between the pier and the boat. "Mornin', guys. Here's to another day of freedom."

Tommy barked a laugh and pushed up the sleeves of his rash guard. "I gotta admit, it's kind of weird knowin' Alex isn't around to help with an odd question or problem."

Alex and Hope had left on their trip two days ago. When Alex had met with Tommy, Jack, and Robert shortly before departing, they had presented a united front that everything would be fine in his absence. And they must have convinced him since there had been no word from the honeymooners.

Robert snorted. *Maybe they're busy with other things...*

Alex had put Jack in charge, which surprised Robert. Now he turned to the boat captain. "So, how come you're not runnin' the show?"

Tommy grinned as he effortlessly slid two tanks into their holders. "Nah. I like bein' in charge of the boat, but the rest of it is outside my wheelhouse—literally!" He burst into laughter as Robert winced at his joke. "Jack will be fine. Not like there's much choice, since you abandoned us."

"I'm here, aren't I?" Robert threw a wetsuit at the big man, who caught it with a laugh.

Jack returned with an armful of regulators. "For which we're both grateful—this is a busy week. We've got a sizeable group of returning guests starting today. I'm taking six and you've got the other half dozen."

Half an hour later, all twelve divers were on board. Jack came on last with his hair sticking up and his jaw set tight. Robert couldn't help a small smile at how concerned he was about doing a good job in Alex's absence.

A tall, middle-aged man with short, dark hair approached Robert. "I see Tommy up there, and I remember you from one of our previous trips, but where's Alex?"

"He's on vacation," Robert said.

"What?" two women asked in unison. They stood behind the male diver, their faces crestfallen. Robert kept from grinning, used to most of the female attention being lavished on Alex, though the former SEAL never cared about that. In all the years he'd known Alex, Robert had never seen him even flirt with a guest. But there was no question who the primary dive guide was.

"Alex is away for a week," Jack said with a tight smile. "But don't worry, we've got you guys covered."

The tall man frowned. "We've always dived with Alex. I wish we would have known."

Jeez, this is the man's first vacation in years. Lighten up!

But Robert just broke into his trademark smile. "He's on a delayed honeymoon with Hope. But he'll be back for your next trip. I promise, Jack and I will take good care of you guys."

At the word *honeymoon*, the two women's mouths dropped open, even more crushed. Tommy climbed down the ladder from the wheelhouse, spreading his arms out. "Hey! Where's the love for me? I'm still here!"

That made them smile. "Ok, Tommy," one woman said. "You're hired. Half Moon Bay wouldn't be the same without your jokes."

"Oh, no!" Jack said, his face wide with horror. "Don't tell him that!"

"Ah, you're jealous." Tommy turned back to the two women. "Ok, just for you two. Where do fish like to get together to sing?" Almost bursting, he waited while they shook their heads. "A... choral reef!" Several loud groans were mixed with laughter, but his joke had the desired effect.

"Come on, folks," Robert called out, grinning. "Let's get a move on. Otherwise, Tommy won't stop."

AFTER RETURNING from the morning trip, Robert stood with Jack behind the counter in the dive shop. They were entering the sites into the computer so each diver would have a record at the end of their trip. The bell above the front door jingled as the general manager, Patti Thomas, walked in, wearing a light-blue polo shirt with her name engraved over one ample breast. Her hair was a natural halo around her head, as much gray as black. "And how was your mornin'?"

Jack glanced up and straightened. "It started out a little rocky but ended up being a fantastic trip. You didn't get a complaint, did you?"

She raised both manicured brows. "No, not at all. I wanted to make sure everythin' was goin' smooth down here."

Robert grinned, leaning on the glass counter. "Makin' sure we don't mess up, huh?"

"I'm just doin' my job here. I can run the resort fine in Hope's absence. But the dive operation is a different story."

"Which is why you're so lucky to have stellar team members like Tommy, Jack, and me."

She finally broke into a grin, and Robert relaxed. "Oh, fine, Robert Davis. What was the problem earlier?"

Jack grinned sheepishly, rubbing a hand through his hair. "The group wanted to dive with Alex. Two women were very disappointed he wasn't here, and then their hearts solidly broke when they found out he's married. It got a little uncomfortable. But don't worry, Tommy told one of his awful jokes and smoothed it out."

Patti laughed. "I can only imagine. Are they goin' out again this afternoon?"

"Yep," Robert said. "All twelve. And happy as can be after a full mornin' of Jack and myself leadin' the dives."

"Sounds like you gentlemen have it handled. Let me know if you need anythin'."

Jack exhaled a sigh after she left. "Great—Patti's checking in on us. I really don't want to screw this up, so I need to look over tomorrow's schedule. The group told me several animals they want to see, so I need to plan the dives."

"All right. I'm gonna get lunch. You want to come?"

Jack shook his head, frowning as he typed on the keyboard. "I'm not hungry. I'll grab something before the dive."

"I'll see you in a bit, then." He clapped Jack on the shoulder. "And would you relax? The resort can still operate without Alex and Hope." As Robert left the building, Sara was coming down the steps from the spa. "I'm glad I ran into you," he said. "Would you please go in there and calm your boyfriend down? He's stressin' out over nothin'."

She smiled, flipping her hair over one shoulder. "Yes, he's a bit keyed up about filling Alex's shoes. Don't worry, I'll sort him out." With a wink, she disappeared into the dive shop.

Robert walked into the restaurant kitchen, where executive chef Gerold Harrigan was at the grill, but the employee table was empty. Since Heather worked a later shift, she didn't eat lunch there. "Can you grill me a blackened fish sandwich?"

The chef nodded and opened the large walk-in refrigerator. He removed a white-wrapped bundle and opened it before sprinkling it liberally with blackening seasoning. Gerold tossed it on the grill, flames leaping. "You're in luck. I got some really nice mahi-mahi in this mornin'. Does your dad still sell to Frank?"

Frank Walker had been Half Moon Bay's fish supplier for years. "Yeah. Pop said he ran into a big school of mahi yesterday, so that's probably his."

"He still givin' you a hard time about not goin' into the family business?" Gerold flipped the fish and scooped out a serving of fries from the fryer.

"He's still tryin' to recruit me. We're kind of at an impasse right now. He's got two boats, but he won't let Eddie captain the other one because he's got his heart set on me takin' it over."

Gerold assembled the sandwich and slid it in front of Robert. "That's rough. Hope it all works out for you."

"Thanks."

Robert took a bite of his fiery sandwich, turning his mind back to Heather and what would be a good reason for approaching her. By the end of lunch, he had it worked out. Grabbing a mint from the bowl on the employee table, he popped in it his mouth and headed for the pool bar.

When he got there, Patti sat at a corner table under the roof, writing on a yellow legal pad while Heather served drinks to two guests in the pool. Heather came around to his side of the bar, her eyes widening when she saw him, which gave him a small thrill. "Hi, Robert. What brings you here?"

He leaned casually on the bar. "Hope mentioned she wanted to hang two of my photos here, and I wanted to get an idea of the space available." He already knew there was room on both sides of the liquor bottle display for two large prints, but he didn't want to look too obvious.

"Can I get you something?"

His smile widened, and her cheeks turned a soft pink. *Don't think we're quite ready for what I'd really like.* "Coke would be great." She brought a can to him, and he tried to think of an opener, finally settling on the mundane. "How are you likin' St. Croix?"

Heather smiled. She had a long, straight nose, and her red hair was wrapped in a neat bun. "Things are going really well now. I'm moving in with Hope's friend Cindy in a couple of days, and it will be nice to have a space all my own. I've been crashing with a friend for the last month."

"Cindy's easy to get on with."

She laughed. "I swear. Everyone knows everyone on this island."

"Not quite, but Cindy's been on the dive boat several times."

Heather stared at the blank portion of the wall and paused before turning back. "I hear you're a pretty talented photographer."

He shrugged. "It's mostly what I do for a livin' now. But Hope has been instrumental in gettin' me started. She's displayed a bunch of my photos around the resort."

"I've seen those! They're in the restaurant and lobby. You do beautiful work, Robert."

Warmth spread through his chest. "Thank you. It's been a

passion of mine for a long time. Makin' a livin' from it is a dream come true."

"That isn't the only way you make your livin', you know," Patti said from the corner, but a small smile played at her lips. "Don't you have an afternoon dive to prepare for?"

Laughing, he checked his watch. "Yeah, you're right. I need to get back." Turning back to Heather, their gazes held for a long moment. "It was good seein' you again," he said, and an enticing shiver ran down his back when a tiny smile fluttered across her lips.

"You, too."

The sun was just a bit brighter and Robert's steps lighter as he headed back to the pier.

Chapter Eight

DUKE, a black and white border-collie mix, tugged at his leash, practically dragging Heather to the fenced-in dog park behind Pet Paradise. She barely got the gate re-latched before he jumped on her, eager to retrieve the ball he knew was in her pocket.

"All right, all right." She unclipped his leash, and he immediately tore across the enclosed area. The dog careened around the perimeter with his tongue hanging out, the picture of canine happiness. "Duke, you are going to need an active family with lots of outdoor space!"

Hearing his name, the dog ran back to her, sitting at her feet with his tail whapping the ground. It didn't take a genius to know what he wanted, so she removed the tennis ball from her pocket and threw it. Duke was the third dog she'd brought to the fenced-in park that morning. Her first half hour had been spent petting cats and enjoying the serenity that came from stroking the warm, purring bundles as they stretched out on her lap.

But now frustration edged in on her good mood. The shelter was full of well-behaved animals who needed homes. But in the weeks she'd been volunteering, few had been adopted.

After fifteen minutes of frolicking, Duke deposited the ball at her feet and lay on the grass, panting heavily. "Ok, that's our signal to head back." After returning him to his kennel, Heather joined Donna in the reception area. "Duke should be ready for a nap now."

Donna laughed, sitting back in her chair behind the desk. "For a little while, anyway. He's a bundle of energy. I've got a lead on Beau, though. A family is coming to look at him this afternoon." An adorable chocolate-brown, floppy-eared puppy, Beau was a sure thing.

"Oh, good!" Then Heather hesitated, not wanting to criticize Donna. "I was hoping the animals would get adopted a little faster."

The owner sighed. "It's a constant uphill battle. I try to update our Facebook page and keep adoption fees as low as possible, but we always have more pets than people. If you have any ideas, please let me know." Then she laughed ruefully. "As long as it doesn't cost money. I'm barely keeping this place open as it is."

"I'll give it some thought. Maybe we can come up with something together."

The shelter wasn't far from Heather's new home, and within minutes she was parking in a dirt driveway. The neighborhood was quiet and peaceful, and a smile rose on her face as she studied the one-story light-blue house. She unlocked the front door and walked into a large living room. Dual master suites sat at each end of the house, with the living room and kitchen between. It wasn't fancy, but Cindy was clean and organized, and in the week since Heather had moved in, the two women had easily adjusted to each other. Heather even had a private patio off her bedroom.

She took a shower, leaving her hair down to air dry and changing into a comfy blue floral sundress. Her gaze paused at a dogeared book on the nightstand. She'd finished the novel Sara had lent her, and now made a mental note to call her about returning it.

The bedroom had contained a queen-sized bed already, and a quick trip to the thrift store had supplied Heather with a nightstand and a small patio set. She laughed out loud at what her mother would think of her shopping in a thrift store. As if it had been a signal, Heather's phone rang, Laura Galen's face lighting up the screen.

She answered with a smile. "Hi, Mom. I was just thinking about you."

"Good thoughts, I hope?"

"Of course. What are you up to?"

"I'm at the house in Maui. Your father was here for several days, but he just flew back to Palo Alto this morning for an emergency meeting of some sort. So you and I are both in the balmy tropics alone."

"There are worse places."

"Oh, I'm not complaining. How are things there?"

"Good. I moved in with a roommate. I really like her, and I've got my own suite."

Laura hesitated on the other end. "Heather, I know you want to make it on your own, but if you need money, please just say so. You don't have to get a roommate!"

Her parents were supportive, but neither had been born wealthy. Heather knew they struggled with her desire for independence. "Honestly, I enjoy living with Cindy. She's a local, born in St. Thomas, but has lived on this island for over ten years. It's good for me to experience other people. Not just rich white snobs."

"Is that what you think we are?"

"No, of course not. But you can't deny you hang out with plenty of people who fit that description exactly."

"Well, that's certainly true." Light laughter came through the phone. "Dad and I have perfected a secret code to rescue each other at cocktail parties when we're desperate. We'll definitely need it the next time we run into the Carringtons. Or we might just dump our drinks in their faces."

"I know the feeling, believe me. And after Grant and everything that happened afterward... I needed to make a drastic change."

"I understand, honey—a new location was a good idea. But I miss you. Maybe we'll come visit you someday."

Heather broke into a wide smile at the prospect of the Galen armada invading cozy St. Croix. "I might just hold you to that, Mom." Her eye fell on Sara's book again. "I'd better go. Enjoy Hawaii."

After hanging up, the silent house creaked around her, reinforcing her homesickness. Cindy went for a long run after she got off work, so Heather wouldn't have company for a while. She dialed Sara. "Hey, I have that book I borrowed, and thought I'd drop it off. Will you be home for a while?"

"Oh yeah," Sara replied. "We're just hanging out. But you can give it to me at work if you'd rather not drive out here."

"I know, but I'm a little homesick and feel like some company. But I don't want to intrude."

Sara laughed, and something about her tone made Heather take notice, recalling that she liked to stir the pot. "Oh, don't worry about that. We're out on the beach, so when you get here, just come straight through the house and join us. We'll save you a drink." She gave Heather directions.

As she backed out of the driveway and headed toward Sara's, Heather disregarded any schemes Sara might be cooking up. *She might be a little nosy, but I could stand to make a friend or two. Now if I could just get the pet adoption conundrum solved...*

Robert relaxed in his chair, staring at the ocean waves splashing on the beach as Jack sat down next to him and clinked his beer bottle to Robert's.

"You lookin' forward to Alex taking the reins again soon?"

"Yeah. He does more behind the scenes than I thought. Running the dive operation is like juggling five things at once."

"You did fine, though." Robert looked back at the single-story weathered house. "You like livin' here, then?"

Jack's face relaxed. "Being so close to the ocean is incredible. And the company's not bad either."

"I'm glad to hear that," Sara said as she approached and sat down, placing her phone on the coffee table. "Nice to know you're not saying terrible things about me when I'm not around."

Jack leaned over and gave her a quick kiss. "No way. We wouldn't be here if it wasn't for you."

"It took both of us, I think."

"This is an incredible cove," Robert said, then inspected the shallows, shading his eyes with one hand against the setting sun. "Looks like there's a reef out there. Have you guys dived it?"

"Not yet," Jack said. "It's on the list, along with a thousand other things."

A flash of yellow zoomed by as Cruz ran down the beach, then dug frantically into the sand, and Robert laughed. "Looks like Hope's dog is settlin' right in."

"Mostly," Sara said with a small frown. "He loves Jack—and tolerates me. But he hasn't run away after getting neutered, which was Hope's concern."

"Looks pretty happy to me." Robert turned to Jack. "Maybe he won't want to go home."

Jack shook his head. "I'm a dog guy, always have been. But

Cruz is Hope's dog. A week away, or getting fixed, won't change that."

Loud yelping interrupted their conversation as Cruz skittered out of his hole, whipping his head back and forth. A large crab dangled by one pinching arm from his nose, and the dog wheeled around and headed toward them at top speed, crying piteously the whole time. After one final shake of his head, the crab went flying into the ocean and Cruz dove behind Jack's legs, whimpering. Bending down, Jack peered at the dog's nose, but there was no obvious damage, and he gave Cruz's ribs a solid pat. "I told you that would happen if you kept trying to dig up crabs, silly dog. Now maybe you'll listen."

Sara's laughter quieted, and she shook her head. "I doubt it. Hope has told me that's one of his favorite sports. He gets pinched occasionally but can't seem to stop."

Cruz rubbed his nose with a paw several times before settling at Jack's feet and closing his eyes.

Sara fished a beer out of the ice-filled cooler, then said with exaggerated casualness, "Heather's on her way over. She wanted to return a book and couldn't resist the siren song of beers on a beach."

She slid her eyes to Robert as she said this, and he made sure his face stayed expressionless, though his heart had gone from a trot to a gallop at Heather's name. "Who can resist that?" Robert knew about Sara's love of stirring the pot, and he didn't want to give her any ammunition. He had been about to leave, but this news decidedly changed his mind.

Sara gave him a long, level stare before breaking into a charming smile. "I hope you're not planning on running off. There's plenty of beer."

"I'm in no hurry. April's workin' tomorrow at Half Moon Bay, and I don't have a photo shoot until late mornin'.

"Yeah," Jack said, opening a second bottle. "Unlike some of us who have to work at the crack of dawn."

"Do you really have to get there so early?" Sara asked. "Is there that much extra to do?"

Robert grinned. "Nah, he's just worried about somethin' slippin' through the cracks."

Sara sighed. "Honestly, Jack, it's a dive resort, not brain surgery. Everyone's walking on eggshells, afraid Hope and Alex will come home to a disaster. Even if things are running a little rougher than usual, is it the end of the world?"

Jack laughed. "Ok, if the dive trips get all screwed up, you can tell Alex all about it."

"Well, you took the blame last time, so that would only be fair. And anyway, it's a moot point! Things have been fine."

"It might not be rocket science," Robert said. "But guests have spent a lot of money and they have limited time. So yes, it matters."

"Hope and Alex have no idea how lucky they are to have us on staff," Sara said. "So conscientious! We'll have to—"

She was interrupted by a "Hello!" as Heather came across the porch and descended the stairs onto the sand. Robert's heart skipped a beat as she walked toward them, and his breath caught. Her hair hung loose, a flat, glossy molten sheet that flowed halfway down her back. She wore a blue sundress with white and pink flowers, and he couldn't tear his eyes away. A smile lit up her face as her gaze swept over them. When she met Robert's gaze, she nearly stumbled, the smile slipping momentarily before growing even larger.

She wrenched her eyes away to hand Sara a battered paperback book. "Thanks. I enjoyed it a lot."

"You're welcome. I'll get you the next one in the series before you leave. Sit and have a beer!"

Sara pointed to the last open chair, which was next to

Robert. Heather unfolded her long body into her seat, sweeping her blazing river of hair over one shoulder. He ached to run his hands through it. Jack opened a beer and handed it to her as she took in the picturesque cove. "What a setting! You guys might never get rid of me."

"We're still getting used to it too," Jack said.

Once again, she moved her eyes to Robert's, and they held. "Hi, Robert. How are you?"

He smiled, entranced. Her nose was slightly too long, but that only made her more striking. "Doin' great. Just enjoyin' the end of the day."

"Sorry about the mess in the house," Sara said. "Hope you didn't trip over my easels."

Heather startled slightly, as if surprised Jack and Sara were there, then turned to the stylist. "I didn't realize you were an artist. Those are fantastic! And you sketch too?"

"No, those are mine," Jack said, smiling sheepishly. "Just chicken scratch."

She laughed. "Oh, that's all, huh? I'm definitely outclassed in this group—can't even draw stick figures, and I'm here with three artists! I absolutely love art, even though I don't have any talent myself."

"There are lots of galleries on the island," Sara said. "We should go sometime."

A shadow crossed Heather's face, but it was quickly gone. "I'd love to. Thanks."

"How was your day off?" Sara asked.

"Good. I'm getting settled into the house and spent several hours at the pet shelter. I volunteer there once or twice a week."

That only impressed Robert more. "The one in Frederiksted? Or the East end?"

Those green eyes turned toward him again. "Frederiksted."

Then she frowned. "There's a lot of pets there, but the adoption rate is really slow."

"Do they advertise much?" Jack asked.

Heather shook her head. "The woman who runs it doesn't have much extra cash. I'm trying to think up a fundraiser or something like that, but it all costs money. Back home, I used to help at a shelter—that's what gave me the idea to do it here. We had a pro who would volunteer a couple times a month and do beautiful photo portraits of the animals. That really made a difference. Professional pictures are critical—" She stopped mid-sentence and her mouth dropped open as she swiveled her head toward Robert.

He was looking straight back, but didn't miss Sara's wide grin as she said, "Oh, too bad there's no talented photographers on this island."

Heather leaned forward, setting her bottle on the coffee table. "Robert! Is there any chance you might help? Even half a dozen pictures could get us started."

He wouldn't have refused if she had asked him to jump off a building, but photographing animals sounded fun. "I'd love to. But I'll need an assistant. Someone to keep the dogs and cats well-behaved and photogenic."

He was rewarded by an enormous smile that sent his pulse racing. "I think that can be arranged."

Robert reached into his back pocket to retrieve his phone. "Guess I'm gonna need your phone number then, aren't I?"

Chapter Nine

JUST AFTER 7 A.M., Heather almost leaped out of bed, excited about the prospect ahead. The day further improved when she padded out to the kitchen to find Cindy had already brewed coffee. Heather's roommate sat at the table with a steaming mug in front of her, plaiting her tiny braids into a long tail. She glanced up, surprise slackening her face. "You're up early."

"Yeah, I know. This was the only morning Robert was available, so I'm helping him photograph the animals at nine. We should have plenty of time, since I don't have to work until noon."

A small smile tugged at the corners of Cindy's mouth, making Heather doubt she had sounded as nonchalant as she hoped. "I'd be surprised if his photos don't make a difference. There's a guy in my running group who's thinkin' about a dog to run with. I'll mention the shelter to him and see if he's interested." She crossed her arms on the table. "This is a smart business move on Robert's part. Even though he's doin' it for free, it's still good publicity, and makin' a fresh start is hard when you're a local."

Heather sat across from her, cradling her mug in both hands. "What do you mean?"

"A lot of long-time island families are very protective of their—our—heritage and traditions. Earning them was a hard-fought process. So, when a child doesn't want to carry on the tradition, it can create some tension."

"Hard fought doesn't begin to describe it. Was it that way for you? Is that why you moved to St. Croix?"

"Partly. My family in St. Thomas has owned and run a restaurant in Charlotte Amalie for generations. By the time I graduated high school, I just wanted somethin' different, so I moved here. I enjoy doin' my own thing, while still bein' close to home. I'm the first in our family to go to college, so my folks are proud of my new degree and job."

Heather smiled. "They should be. I can understand what you meant about wanting to make your own mark. That's why I'm here too."

Cindy nodded, then her text tone sounded, and she picked her phone up. A broad smile rose on her face.

"Good news?"

Still smiling, Cindy handed over the phone. "It's from Hope. Today is their last day, and they're relaxin' on the beach."

In the photo, the couple sat on a chair, with Hope leaning back against Alex's chest. A backdrop of turquoise water lay behind them, and both her arms encircled her bent knees. Alex must have taken the selfie. Their smiles could have cracked their faces, and Heather laughed. "Someone's having a good time."

"She's texted a few times. Their first couple of days were at a fancy hotel, then they moved on to a family resort on a small key. They've been divin' and spent a day in Key West."

Heather lingered over their smiling faces. *Hope and Alex are proof that some love stories have a happy ending.* "The resort has been quieter without them."

"They're probably not ready to come home! If anyone deserves a little happiness, it's those two."

"Alex has been through a lot."

Cindy darted a glance at her before picking up her mug. "So has Hope. Her story just isn't as... public. Though that wasn't Alex's doing."

"How did you and Hope meet?"

"Through the runnin' club. She bought some shoes at the store where I used to work, and we got to know each other on weekly group runs."

Heather shuddered. "Better you two than me. Walking and playing with the shelter animals gives me plenty of exercise."

Cindy drained the rest of her coffee. "I need to get ready for work. Have a good time at the shelter." As she left the room, she grinned and threw over her shoulder, "And have fun with Robert too."

JUST BEFORE 9 A.M., Heather and Donna were standing in the reception room of Pet Paradise when Robert walked in the front door. Two cameras were slung over one shoulder and he carried a thick roll of black fabric under his other arm. He flashed them a bright smile that made Heather's knees weaken. "Good mornin', ladies! I hear there are some pets that need homes."

Donna rushed forward to shake his hand. "Oh, thank you, thank you! When Heather told me you were willing to do this, I could hardly believe it."

Extricating his hand from hers, Robert just shrugged. "I'm lookin' forward to it. It's a win-win for all of us." Then his smile took on a different glint as he turned his attention to Heather. "How are you this mornin'?"

"Excellent. I'm excited to see you in action."

Robert's chest rose with his sharp inhale, and she gave him a tiny smile in return. Just then, the phone rang, and Donna returned to the desk to answer it. "I'll let you two get to it. Just yell if you need anything."

Heather turned back to Robert. He wore a red T-shirt that contrasted his dark skin spectacularly.

"Where do you want to set up?" she asked.

"Let's start with the dogs. I'd like to do two scenes. First, indoor with this black backdrop. Then we can move outdoors and film more dogs there. We'll use the indoor setup for the cats and any other critters you think I should photograph."

She nodded, then grinned. "I'm glad you said photograph and not shoot."

Robert laughed as they crossed the room. "Yeah, I try to be careful how I use that word. One time, I made the mistake of sayin' that I shot a bride, and it didn't go over well."

They moved to a storage room she had cleaned out, and Robert studied the area. "This will do. If you'll drape the backdrop, I'll get a couple of lights from my car. We'll be started before you know it."

Fifteen minutes later, Heather led Butch, a tan Mastiff-cross with a black muzzle, into the small room. She didn't quite trust him in the open area Robert wanted to use outside. The photographer gave a low whistle when she entered. "That's a big boy."

"Yeah. If he took off, there's no way I could hang onto the leash. So he's a good one for inside pictures." She led Butch onto the black fabric, which she had tucked behind a whiteboard, and let roll across a portion of the floor. The massive dog sniffed the drape with interest before agreeing to sit in the middle.

Robert adjusted the two accent lights to illuminate the scene to his satisfaction, then stood in front of the dog. "Will he be ok if you take off the leash?"

She arched a brow. "If he really wanted to run off, you think the leash would help?"

They both laughed and Heather unclipped Butch, telling him to stay as she joined Robert's side. She waited until the photographer was ready, then placed her hand in her pocket, where her secret weapon was. Holding her breath, she gave two quick squeezes of a squeaky toy. Butch cocked his head and froze, staring straight at them, and Robert depressed the shutter, clicking off a long series of shots.

A big grin cracked Heather's face. "That was perfect!"

"Yep. That should be all I need. Keep doing that and we should get through this quickly. You want to grab the next victim?"

They both broke into laughter as she returned to Butch. Minutes later, she was back with Peanut, a small dog of indeterminate heritage, and the process was repeated. As he photographed more dogs, the scent of the black fabric became more enticing, and her squeaky toy was accordingly less effective. A black Lab proved particularly difficult to distract, but Robert finally got several shots with Heather doing jumping jacks behind him, squeaking her toy madly.

He dropped the camera, so it hung from his neck. "Maybe we should try outdoors now."

Her breathing calmed. "While we're in here, let's photograph some cats. That way, we don't have to come back."

"Good idea." He pointed to a milk crate in the corner. "I'll set that under the drape, and you can place them on it."

Heather entered the Cat Shack, evaluating her prospects, and finally chose an older tortoise-shell calico. Snickers was calm and affectionate—the perfect candidate for adoption. She scooped the cat into her arms and carried her into their makeshift studio, enjoying the cat's soft purring. Then she frowned. "I don't know if a squeaky toy will be effective with her. Most of the dogs knew the command *stay*, but that won't exactly work now."

Robert bit his bottom lip before shrugging. "Just set her on the milk crate and I'll work fast."

But as soon as Heather set Snickers on the black cover, the cat smelled the canine scent permeating the fabric. Screeching, she bolted across the room with her tail puffed out and sat in the corner, staring crossly at Heather as she lifted a front paw to wash her face. "Oh, no! Cats hate the smell of dogs. I never even thought about that."

Robert was bent over in quiet laughter. "Yeah, neither did I. This won't work—I have another black backdrop, but it's at my house. Maybe we should just photograph the dogs this time. I can come back later this week to take pictures of the cats."

Heather returned his smile, happy to hear he wanted to return. "Lessons learned, I guess. Do you need the lights outside?"

"No. Can't improve on natural light."

Snickers was only too eager to escape the studio and return to her familiar enclosure, so Heather's next stop was Lucky's kennel. He had become her favorite. She clipped a leash to the black and brown dog, who danced around her, thrilled at the prospect of going outside.

"Looks like you two know each other," Robert said as they entered the bright sunshine.

"Lucky was the first dog I met here, and I've got a soft spot for him."

"Then he's aptly named," Robert said with that dazzling smile, and she couldn't help but laugh.

He evaluated the area, then pointed to the grassy meadow in front of several shade trees. "Why don't you take him over there? The trees will make a great background."

"Sure. You want me to stop right in front of the trees?"

"No. About halfway—I'll tell you when. That way I can blur the trees, and the dogs will stand out more."

This time, Robert needed to keep the squeaky toy under one foot because Heather couldn't unleash the dogs. Lucky was a well-behaved subject, and they quickly got their shots. Next, she trotted back with Duke, the energetic Border Collie. She and Robert worked out a system of posing the dogs and photographing them before they became too distracted. Within an hour, they had worked through eight more.

With a little time left before Heather needed to leave for Half Moon Bay, they returned to the inside studio, where Robert photographed three guinea pigs and four iguanas who didn't mind the doggy smell. The final iguana, Igor, was a massive specimen who spread out on the black cloth like a king on his throne, staring imperiously at Robert. The photographer was grinning hugely. "Ok, got it. He's the last one?"

Heather clipped a leash to the iguana's collar. "Yep. We're done. Come on, Igor."

Robert burst into laughter when the iguana obediently waddled at Heather's side as she moved toward the door. "I was too shocked to react when you walked in with him, but that's the funniest damn thing I've ever seen."

Grinning, she looked over her shoulder at him. "He's very leash trained and loves going for walks on the warm sidewalk behind the shelter. I'll be right back."

When she returned, Robert already had the two lights broken down and was rolling up the black tarp. "I'll remember to bring both backdrops next time."

She gave him a small smile. "I'm glad there will be a next time."

"This was a blast! I can't wait to do it again."

She looked at her watch reluctantly. "I'd better get going.

You'll email me a link to the files? I can take care of uploading them to the website and Facebook page."

"I'll have the best images ready in a couple of days. I'll let you know."

She moved toward the door, hesitant to leave. "Thanks again. See you soon."

His arresting light brown eyes held hers. "Count on it, Heather."

Chapter Ten

ROBERT SAT in his home office, a faint smile on his face as he scraped his hand over the stubble on his head and made a mental note to shave it in the morning. He opened his imaging software to work on the photos he'd taken at the shelter. There were plenty to choose from. He brought up the first picture, which was of the giant Mastiff-cross Duke, and laughed out loud. The lighting was beautiful, the tan dog vivid against the black backdrop. Duke stared alertly forward, his head cocked. Robert tabbed through the next several images, then transferred the winner to a separate folder.

A few pictures needed retouching, where the illumination wasn't quite right, but he had taken some great shots. His smile widened when he opened the outdoor photos, pleased with the aperture and focal length settings he'd chosen. The first picture was of the brown and black dog Heather liked so much. Sunlight reflected off his short coat and the gauzy backdrop of trees only made him stand out more.

Working quickly, it took Robert less than two hours to sort through the images, adding his watermark to the lower right corner of each. Shaking his head and grinning, he ended with

Igor, staring magnificently into the camera with his green, yellow, and orange colors almost fluorescent.

After transferring the best image, Robert went back to the outdoor shots. He had taken several wide-angle pictures, intending to crop them so just the dog was visible, since Heather was in quite a few. He tabbed through several images before he stopped, transfixed. She was holding the leash and trying to stay out of the frame. In most of the photos, she was fully focused on the dog. But in this one, she stared into the distance with a wistful expression.

Robert duplicated it and cropped the dog out, isolating Heather in the frame. He kept enlarging it until the photo showed her from the shoulders up, highlighted against the soft trees. She hadn't worn makeup and her hair was tied back in a ponytail, but she was one of the most attractive women he'd ever seen. He added the photo to his image folder so it would sync with his phone.

That one was a keeper.

Bringing himself back to his task, Robert typed out an email to Heather and provided a link where she could access and download the files. Then he hesitated. He wanted to see her again—hell, he wanted to ask her out.

"Be a man. Ask her on a date in person." Alex and Hope had returned, and Jack was taking a couple of days off, so Robert would be working at Half Moon Bay for the next two days.

He retrieved a bottle of soda from the fridge and sat on his front porch to enjoy the twinkling lights of Frederiksted. Though he had no desire to adopt a pet, he hoped the photos would help. Donna had certainly been grateful, and he'd be interested in continuing the project even without Heather's presence. But with her there, the possibilities were endless.

THE NEXT MORNING was sunny with a soft breeze, and Robert went around *Surface Interval* after the second dive, handing out slices of Hope's banana bread.

"Hey!" Tommy called down from the wheelhouse as he snugged the dive boat next to the pier. "Save some of that for me."

As Robert jumped off the boat to tie them to the dock, Alex looked up and laughed. "I already gave you yours."

The captain straightened, trying to look prim. "It wasn't enough. I've had to survive on Gerold's treats while you guys were gone."

"Ok, I'll pass it on and try to get you more tomorrow."

Robert jumped back aboard, grinning at Tommy. "Besides, I thought you were tryin' to lose weight?"

"I am! But the idea is to do it slowly, so it doesn't come back. Don't you know anythin'?"

Laughter rang out. "Well, we don't want you to waste away, Tommy," a woman called up.

"See? She gets it." The guests filed off the boat to rest and eat lunch before returning for the afternoon trip, leaving the three men alone.

"Maybe I'll tell Gerold you don't like his cooking anymore," Alex told Tommy with a gleam in his eye.

"Hey now, don't you be threatenin' me. You're supposed to be all rested and relaxed." In fact, Alex had been in an incredibly good mood all morning. He had already been tan, but the results of his trip were clear in his easy smile and relaxed frame.

"Have you even taken a vacation since you moved here?" Robert asked.

"No. I hardly took a day off until Hope arrived. But she didn't need to twist my arm too hard. We had a great time."

Robert had known Alex for a number of years, but the two hadn't become close until Half Moon Bay's boat-sinking disaster, when Robert had helped out after Alex was injured. The tall man had experienced some dark times, and Robert was pleased he'd found happiness at last.

"I'm glad to hear you're not complaining about being bored," Hope's voice came from behind and all three men turned as she stepped aboard, wearing the same relaxed smile as her husband.

Alex elbowed Robert out of the way and bent Hope over backwards in his arms, kissing her soundly. "Definitely no complaints here."

Smiling, Robert rubbed his arm. "Speak for yourself. I think you broke my arm."

A strong pink flush spread across Hope's face as Alex set her back on her feet. "Sorry, Robert. He can be rather single-minded."

"How is it bein' back in the salt mine?" Tommy asked.

Hope sighed with a cheerful smile. "It's good to be back. We had a wonderful time, but there's nothing like home, and I missed the activity."

Alex smirked. "That's only because *you* didn't have to work during the trip."

"What do you mean?" Robert asked.

"A resort we dove at ran into some staffing problems," Hope said. "Alex filled in and led dives for a couple of days."

Tommy grinned. "Not exactly what you were plannin' on your honeymoon, but I imagine you made it work."

"In some ways, it's easier for me to lead dives instead of watch someone else do it."

"Yeah," Robert said and laughed. "That doesn't surprise me."

Alex just shrugged.

"You guys will all have to check out the lobby," Hope said. "We made a purchase on our trip."

"Oh, did it get delivered?" Alex asked.

Their eyes held as Hope slid an arm around his waist. "This morning. Now I have a permanent souvenir of how lucky I am."

"That sounds mysterious," Tommy said. "But I'm very grateful I didn't have to install, wire, or hang whatever it is."

"Nope. No assembly required. Tommy hung the new pictures in the pool bar," Hope said to Robert. "Have you seen them yet?"

He shook his head. "I'll head up there now. I'm curious to see which two you chose."

Hope patted Alex's chest. "Let's go to the house for lunch." She gave him a rather smoldering stare, and his only reply was an easy smile.

The foursome strolled up the pier, with the Monroes splitting off as they headed toward their house at the end of the beach. Robert turned to Tommy. "I'll join you in the kitchen in a few minutes. I'm gonna head to the bar to check out those photos."

"Photos. Sure. See you soon."

Robert ignored Tommy's laugh as he headed toward the bar, the powdery sand shifting under his bare feet.

***

Heather turned off the blender and poured two glasses of Half Moon Dream—with cloves, of course. After adding the banana-dolphin garnish, she pushed them to the woman on the other side of the counter. Over the guest's shoulder, she spotted Robert walking toward the bar. He wore a royal-blue Half Moon Bay rash guard with *Staff* printed on one sleeve and black board shorts. Her breath caught as they made eye contact, and she poured him a large glass of ice water.

He accepted it with a grateful nod and drank half of it in

one shot. Then his attention moved to the two new glass photos hanging on the wall. "Hope told me the new prints were up. I was curious which ones she picked." On the left was a closeup shot he'd taken of Clark. Just his arm was visible, slicing a pineapple, with the beach and ocean beyond. The other print was of a selection of tropical fruits surrounding glasses of Half Moon Hope and Dream, beads of water condensation sparkling on the hurricane glasses.

Heather wiped the counter and shot him a smile. "They're really nice. But after seeing your work firsthand, I'm not surprised."

He leaned forward, crossing his arms on the wooden bar. "So, have you examined the pictures yet?"

Her smile turned into a laugh. "The past couple of days, I've spent hours going through them! They turned out incredible. This morning I finished uploading them to the shelter's website and their Facebook page. Now we sit and wait."

"I put some on my website and my Galendo page. Not sure my fans are lookin' for pets, but it couldn't hurt."

She smiled at his Galendo reference, but stayed quiet. This was not the time to discuss that subject.

"Do you get attached to the animals?" Robert asked. "So it's hard when they get adopted?"

Her smile faded somewhat. "None have been adopted since I've been there, so the answer is no. I'd be thrilled if they found new homes, honestly."

"Not a single one has caught your eye?"

She stilled, staring back at him. "Oh, yes. One in particular. A very charming character—he's hard to resist. But I'm not planning on taking him home just yet. Not sure how he feels about the whole thing."

A corner of Robert's mouth turned up. "I have a very hard time believin' he wouldn't love to follow you home."

Heather returned his sly smile, wiping the counter again. "We'll see. We're still in the *getting to know you* phase, so I'm not sure where things will go."

"There's only one way to solve that, you know."

"Oh? And what might that be?"

"The two of you need to spend more time together. Alone."

She stopped, tapping her fingers on the bar. "You're right. That would clarify the situation."

"Did you have a good time when we went divin'?"

Heather blinked, her face going blank at his change in subject. "I had a great time, especially after being out of the water for so long. I've never been diving in such warm water before. And it was so clear!"

"It just so happens I'm a pretty decent divemaster, you know. There's an incredible wall on the north side of the island, at Cane Bay. If you're lookin' for some more practice, I can help you out."

She leaned close over her crossed arms, matching his posture. "Robert Davis, are you asking me out?"

"Depends."

"On what?"

"Whether you say yes."

She straightened again. "Oh, now that complicates things. All this pressure on me to say the right thing."

"Then say the right thing."

His brown eyes held hers, making her heart pound. "You'd like that, wouldn't you?"

"You have no idea."

She leaned back down, staring at him with a small smile. "In that case... yes."

Robert burst into laughter and laid his head on the counter. "Damn, woman. You sure made me work for that!"

Grinning, she resumed her cleaning. "Don't want you thinking I'm easy."

His smile faded. "That's the last thing I think. When's your next day off?"

She sighed. "Not for another five days."

"Well then, we'll have plenty of time to look forward to it."

After he left to get lunch, Heather watched his retreating form, excitement tickling down her spine. Robert couldn't be more different from Grant. Which was the best comfort possible for her sore, bruised heart.

Chapter Eleven

HEATHER DROVE down the shady access lane to Half Moon Bay Resort, her attention caught by workers cutting a path through the thick brush to her left. They were working on a track parallel to the road, clearing from the resort toward the highway. She tried to decipher the project—the track was difficult to make out. *A hiking trail? Maybe they're trying to keep it natural?*

Making a mental note to ask Hope about it, she parked in the sand lot next to the other employees and headed toward the lobby. She liked to start her shift by walking past the dolphin sculpture Hope and Alex had bought on their honeymoon. A stunning glass figure seven feet tall, the dolphin was placed in the middle of the large room so it could be admired from all sides.

As someone who appreciated art, Heather had been captivated by the sculpture. The artist had captured the dolphin leaping upright out of a frothy wave. The transition from gray back to white belly was seamless and its sapphire eyes glittered. She could understand why the couple had been drawn to it.

Continuing toward the pool bar, she easily tuned out the

noise. The resort's atmosphere differed completely from when she'd started working there. Three in-progress bungalows were a busy hive of activity at the margin where beach met jungle. Palm trees were spaced evenly between the new rooms before they continued northward in a line up the beach. The new accommodations were also cleverly placed to take advantage of the ocean view visible between the beach bungalows in front.

Further in the distance was the other major project. A second construction crew was busy building the large rectangular structure Sara had mentioned as the new spa. Heather entered the quiet, deserted bar and went behind the counter, enjoying the contrast to the busy construction zones. She glanced toward the pier, but the dive boat hadn't returned yet, and Robert wasn't working, anyway. Several days remained before their date, and she was getting more eager. She liked Robert's unconventional approach. Diving was more casual and less pressure-filled than dinner and a movie.

Usually, one of the first tasks of her shift was carrying a case of plastic water bottles to the dive shop to fill the refrigerator there. Heather studied the bar, but the usual case of water wasn't there, so she checked the ice-filled metal chest instead. She was bent over, scrounging between Coke cans, when a loud thump sounded from the counter, and she looked up.

Hope stood on the other side of the counter, having just deposited a large cardboard box on the wooden surface. "Hi Heather, how's it going?"

"Good. I was about to head to the kitchen to get a case of water for the dive shop."

Hope tapped the cardboard box. "Don't bother." Opening the flaps, she removed a blue stainless-steel Half Moon Bay Resort water bottle. "Alex is on an absolute rampage about eliminating single-use plastic in the resort, and I'm in full agreement too. These just came yesterday, and he handed several out to divers this morning. Each diver will get one to use throughout their trip, and we're providing them in the bungalows as a free souvenir. But I'd like to keep a supply available for sale in case guests want to buy more."

She pointed to a five-gallon water bottle set up on a cooler dispenser. "They installed that this morning. There's another one in the dive shop and the lobby."

"Good idea. We already use bamboo straws, and the pool glasses are all reusable." She helped Hope to unpack the box, finding silver, pink, and green bottles, as well as the blue. "I'll line them up on the bar and make a display for the counter."

Hope gave her a sunny smile. "Excellent! The resort is moving into its next phase, and this will help with our environmental focus."

Heather laughed as she lined the bottles up, alternating the colors. "It certainly is moving into the next phase. The new bungalows look like they're coming right along."

"They are. The exteriors are finished, and the crews are working inside. The spa will take longer because it's a much bigger project."

"I was worried the guests would be cranky at having their vacation disturbed, but I haven't had a single complaint. Though I guess they knew about it before they arrived."

"I'm glad to hear that," Hope said. "We send several emails informing the guests before they get here. Not to mention I'm giving everyone a thirty percent discount, so they *should* be happy! But we make sure the construction only happens between nine and five."

"What's the path they're clearing? Hiking trails?"

Hope twitched a corner of her mouth. "Sort of. It's the trail to Half Moon Grotto. On the other side of the highway, there's a really beautiful spring-fed pool. It's got a sandy beach and a gigantic cave to explore. We're keeping the path non-intrusive because we want to make the Grotto available only to resort guests. There's a fence around it and we'll give guests access to a key to unlock the gate."

"Wow. That sounds like a pretty major project."

Hope's eyes took on a faraway cast. "It has been. Very major." Then she snapped herself back to the conversation. "You'll have to check it out sometime. It's worth the trek."

After Hope returned to her office, Heather continued opening the bar, her mind full of visions of Half Moon Grotto. It sounded romantic and private, perfect for two people who wanted to learn more about each other. Once again, she turned her eyes toward the pier...

THE NEXT MORNING, Heather considered crossing her fingers as she opened the front door of Pet Paradise, but that might be overkill. She hadn't been to the shelter since she uploaded Robert's photos, but she had been thrilled with the response to the Facebook post, which had garnered a boatload of comments and positive reactions.

Donna sat behind the desk and squealed upon seeing Heather. She rushed around and enfolded the bartender in a bear hug.

"What brought that on?" Heather asked once she could breathe again.

"I'm just so happy! I can't believe it."

"Is this about the photographs?"

"Oh, Heather! The phone has been ringing off the hook. We've had four adoptions, and five more are in the works. The first was a young man who adopted Duke. He wanted a dog to run with, and Duke was perfect for him! A family came and adopted Peanut, and a man absolutely fell in love with Igor."

Heather laughed, light spreading through her as she recalled Cindy's promise to mention the shelter to her running group. "That's fantastic! What about Lucky?"

"Not yet, but there's a family that's interested in him. Their kids are older, so it might work out."

"Oh, I hope so."

"A lady is coming by this afternoon to adopt a kitten. Do you think Robert can come back to photograph the cats?"

"Definitely. He's just been really busy lately. We'll work out a time to return when I see him again." She grabbed a leash and headed to the Dog House.

As usual, Lucky was happy to see her and they hurried to the dog park, where he bounded after the tennis ball. He dropped it at her feet, tail wagging. "I'm sure you'll find a home. With Robert helping, neither of us can lose."

Late the next afternoon, Robert strolled down the rickety floating dock of the local marina just south of Frederiksted. Two dozen fishing boats were lined up in their slips, and he waved to three fishermen as he passed. Near the end, *Althea* was tied up with her twin *Margaret* next to her, as usual. Both were forty-foot fishing trawlers, clean and well cared for, though showing their age. Margaret was Althea's middle name, of course. Eddie was bent over the engine block of *Margaret,* so Robert didn't bother him, instead boarding *Althea,* where his father was sitting at the console. "Afternoon, Pop."

Bennet looked up from his logbook. "Hi there, son. What brings you by?"

"I was in the neighborhood buyin' a new camera case and wanted to drop by."

"Stayin' busy?"

Robert smiled slightly. His father was baffled that he could make ends meet being a photographer. "Very. I had a fun project last week. Went to Pet Paradise and photographed the animals there."

"You took pictures of *pets*?"

"Yeah, it helps them get adopted. It worked too." Heather had called him the previous evening, exclaiming about the flush of adoptions. He was happy for the pets, but even happier she had called him. He was counting down the days until their date.

Bennett's lined brow became even more creased. "How much does that pay?"

"Nothin'. That's not the point."

"It's always the point." With a smirk, he tossed the log onto the console and stood. "I need to fold the nets. Will you give me a hand?"

"Sure." Robert picked up the large fishing net and began folding it with practiced efficiency. Just because he didn't particularly enjoy fishing didn't mean he couldn't do it.

"I'm short a crewman next Wednesday and could use a hand if you're free."

In fact, he was free, but he was hoping to return to Pet Paradise with Heather to do a photo shoot of the cats. "Sorry. I'm goin' back to the shelter. Doin' that made me feel good. The lady who owns the place needs the help, and I like feelin' useful."

Bennett straightened. "You're useful here."

Robert smiled, trying to deflect the tension as he set the folded net on the deck. "Thanks. Maybe next time."

His father just grunted.

"Divemasterin' is a lot safer than fishin', you know. If the weather gets nasty, the dive charters all cancel."

"Can't argue that."

"Hey!" Eddie's voice called out behind him. "When did you show up?"

Robert turned. "A few minutes ago."

"Yeah. After the work is done, of course." Eddie wore a big smile to take the sting out of his words.

Bennett clapped Robert on the shoulder. "Go talk to your brother. I'm finished here and headin' home."

After they said goodbye to their father, Robert stepped aboard. "Problem with *Margaret*?"

Eddie barked a humorless laugh. "When isn't there a problem with her?" He nodded to a large cooler. "Help yourself to a soft drink."

Robert fished two out and tossed Eddie one before sitting on the closed cooler. "No beer? It's the end of the day."

"Beer in the work cooler? You kiddin'? I *enjoy* livin'!" Eddie, who had inherited their mother's darker skin as well as her large frame, wore a Davis Fishing baseball hat and a pair of yellow rubber bib pants. He smelled vaguely of fish.

"Pop wouldn't approve of it, for sure." Robert glanced around the boat with its forward covered wheelhouse. "Clarence still drivin' *Margaret*?"

"Yeah. I'm workin' on *Althea,* mostly. But Pop let me captain yesterday for one set."

"That's progress."

"I guess. Just have to be patient."

"Mother try to fix you up with anyone new lately?"

Eddie burst into laughter. "Her latest is Chantal, from church."

Robert drew his brows together. "Isn't she like twelve?"

"Nineteen."

"Jeez, Mom."

Eddie shook his head and took a long pull of his soft drink. "I think she's gettin' a little desperate. Good thing Chantal isn't any more interested than I am. I think our mother needs a distraction to get the heat off me. How are things with your California girl?"

"We're goin' divin' tomorrow, so I'll find out."

"At least you have that in common."

Robert bristled. "We have plenty in common."

Eddie's smile grew. "Yeah. Sure. Where's she from in California?"

He hesitated, realizing he had no idea. "Not sure."

"Do you know anythin' about this woman?"

"That's what dates are for, Eddie. I know I like her, all right?"

Eddie crumpled his empty can and tossed it in the trash bag before standing. "Fine, Romeo. I'll leave you to it. I need to get back to that engine."

As Robert returned along the bobbing dock, a smile rose as he anticipated the following day. He had an easy dive site all picked out, and the weather looked perfect. Heather might be from distant California, but he was eager to learn more about her. After all, how different could their backgrounds be?

Chapter Twelve

EVEN THOUGH SHE had been expecting it, Heather still jumped when the doorbell rang, her heart racing. When she opened the front door, Robert stood on her porch wearing a long-sleeved rash guard, board shorts, and a wide smile. "Mornin'!" He handed her a covered Tropical Bean cup. "I got you a vanilla latte. Seemed like a safe choice."

Laughing, she accepted it. "One of my favorites, actually. My friends used to give me a hard time for being vanilla."

His eyes took on a speculative gleam, but he only said, "Ready?"

"Absolutely." She grabbed her beach bag and closed the door after her. Robert opened the passenger door of a late-model white Jeep Compass. The leather interior was clean and upscale. "Nice car."

He laughed. "Don't be too impressed. I bought it from a rental fleet liquidation. Mostly because of the light colors. Dark shades are awful in a hot environment like this."

"I bought my Malibu from a rental company too, just after I moved here."

Robert drove through Frederiksted and followed the road east. "Ever heard of Cane Bay?"

"I've seen signs for it but have never been. Isn't there a beach?"

"Yeah. The area is pretty developed with restaurants and a few resorts and condos. Cane Bay Wall is just offshore, and one of the best dive sites on the island. Plus, you can dive it from shore."

"I'm looking forward to it."

"You ok with a wall dive? Some people don't like the sensation of a wall plummetin' below them."

"I've never done one before, but I think it should be ok. Does the wall go that deep?"

He grinned. "Only 37,000 feet."

A sense of vertigo made her stomach turn over. "Oh. Wow."

Laughing, Robert held a hand out. "Don't worry, it doesn't go that deep until further offshore. But there are parts of the dive site that still drop hundreds of feet. Since you're open water certified, we'll stay around sixty feet."

"You have my gratitude. Maybe we'll save the thirty-thousand-foot dive for next time."

"I'll see if I can find a submersible." He grinned as she shuddered. They drove along the north shore road, and Robert turned right onto an unnamed dirt track. "How come you didn't take the advanced class with Hope, Sara, and Zach?"

"It was right after I started at Half Moon Bay, and I had enough going on just learning the job. Maybe I'll take the class someday. Do employees get a discount?"

"I'm sure Alex would do it for free. If it involves divin', he'll help anyone who works there."

"You've never wanted to become an instructor?"

"Not really. I learned to dive when I was in my early teens and worked my way up. But I found my niche with divemaster."

"You got certified here on the island, I take it?"

He laughed as he pulled into a small dirt parking lot, then backed into a stall facing the beach. "I didn't get officially certified until much later. I got together with a couple of friends, and we borrowed some tanks. We taught ourselves to dive, along with some help from a buddy's older brother." He ran a hand over his shaved head, the smile lingering. "When I was twenty, I wanted to find a job leadin' dives and talked to a guy who owned a shop. He basically read me the riot act. So I got certified for real, then continued all the way up to divemaster."

Heather was laughing too. "Oh good! I feel better knowing I'm with a professional."

"I can show you my license if you want."

"That won't be necessary." She smiled, already completely comfortable with him. "Sounds like you've been doing this for a while."

He opened the driver's door. "I have. I love bein' a photographer, but I can't see myself leavin' this behind. Come on. I'll show you the site."

Heather studied the quiet space as she exited the car. It was mostly scrub brush and spindly trees mixed with sand. "I thought you said this area was built up."

"This is the local end, which is usually pretty deserted, so I like to dive here. After we've finished divin', maybe we could get lunch at a restaurant down the beach a bit? It's real casual."

"That sounds great." She liked that he'd given a lot of thought to their date but kept the situation low-pressure. He also wasn't coming on to her full steam, but letting things develop naturally.

They emerged onto a white sandy beach with a light breeze blowing in their faces. Small waves tumbled onto the shore. Robert pointed to the aquamarine water. "We'll enter to the left and surface swim out a couple hundred yards. At that point, we'll be on top of the wall and descend. Anything in particular you'd like to see?"

Heather thought of all kinds of replies to that, but didn't blurt any of them out. *First date! Remember that.* The glint in his eyes told her his words had been deliberate, but she was determined not to get too carried away. Instead, she answered his question honestly. "I've never seen a shark. I think that would be pretty cool."

"Well, I can't promise a shark. They aren't nearly as common as people think, but we've got a chance to see one because of the deep water off the wall. Keep your eyes peeled."

They returned to his car, and he opened the rear hatch to reveal two tanks with dive equipment stacked on top, along with a wetsuit. Heather hadn't asked for any details about the logistics involved with a dive date, content to let Robert surprise her. "Oh good. You brought me a wetsuit. Is this your gear?"

"No, it's Half Moon Bay's. I told Alex I was divin' with a friend. Didn't think they needed to know our business."

With a grin, he handed her a BCD and regulator and set her tank on the sand while he assembled his own kit. She was pleased he assumed she was competent to put hers together, which she quickly did. Turning to her wetsuit, she pulled off her T-shirt and board shorts. Her wardrobe choice had been the result of some thought. Her only swimsuits were two-piece, but there was a definite difference among them. A string bikini on a first date would send an entirely different message than what she wanted, so she'd picked out a sporty yellow and black one.

As she pulled on her wetsuit, she turned to Robert. "No wetsuit for you today?"

"Nah. For only one dive and in warm summer water, I prefer to go without."

He helped her into her tank, and they walked to the shore, where Robert gripped her upper arm to steady her as they entered the ocean. The waves presented little barrier, but Heather wasn't about to turn down his help. All it would take was one wave at the wrong moment to result in a face plant, with sixty pounds on her back preventing her from getting up again. Not a good image for a first date. The neoprene fabric of her wetsuit was thin enough that she could feel him tracing his fingers down her arm before letting go. She turned to him, and they shared a smile, a bolt of electricity running through her.

After donning their fins, they flipped onto their backs and kicked at a leisurely pace until Robert stopped to peer into the water below. "This is good. Ready to descend?"

"You know where we are just by looking from the surface?"

"Oh yeah. I've dived this hundreds of times."

With that reassuring statement, Heather nodded and gave him a grateful smile, eager to get started.

But Robert wasn't quite done with the briefing. "I'll keep an eye on our depth, but make sure you pay close attention. In clear water like this, it's very easy to lose track of your depth on a sheer wall."

"I'll try to stay above a thousand feet."

He laughed at that and placed his regulator in his mouth. After getting her confirmatory ok signal, he gave her the thumbs-down to begin their dive. The bottom was at twenty-five feet and Robert led them down a narrow sand shoot. It descended at a steep slope, and Robert leveled off at sixty feet. There was no current, and Heather relaxed, enjoying the weightless environment. The sandy chute soon ended, giving way to a coral-encrusted reef that continued at the same slope.

Heather was reassured at being able to see the coral directly below. This wasn't as sheer as Robert had made it sound. The reef was a vivid mixture of colors. She'd never seen anything like it. Bright green whip corals protruded into the water, corkscrewing in ever-decreasing circles as their length increased.

Robert stopped and inspected one closely, finally beckoning to Heather, who grasped his arm to steady herself. He held his index finger and thumb an inch apart and pointed to the coral. At first, she couldn't see the tiny fish. It was nearly translucent, and as Robert waved his finger at it, it hopped an inch further down the whip coral, making Heather laugh.

They continued along the wall. Lacy white sea fans competed for space with brain coral and lavender tube sponges, and tropical fish swam all around and through them, countless varieties. Heather was so engrossed in the lush reef she hadn't checked the slope for quite some time.

The wall was now a sheer vertical cliff, albeit a cliff wild with life. She stared downward, and the wall disappeared into the hazy depths with no bottom visible. Her queasy stomach flop came back at the sight, and she quickly glanced at her dive computer, exhaling a relieved sigh after verifying they were only at fifty feet. Robert gestured with an ok signal, and she returned it, but gave one final long look below, wondering how deep it went.

Better not drop anything...

They continued, slowly finning along the lush, intricate wall. She had no idea so many colors and types of coral existed. Her previous experiences had been in California, a very different environment, with tall green kelp beds and much fewer fish.

Robert squinted below, studying something. Then he turned to her, his eyes round, and whipped his outstretched hand vertically to his forehead. He tapped the index-finger side of his hand several times against his brow, alight with excitement. Divers had an incredible amount of hand signals for communicating underwater, and even non-divers knew the sign for shark.

Heather followed his pointing finger to a six-foot gray shark swimming casually by ten feet below them. Two more swam just behind. She couldn't help the shout that escaped at seeing her first shark, never mind a second and third. But they ignored the two divers and continued swimming away. On impulse, she grabbed Robert's hand and squeezed. He tightened back, but held on as he turned to lead again, brushing his thumb over the back of her hand. A warmth radiated through her chest, sheer happiness at what she was doing and who she was with.

After a few minutes, Robert let go to rise several feet above her. *Why is he ascending?* Confused, Heather looked at her dive computer and was startled that she was at nearly seventy feet. Now understanding his warning about the depth being deceptive, she added air into her BCD and slowly drifted back to Robert's side, precisely at sixty feet.

At the thirty-minute mark, Robert turned them around, and they angled up to thirty feet, now heading in the opposite direction. They drifted together side by side. Time didn't exist—she was totally absorbed in her surroundings. Robert tapped her shoulder and led her up the wall and into the shallows at some seemingly random point. They were now on a broad sandy flat with coral formations scattered about and grass swaying in the gentle surge. The isolated coral heads were a hotspot for juvenile fish, who rushed into crevices anytime danger threatened.

As they were passing one large, oval-shaped formation, Robert gave an excited shout through his regulator and grabbed Heather's hand again, pulling her toward the big outcropping. She quickly saw what had drawn his attention. Before them was a huge black turtle with long parallel ridges running down its shell. It lay mostly on the sand, using its front flippers to brace itself as it ate a purple sponge.

Keeping hold of Heather's hand, Robert slowly approached. She hardly dared to breathe as they crept ever closer to the massive turtle. It bit off a large section of sponge, chewing it calmly as it swiveled its head to stare at them. After swallowing, it turned back to its lunch, tearing off another bite.

They were only a couple of feet away, and the sound of the turtle biting into the sponge was clearly audible. Heather was stunned, her heart pounding at the thrill of being so close to a wild creature, with her hand encircled within Robert's.

He let go to point at his palm, asking how much air she had. She glanced at her computer, and her stomach sank at what she reported back to him—only six hundred psi left. With a sad smile, he indicated for them to start their three-minute safety stop. They continued slowly swimming toward shore along a finger of coral as they ascended to fifteen feet. Heather peered into crevices and watched sunbeams shimmer in the water as they closed in on the shore.

When their three minutes were up, Robert flashed her a thumbs-up to surface. Regret twisted her heart for a moment. The dive had been incredible, and she was sad it was over. But elation quickly overcame any sadness she was feeling.

The dive might be finished, but our date isn't...

Chapter Thirteen

ELATION ROSE through Heather's body as she removed her regulator and tugged her mask down around her neck. "Oh, that was incredible! I loved it. What kind of turtle was that?"

Robert grinned as they walked toward the shore. "Leatherback! We have lots of green and hawksbill turtles here, but leatherbacks are much less common. You got your sharks too."

"Three of them!" She broke into stunned laughter.

After getting directions to the restroom, she retrieved her beach bag and was pleased to find a shower available. Even with no shampoo, she was able to wash the salt out of her hair and braid it before redressing with clean undergarments she'd thought to bring. When she returned to the car, Robert had already changed into a polo shirt and black cargo shorts.

"How does lunch sound?" he asked.

"Fantastic. I'm starving."

The sun was high overhead, but a steady breeze tempered its heat. As they walked down the beach to the restaurant, Robert grasped her hand again. Confidently, he laced his fingers through hers as if it was the most natural thing in the world.

Heather ducked her head and smiled, amazed how at ease and alive she felt with him. A new relationship should be the last item on her agenda, yet here she was.

They approached Cane Bay Beach Hut, which was much more than a hut. An expansive open-air restaurant spread out before them, raised on blocks for a superb view of the north shore. At the end of a flagstone path, a menu was locked inside a glass case. It was only 11:30, and the path was deserted.

"You can check out their menu," Robert said. "See if it works for you."

Heather perused multiple pages of offerings, finding it difficult to imagine anyone not being satisfied. "This looks great. What do you want?"

When she turned, he stood completely still, staring right at her. He held her with his eyes. "More than anything, I want to kiss you. Right now."

She gave him a small smile. "You're not supposed to kiss the girl until the end of the date."

"I'm impatient. And I really like you."

"I'm glad to hear that, because I feel the same way."

Her breath stilled in her lungs as Robert moved toward her. He pressed his hand softly against the side of her face and touched his lips to hers. They were full and warm. He kissed her with a gentleness that made her step closer, and she wondered if he would deepen the kiss. He didn't, and she was surprised at her disappointment.

Finally, he pulled away and nodded. "Now that we've got that out of the way, we can enjoy lunch without all the jitters."

She laughed out loud. "That's one benefit I never thought of."

He grinned back. "I would have been a mess. Probably wouldn't be able to eat a thing, and I'm famished."

"Well, let's get to it. Shall we?"

Taking his hand, Heather trotted up the stairs. As the hostess led them to their table, Robert traced his fingers up and down her back, sending a quiver through her. They passed a tourist couple seated side-by-side in a booth. When they looked up, Heather smiled at them, an automatic habit from working the bar for so long. She was met with two frosty, stone-faced expressions. Heather nearly stumbled at the hostile reaction.

What the hell is their problem?

As they continued across the floor, Heather realized exactly what the couple's issue had been—her back was still warm from Robert's soft touch. They sat at a table next to the beach, and Heather murmured quietly, "I can't believe how those two people looked at us. Guess they don't realize it's the twenty-first century."

He waved a hand absently, frowning. "Don't let it get to you. It comes with the territory, even here. You can't let a couple of jerks ruin a wonderful day."

That brought a smile to her face, though she was still flustered. She breathed out a big lungful of air. "You are absolutely right. And this morning has been fantastic."

They spent the first half of lunch discussing the dive, and she learned the tiny fish on the spiral of green coral was called a whip-coral goby. "How deep have you gone there?"

Robert shrugged. "There's a cool purple stone fish that lives at about 110 feet. They hardly ever move, so that fish is worth goin' down there for. But most of the light is between thirty and seventy feet. That's the sweet spot."

"Thank you. That was the best dive I've ever been on."

"I enjoyed it too." He took a sip of his Leatherback. "So, what brings a California girl to the Caribbean?"

Heather thought for a moment. She certainly wasn't going to tell the whole sordid story on a first date, but she refused to be less than honest, either. "I'm trying to become my own person, succeeding—or failing—on my own."

"Failing? Looks like you're doin' great to me."

A titter of laughter escaped. "You didn't know me before I worked at Half Moon Bay." She told him the story of how she got fired from Serenity. "And I *was* late a couple of times. Both were because of circumstances beyond my control, but I would've had a difficult time fighting the termination. And life's too short for that."

"Doesn't make it right, though."

"No, that's true."

"So you came here to escape your family?"

"Escape? No. I love my parents very much, and I'm incredibly grateful to them. But I want to be my own woman. I love that no one here knows who I am."

He cocked his head. "Who you are?"

She gave a brave smile. *Here we go.* "My parents are very wealthy. Not flying-first-class affluent. I mean a-fleet-of-private-jets wealthy." She paused, but his only reaction was two raised brows. "The other day, when we were talking about the photos, you mentioned Galendo. My dad created that, and I've been living in a bubble my whole life because of it. I have no interest in software engineering or computer science. I know this sounds trite and spoiled. But for the first time in my life, I introduce myself and get no reaction from the Galen name. People like me based on my own merits. Or lack of them," she added with a smile.

"I don't think that sounds trite or spoiled. I'm tryin' to create my own life too, so I understand what you're sayin'."

She dropped her shoulders and relaxed, trying not to make it obvious. She had been worried Robert would be intimidated by her history. But so far, he was handling it fine.

"And mixing drinks is such a grand passion that you moved several thousand miles to do it?"

Heather burst into laughter, leaning forward. "No, it's a way to earn money. Same as most people's jobs. I really enjoy it, and the people, but it's not my passion."

He stared steadily at her. "And what is your passion?"

She met his gaze. "Art."

This time, he couldn't hide his surprise as his face went blank. "Art? Really? You mentioned likin' art at Jack and Sara's, but said you didn't have any talent."

"You're a good listener."

"When someone is worth listenin' to, yes."

"In college, I majored in art history, and I tended bar all the way through. When I left San Francisco, I knew I could work as a bartender here. And you remember correctly. I have a great eye for art, and I know a lot about it, but don't have any personal talent. Eventually, my dream is to manage a gallery here on St. Croix. Maybe own one someday, but I need more experience first." She was skating on very thin ice here, getting perilously close to the subject she wasn't ready to discuss.

"There's no shortage of galleries on the island. I'm sure you'll get what you want."

"Thanks, I hope so. What about you? Have you always wanted to be a photographer?" He told her about Hope helping him turn a hobby into a business. "What do your parents do, anyway?"

"I'm from a pretty traditional Cruzan family. My father is a fisherman and my mother mostly stayed home with my brother and me. She worked some as a librarian. Pop owns two boats, and my brother Eddie is hopin' to take over the family business. I'm a lousy fisherman." He said this with a smile, but his eyes were tight.

"We're both trying to make our own ways in the world. I'd say we're getting off to a good start."

Their server had cleared the plates some time ago and now dropped off the bill. Robert snatched it away before Heather could move. "I'll get this. I'm kind of old-fashioned that way. This is a first date, after all."

Heather smiled at him. "Thank you. This has been the best first date I've ever been on."

He laughed. "You're way too easy to please, then."

"I mean it. After what I just told you, some men wouldn't want a second date. They'd be too intimidated. I hope that's not the case here."

"Then they're stupid. I respect what you're tryin' to do. And I think you just told me you want a second date."

She arched a brow at him. "You've forgotten already? I take back what I said about you being a good listener. We already have one—you agreed to take pictures of the cats."

"Oh ho! She sees my bet and raises me. I didn't realize my offer to photograph lonely pets in need of homes was subject to such strict conditions."

"Not so strict. All I ask is dinner after the photo shoot."

Robert grinned. "How's that goin' to work? You're always at the bar until late."

"Hmmm, that does present certain difficulties. But I didn't think you'd give up so easily."

"Who said I was givin' up?"

"I believe the floor is yours, Mr. Davis."

The server brought the finalized bill back, and Robert was quiet as he signed the slip. Then his face lit up. "Brunch! Right after the photo shoot. Ha! Top that."

She laughed, loving his warm smile. "I think we've come to an agreement. Brunch it is."

. . .

As he walked Heather to her front door, her nerves came back. Which was silly, considering they'd already kissed, and the date had been a smashing success. She climbed the stairs, digging into her purse to remove her keys, and turned. "I really had a great—"

Robert stopped her sentence with a kiss, devouring her lips as he wrapped both arms around her shoulders. This kiss was completely different from their first—wet and full of hunger. She met him, encircling his waist as she pushed against his rib cage. Opening his mouth, he brushed his tongue over hers, igniting every cell in her body. Even though she wanted more, Heather pulled back and pressed her palm against his chest as they both breathed hard. Her heart beat fast, from more than just desire. "First date, right? Let's take things slow."

He stepped back, concern flickering in his eyes. "Of course. I'm not lookin' for a one-night stand here, if that's what you're worried about."

She used the hand pressing against him to stroke up and down his chest, realizing she might have overreacted a bit. She couldn't help it. "No, I'm not worried about that at all. My... last relationship ended badly and I'm a little unsure of myself. I'm sorry."

He stroked a finger down her face. "Don't apologize. Mine didn't go so well either. We'll take this nice and easy. For both our sakes." He kissed her again, short and tender this time. "I can go back to Pet Paradise on Friday. Are you free that mornin'?"

"Yes. I'll see you then."

"Count on it." After a nod, he trotted down the stairs, then froze at the bottom. Turning around, he ran back up and cupped her face in both hands, kissing her deeply, his tongue softly probing. Before she was ready, he ended the kiss and stared into her eyes. "I had a really great time today. See you Friday morning."

Chapter Fourteen

ROBERT SPENT the following afternoon retouching the photos from that morning's shoot. The subject had been the six-month-old daughter of his very first clients. Robert had photographed the local couple's engagement, wedding, and their child's newborn pictures. The busy day had the added advantage of keeping his mind off Heather. Her delicious mouth, and that molten river of hair, though he still hadn't been able to really touch it. But also, what she'd told him about her family.

With a start, he realized he'd been daydreaming about her for several minutes and turned back to his computer. But fatigue was setting in fast. He was thinking about stopping for the day when Alex called.

"I just spent two hours with the regional scuba agency rep," Alex said. "And I desperately need a beer. You busy?"

Perfect! I could use a distraction. Even though he'd enjoyed the previous day tremendously, the implications of what Heather had told him lurked constantly in his mind. Alex would make a good sounding board. "I'm just finishin' up. Where do you want to go?"

"Let's meet at The Refinery. I can be there in thirty."

Robert found a parking space near the industrial-themed bar in Frederiksted. As he walked up, most of the patrons were sitting on the patio. Not wanting to be in a crowd, he opened the heavy front door and chose a quiet table in the corner. Black exposed ductwork complemented the red brick walls surrounding the booth he slid into.

As soon as he sat down, Alex walked in the door. His light hair was ruffled, like he'd raked a hand through it. His face was lined and tense as he held up two fingers to the bartender, who nodded, then he sat across from Robert.

"Rough meetin'?"

Alex briefly squeezed his eyes shut. "As part of the resort expansion, I'm getting the dive shop reclassified with the agency as a five-star facility. I did everything humanly possible to complete the process without an in-person meeting, but it was just impossible. So, I got to spend the afternoon with my *wonderful* friend Cody in Christiansted."

Robert raised a brow, surprised. "You're not goin' to be orderin' through Gordon anymore?" Alex had steadfastly supported Gordon at Emerald Isle Scuba for years, even after being shot in the shoulder after leaving his shop. Alex was nothing if not loyal.

Now the former SEAL gave Robert a rueful look. "I was informed Gordon's shop was no longer cost-effective and we have to order everything ourselves."

Robert grinned. It never ceased to amaze him how this formidable man, who had knocked a behemoth of a guy uncon-scious with just a few punches, became as docile as a purring cat whenever his wife suggested something. As long as he wasn't feeling stubborn, anyway. "Guess Gordon's no match for Hope, huh?"

"No, he's not. At least not when her mind is on business."

"I take it you had trouble changing the status of the dive operation?"

The server brought two draft beers, and Alex shot her a quick smile. "Bless you." After a long drink, he returned his attention to Robert. "No, that part went fine, once I finally figured out what he needed. The problem started after that. I met Cody, the rep, last year at an instructor's meeting. He made a big deal out of my military background, and I almost walked out before Mark from Ocean Surf Resort shut him up."

Robert didn't know where Alex was going with this, but he couldn't wait to find out.

"This afternoon I thought we were all done, and was getting ready to make my escape, when he dropped this absolute turd of an idea on me. He was very proud of himself." Alex leaned forward, both hands pressed against the tabletop. "Cody said, 'I've got this great idea I want to run by you. Why don't you work up a recreational scuba specialty course that would mimic SEAL training? There are plenty of men—and women—who think they're hotshots. This would give them a chance to strut their stuff.'" Alex took another long drink before slamming the bottle on the table. "Thanks for listening. I need to get this off my chest and I'm sure Hope is already sick of me ranting about getting rid of the plastic."

"Of course." Robert took his own drink while deciding how to respond. Alex obviously hated the idea, but Robert was curious as to why, exactly. "He's probably right that you'd get a lot of interest. I take it you're not in favor?"

Alex had been lifting his glass. Now he froze with it halfway to his mouth, eyeing Robert narrowly. "Are you kidding? It's a terrible idea!"

"Explain it to me, then. As someone without your experience."

Alex deflated, his face softening. "Two reasons, though I

could probably come up with a hundred more. First, recreational and military teaching are pretty much polar opposites. My job as a recreational instructor is to do everything possible to ensure the student succeeds. The job of a SEAL-candidate-class instructor is to make those guys give up. Everyone thinks the biggest and strongest guys are the ones who make it through. That's wrong." He tapped his index finger on the table, emphasizing his point. "It's the ones who won't quit. Who persist, and categorically *refuse* to give up. Despite every obstacle being thrown at them, day after day."

Alex spoke as if he were referring to friends, with no acknowledgement that *he* had been one of those men who had refused to surrender. He stopped for another drink before continuing in a less-impassioned voice. "I've taught both, so I should know. I did fill-in work as an instructor for BUD/S classes—that's SEAL candidates. It's what I thought I would do when I couldn't command active-duty troops anymore. But that's another conversation entirely."

He sighed. "My point is that the worst possible thing you could do to a recreational diver is tear down their confidence. Look, I'm a biologist too. You've seen what's happening to the ocean, and how reefs are degrading. The more people we can interest in restoring and maintaining these waters, the better."

Robert was fascinated. He had known Alex was a SEAL for quite some time, but it hadn't been until the wedding reception that he'd discovered Alex led the mission that had resulted in the deaths of half his platoon and nearly killed him. "You don't need to convince me, man. You said there were two reasons. What's the other one?"

Alex stiffened, his eyes becoming flinty. "It takes about two years to train a SEAL completely, so he's ready to go into combat with his Team. The selection class people are familiar with is just the first few weeks. It's a very long, very brutal road."

He paused, obviously searching for words. "I'm sure there are former SEALs out there who wouldn't mind doing this. That's fine—their experience was different from mine. But creating some vacation-SEAL-wannabe class would make a mockery of everything I believe in. Of what we fought—and died—for. Cody only had ears for what it would do for tourism, though."

"What did you say to him?"

Alex whipped his head up, and a slow smile crept across his face. His expression was far from pleasant, and Robert suppressed a shiver. "I told him if he really wanted me to do this, I'd make sure he was the first one in the class."

Robert covered his unease by breaking into laughter, which caused Alex to join in too. "I take it he didn't accept?"

Still laughing, Alex pressed one palm against his eye. "No. I pretty much scared the shit out of him, and he called the whole thing off. God, he pissed me off."

Robert finally got his laughter under control enough to ask, "You didn't explain any of that to the agency guy?"

Alex waved a hand absently, then got the server's attention for another round. "No, he isn't worth my time to explain it."

Robert drained the rest of his beer, touched at Alex's simple statement. Until recently, Alex had always deflected personal inquiries, and he had never opened up about his SEAL days like this. The server brought their new beers. "Feelin' better now?"

"Yeah, I do. Thanks." Alex held up his beer in a toast. "A fresh round deserves a subject change. Please."

"Fine by me."

Robert was taking a cold drink when Alex asked, "So how was your *dive* yesterday?"

The emphasis he placed on the word made Robert dart his eyes toward him. Alex had his hands clasped on the table and wore a wide grin, his anger apparently forgotten. There was nothing threatening about his almost-smug smile.

The divemaster set his bottle down with a long sigh. "Who told you?"

"Selena saw you two strolling hand-in-hand down the beach. She told Sara, who told everyone." That made total sense, and they both broke into laughter. "I wondered why you wanted to take two kits home. Hope gives me a hard time about being clueless about relationship signals, but I finally figured it out."

Robert fixed a bland look on his face. "Heather and I had a very nice dive."

"Nice? That doesn't sound promising."

"Since when are you so interested in my love life?"

"I've turned over a new leaf, remember? Besides, it's a lot more fun *not* being the object of attention." Alex's smile faded. "I'm serious, though. Your dive went well?"

Alex being open made Robert want to give too. *I wanted to talk to him, after all...* "Really well. We had a great time."

"See any sharks?"

Robert smiled, delighting in the memory. "Three! Heather had never seen one before. She was pretty psyched."

"It's always a good sign when they're not terrified."

As Robert stared at his bottle, his smile lingered. "The morning was... special. We really connected..."

"You didn't say it, but I'm hearing a big *but* there."

He gave Alex a measured look. "Do you know anythin' about her family?"

"Hope mentioned they're pretty wealthy. IT or something?"

"Way more than that. Her father is Tim Galen, as in the Galendo empire. I use that app *every day* to post photos, and I just went out with its creator's daughter. We're from totally different worlds, Alex."

"I thought she was distancing herself from them."

"She is. She's trying to make her own way, and not rely on what her parents created."

A tiny smile rose on Alex's face. "Sounds like someone else I know."

"We have a lot in common. Heather hasn't dived much, but she loved yesterday, and we also both love art. She volunteers at a pet shelter, for God's sake. She's amazin'. And... I'm the son of a fisherman. A divemaster tryin' to be a photographer. I've lived on this island my whole life—how can I measure up?" That last horrible argument with Leticia flashed into his mind, and he pushed it away forcibly.

"I'd say plenty."

Robert shook his head and hunched his shoulders. "I can't believe I'm even thinkin' about this."

"Is it any more unbelievable than a dive guide marrying a resort owner?"

"You're a lot more than that."

Alex's voice was soft, but he spoke firmly and met Robert's eyes with a steel stare. "So are you."

HEATHER ARRIVED home at 10 p.m., surprised to find Cindy sprawled on the couch, watching a cooking show. "You're still up!"

Cindy sat upright and muted the television. "I had to leave early this mornin', so I haven't heard about your date! But how was work?"

Heather was on cloud nine all day. Nothing could phase her, which was good because it had been an incredibly busy day. Charlotte, a server from the restaurant, had helped her through the dinner rush, but Heather was looking forward to Clark's imminent return. His son was doing well, and he expected to be back at work within two weeks. She sat on the couch facing Cindy. "The day flew by. The bar at the restaurant is almost finished, which will save a lot of effort during meals. I had a couple of locals in tonight who weren't real happy about the 9 p.m. last call."

"That is pretty early for a bar."

"Once we have Clark back, I have a feeling our hours will expand. I'm enjoying the early nights while I can."

Cindy tilted her head and tucked one of her pink braids behind an ear. "For someone who just finished a grueling shift, you sure look happy."

Heather beamed. "It was a good day."

"I think I got my answer about your date before we've even discussed it."

"Yesterday was even better."

"Girl, you need to tell me more than that! I waited up, you know."

Heather laughed and draped an arm over the top of the couch. "Our dive was so much fun. It was casual and thrilling and I felt so comfortable during all of it. And secure too. He brought us back to the exact same place we descended!"

"Robert's been leadin' dives for a long time. I dove Cane Bay once with a friend, and we did a terrible job navigatin'. We had to surface swim back to where we started because we ran out of air."

"We had lunch at the beach restaurant there afterward. He's very easy to talk to, even when I was nervous about telling him my background. Robert is a lot different from anyone else I've ever dated."

"Is that a good or a bad thing?"

"Oh—good for sure. I hope he believed that I'm serious about supporting myself without any help from my parents. I think he did." She picked at the fabric on the couch, trying to come up with the best way to word her next question. "Have you ever dated anyone who was really… different from you?"

Cindy smiled slightly. "Interracial, you mean?"

"I was trying not to be too blunt, but yes."

"Yes, several times. My last boyfriend was white. He was a complete asshole, but his skin color didn't have anythin' to do with that. Assholes come in all colors."

"They certainly do. I'm really attracted to Robert. I felt an instant connection the very first time we met, and he did too. But I've only dated white men before—the circles I traveled in were *not* multicultural. I'm worried I might say or do something wrong."

Cindy shrugged. "The best thing you could do is not make a big deal out of it. After you've been together for a while, you won't even notice it anymore. But other people will—you should be prepared for that."

"Yeah, we got the stink-eye from a couple in the restaurant. It pissed me off, but Robert said pretty much what you did."

"Sounds like this wasn't a onetime thing."

"No. We're meeting up at the shelter, then going to brunch after. I can't wait to see him again."

"Ooh. Was there a goodbye kiss?"

Heather laughed out loud. "There was a mid-date and a goodbye kiss!"

"There's nothin' like those first early get-togethers. Thrillin' and terrifyin' at the same time. Your parents will be ok with you datin' Robert?"

"Honestly, I can't imagine them minding at all. I'd like to meet Robert's parents someday."

"Do you know what his family is like?"

"His father owns two fishing boats and his mom mostly stayed home. They sound like hard-working, salt-of-the-earth people. I think I'll get along well with them."

Cindy smiled but didn't reply. A cloud crossed her eyes for a moment, then it was gone, like she had something less than pleasant to say but didn't want to ruin Heather's euphoric mood. "Well, now I can finally get some sleep. Don't have to stay up half the night worryin' that he picked his teeth the whole day or somethin'. You'll have to tell me about Date Number Two when the time comes."

Chapter Fifteen

ROBERT SHUT off the ignition and smirked at the Pet Paradise sign, which was bright purple to match the building. The name was written in loopy black font, outlined with turquoise. Photographing shelter pets was something he never would have thought of, but he had enjoyed the previous session tremendously. Watching Heather with the animals had made it even more fun. A side glance confirmed her car was in the parking lot, and he popped the rear hatch of his SUV. Slinging his cameras over one shoulder, Robert picked up the roll of black fabric. After cleaning it as best he could, he was curious how this would go, since cats weren't known to be as obedient as dogs.

A blast of air conditioning hit him as he walked in the front door. Donna and Heather leaned over the computer at the reception desk and looked up in unison. They both smiled, but only Heather's face made his heart thump.

"There he is! Lucky's been adopted!" Donna screeched, then frowned. "Of course, we've had three more dogs come in. But, no matter. We'll figure it out."

"Looks like you're ready for action," Heather said, with a slight purr in her voice that made the hairs on his arms rise.

"Very ready for action. Shall we?"

She led the way into the makeshift studio room, where two milk crates were stacked under a soft cat bed. A chair sat next to the formation.

"I thought we'd try something a little different," Heather said. "Can you drape the fabric over the bed, and I'll sit in the chair next to it? We'll let the kitty get comfortable while I pet it, then you can take pictures when I remove my hand."

He laughed softly. "I've been wonderin' how you'd get a cat to behave, but that just might work."

After setting up, Heather returned with Snickers once again. This time, when she set the calico down on the black fabric, the combination of soft bed underneath and lack of dog smell convinced the cat to sit happily enough. Heather took a seat in the chair and continued stroking her back. "Are you ready?" she asked softly without disturbing her movements.

Robert lifted the camera to his face, pleased with the settings he'd chosen. "Ready whenever you are." He matched her quiet tone. The accent lighting glimmered on Snicker's coat as Heather moved her hand away, and Robert depressed the shutter. The clicking sound caused Snickers to flick her ears forward, looking straight at the camera for a long moment. Then she turned to Heather with a meow.

Robert laughed gently. "I don't think she's happy you stopped, but I got what I needed."

They repeated the process with four more cats, and it worked wonderfully, though Robert had to work fast with a gray tabby who kept jumping out of the bed. But he was successful, and Heather quickly rounded up the cat, who was content to rest in her arms.

Lucky cat...

She stroked its back absently as she turned to Robert. "There are two litters of kittens I'd like to photograph, but I'm not sure the best way to go about that. Any ideas?"

He thought for a moment. "Got any balls of yarn around?"

"Yes. Lots."

"Bring two in different colors, then just put the kittens in the bed. It has tall sides, so that should contain them long enough for me to take a few shots. The yarn will look cute with them."

Heather placed one red and one blue ball of yarn in the bed, and they really popped against the black background. Shortly after, she returned with an armload of squirming, mewing kittens. Robert had to keep from laughing out loud, not wanting to startle them. Five in all, there were two black and white, two solid gray, and one gray tabby.

"Ok. Just set them in the bed, then move back quick," Robert said. "I don't think we'll have much time."

She did, and a confusion of adorable kitten antics ensued. Robert gave up trying to hold his laughter in as they crawled all over each other and the yarn balls. A gray one jumped around madly, chasing an errant line of red yarn.

Robert lowered his camera. "That was awesome. One of those might be the new cover image for the shelter's Galendo page."

She gave him a quick smile before rounding up the kittens again. The second bunch was just as cute, a mixture of orange tabbies and white kittens with black spots. One made it all the way out of the bed, clinging to the draped fabric by its claws before Heather could rescue it.

As she returned the kittens to their enclosure, Robert started disassembling his light, and rolled up the fabric. Heather returned, brushing a hand down the sleeve of the shirt she wore.

"I'm glad I thought to wear long sleeves. Otherwise, I would have gotten plenty of scratches."

He grinned. "A true artist is willing to suffer for her passion."

"You're the artist, not me. Remember?"

"That mean you're goin' to make me suffer?"

She snapped her head up at that, then slowly strolled over to him, meeting him eye to eye. Her height gave her an assertiveness that was incredibly sexy. "Not unless you enjoy suffering."

"I don't think we know each other nearly well enough to answer that."

She arched a brow, but her eyes were dancing. "We need to work on that, then. And I believe you promised me brunch." Her nose wrinkled adorably. "But I have to admit I'm not really in the mood for a fancy spread at some posh hotel. Does anyone do an informal brunch around here?"

"Yeah. Me."

A slow smile appeared on her face, and she took a step closer. "And what does that mean?"

His breath was deepening by the second. "It means I'm no gourmet, but if you want to come over to my place, I can whip up some eggs and bacon. And this will be faster too—don't you work in a couple of hours?"

Regret flickered through her green eyes. "Yes, though I wish I didn't. I think I'd have much more fun with you."

Her hair was in a ponytail, and he cupped the back of her head beneath the gathered strands as he bent to kiss her. Opening his mouth, he flicked his tongue over hers. She tasted slightly of toothpaste. With one hand, he slowly drew the elastic ring from her hair, at last running his hand through the long, fiery strands.

He broke the kiss so he could watch as he slid his fingers

through a second time. "You have the most incredible hair. I've wanted to do this since the first time I saw you."

She closed her eyes and leaned into his touch. "When we met during my interview, I couldn't look away from you."

"I felt it too." *Like a blindfold had been ripped off, and I saw what I really wanted.*

Heather opened her eyes and straightened. "Getting fired from Serenity might have been a blessing."

"From my perspective, it certainly was. Come on—let's head to my house."

Heather followed Robert, her anticipation growing with each mile. Too bad she only had an hour before work. Every time they kissed, Grant became a more distant memory—and good riddance. Robert's SUV climbed steadily into the foothills east of Frederiksted, winding over a narrow asphalt road. They ended in a neighborhood with large lots and older one-story houses. He turned onto a dirt track and stopped next to a tan house with white trim. The front door was painted a cheerful lavender, and several bougainvillea were planted against the house, their pink and yellow blossoms bright against it.

Heather exited her car, a delighted smile on her face as she gazed around the serene setting. An occasional rooster crowed, but it was quiet, with only the infrequent car passing on the road behind them. "I love it! What a wonderful neighborhood."

He gave her a small smile and shrugged one shoulder. "The house isn't much, but it's got a terrific view."

Robert pointed behind her, and she turned. Her mouth dropped open. Colorful Frederiksted spread out below, with the azure Caribbean Sea beyond. "Oh my God! That's incredible." Then she stopped, cocking her head. "Wait a minute—I've seen that view. Isn't there a photo of this in the lobby at Half Moon Bay?"

Robert laughed. "Yes. A sunset shot I took after the town lights had come on. Good eye."

She turned back with a sly smile. "Told you. I have an excellent eye for art."

The front door opened into a long hallway. As Robert led, Heather peeked into a guest room and a home office on the other side. His desk was dominated by a dual-screen computer and photos were scattered everywhere. She couldn't resist a nosy peek as they passed a large room with a king-size bed, obviously the master bedroom. Neat and well-kept, the bed was made, its light-blue comforter snugged under two plain white pillows.

Hurrying to catch up, she emerged into a large living room with the kitchen to the right. The house was older, and could use some renovating, but it had a very welcome, lived-in vibe.

"Hungry?" he asked, heading straight for the kitchen.

"Yes! I just realized how much. How long have you lived here?"

Robert opened the refrigerator and removed a carton of eggs and a pack of bacon. When he set them on the counter, there was a new tightness in the set of his shoulders. "Eight years." He glanced at her quickly before cracking several eggs into a large glass bowl and proceeding to whisk them. "My wife and I bought it, and I received it as part of the divorce settlement."

Her stomach gave a small lurch. "Oh. How long ago was that?"

"We divorced about four years ago. She moved to St. Thomas. Wanted more excitement in her life than this sleepy island could provide." He said this matter-of-factly, but pursed his lips together afterward.

"I'm sorry. That had to be rough."

He gave her a half smile and shrugged. "It was. She wasn't much interested in workin' things out with me and left the island. It was for the best."

As usual, he was being even-tempered, but Heather could see the pain tightening his eyes. *She was a fool, Robert. But I think you see that now.*

He removed two frying pans, placing them on the stove and igniting the gas burners. "What about you? Ever been married?"

The oxygen left the room. Suddenly, she felt dizzy and closed her eyes. It was a natural question, and one she would have to get used to answering. "No... never married."

When she opened her eyes again, Robert was staring at her, his expression inquisitive yet kind. "Are we talkin' about the relationship that ended badly now?"

"Yes." She studied her hands, clasping them so they wouldn't tremble. The next thing she knew, Robert was right in front of her. He brushed a knuckle over her chin.

"You don't have to talk about it. Slow, remember? I think a subject change is in order. Why don't you tackle the bacon while I make us an omelet?"

She smiled at him gratefully and brushed her lips over his. Then, moving to the other side of the counter, she opened the package of bacon and placed several strips in the frying pan.

"You happy Lucky got adopted?" Robert asked.

"Oh, that was great news! And hopefully now more cats will find new homes. Donna let it slip this morning that she'd been able to pay off some past-due bills. It doesn't sound like the shelter is doing too well financially."

Robert added some cut-up bell pepper to the egg batter and poured it into the skillet with a sizzle. "I can't imagine there's a lot of money to be made in runnin' a shelter."

"No, I'm sure you're right. She says the new photos are

really helping, so that makes me feel better. But this is an awkward place for me."

He looked up. "What do you mean?"

A blush crept over her face as she turned over the bacon. The delicious scent made her stomach growl. "I feel guilty. I'm trying to make my own way, yet I could solve so many of Donna's problems with a single phone call. Galendo has an entire charitable donation department."

Robert flipped the omelet. "You shouldn't feel guilty about that. I haven't seen any other people in there volunteerin'. You *are* a big help to her. And you're smart too. I'm sure you'll come up with somethin' else if she needs more help."

"You're pretty incredible, you know that?"

He barked surprised laughter. "I don't know about that, but thank you. But let me remind you, I'm not the one feelin' guilty even though I'm donatin' my valuable spare time to a good cause. You're the incredible one."

Heather reached out and pressed her hand to the side of his face. His skin was smooth from a recent shave, and she leaned in, giving him a long, deep kiss. Whenever their lips met, taking things slow became the last thing on her mind. Robert kissed her back, tracing his index finger across her collarbone. His light touch sent a jolt through her, and she pushed hard against him, twining her tongue around his. With a feather-light caress, he traced his fingers down from her collarbone to circle her breast. Heather moaned slightly, and he quickly slid his hand under her shirt and up, sliding his thumb under the cup of her bra. She tightened her arms around him, and his breathing deepened, matching hers now.

She pressed her hand against the front of his pants, discovering he was as aroused as she was. Robert gasped at her soft squeeze as she breathed in his ear, "Maybe we should skip brunch."

He froze in her arms, then pulled back with a headshake. "No, not yet. You need to take this slow. Let's do that."

She ground against him, and his nostrils flared. "Forget slow."

Robert laughed softly. "Let's not rush this." But instead of stepping back, he leaned in and kissed her again, raking his mouth over hers.

Then the bacon next to them emitted a loud, sizzling *pop* and they broke apart, laughing.

Robert gave her a regretful smile and took a determined step back. "Ok, that must be fate—let's eat. Besides, you need to go to work." His light-brown eyes held hers steadily. "I don't want a quickie with you, Heather. We'll know when the time is right."

Chapter Sixteen

JULY...

Robert smiled as a flying fish soared through the air, disturbed by the frothy water as *Surface Interval* sped by. They were nearly back to Half Moon Bay Resort. He stood under the canopy, and was unhooking scuba gear when his text tone went off. Quickly moving to the dry area, he read the message, then grinned at Alex, who was removing equipment in the stern. He moved past the cluster of divers who were demolishing a plate of Hope's cookies so he wouldn't need to shout.

"Looks like you're goin' to have to wash the gear alone. Your wife just texted and invited me to lunch."

Alex rolled his eyes. "Figures. She never wants to have lunch with me. You enjoy a leisurely lunch while I work myself to the bone in the blistering sun."

"Job security, man. She's just makin' sure you earn your keep."

A broad smile came to Alex's face, and he opened his mouth, then hesitated. Finally, he just shook his head. "I'm not even gonna say it. Tie us up and take off. Warn Hope she's going to pay for this tonight."

Both of them laughed as Tommy moved the boat sideways to the dock. Robert hopped off and tied it up. With a last wave at Alex and the captain, he headed up the pier, already anticipating seeing Heather at the bar. He'd been busy photographing a wedding in the week since they'd taken pictures of the cats, so he hadn't seen them yet. He was thinking about asking her over to pick out the winners together.

As Robert trotted down the steps onto the white sand, his mind turned to their short breakfast make-out session. He was more than ready to take things to the next level, but he needed to be confident she was ready too. He'd been in the drugstore in Christiansted the previous evening and picked up a box of condoms. Just in case.

His wide smile faded slightly when he remembered her requests to take things slow. She hadn't been holding back the other morning, though he was glad they'd been interrupted. He didn't want to rush through their first time together. And he was worried about doing something inadvertently to give her pause. Though that was difficult when he didn't know what the problem was, other than a failed relationship. But it was clear she was still suffering the effects.

The soft calypso sounds of a Cruzan steel-drum band echoed from the pool bar, and Robert's smile returned, surprised Heather knew of them. The group was a local secret and only sold music directly from their gigs. With his heart going from a trot to a gallop, he rounded the corner by the pool and lifted his eyes to the bar.

Clark stood behind the polished wooden counter, slicing limes.

Robert's momentary disappointment quickly turned to happiness. "Clark! Welcome back."

The thin man snapped his head up, a wide smile making his silver tooth glitter. "How's it goin' Robert? I'm glad to be back."

"Your son doing well?"

"Frisky as a puppy, and twice as active." He placed the limes in a bowl and shut it in the refrigerator. "The surgery and recovery took longer than we expected. Eli got an infection that kept him in the hospital an extra week, and we stayed on St. Thomas longer, just to make sure he was all healed. But he's doin' great now."

"I'm really glad to hear that. It hasn't been the same without you."

Clark gave him a huge, sly grin. "Yeah, that's what I heard."

"What's that mean?"

"You know exactly what I'm talkin' about. I'm happy for you. I like Heather. She texted me several times to ask how Eli was doin'."

"Thanks. We've only been out a couple times. Where is she?"

"Hope called her this mornin' to give her the day off since I came back."

"I'm sure she appreciates that. She's been workin' hard."

"Yes, she has," Hope's voice came from behind, and she joined Robert's side. "Charlotte has been helping during the rush times, and the bar in the restaurant is done. We're just waiting for the final inspection, so we'll have plenty of work for both of you in just a few days."

Clark laughed. "I hardly recognize the place!"

"I moved quickly this time. The three rooms on the north side are almost finished. I'm calling them rainforest bungalows since they're surrounded by tropical foliage, and the spa building is coming along. I'm starting the outdoor shower construction in the beach bungalows. Once that's done, we'll repeat the whole process on the south side."

Clark's face went blank. "Outdoor showers! Who wants to take a shower out in the open?"

Hope raised a brow at him. "They're completely private, Clark! Surrounded by a high wall, but very tropical with lots of green plants and flowers. Outdoor showers are very popular."

"If you say so."

"What are the new bungalows like?" Robert asked.

Hope had narrowed her eyes at Clark until he burst out laughing, then turned her attention to Robert. "They're exactly the same floor plan as the current ones, just behind them, in the jungle instead of the beach. But since they're positioned between the rooms in the front row, they each have an ocean view. Only the beach bungalows will have the upgraded bathrooms with the outdoor shower."

Clark's eyes took on a dreamy cast. "Rainforest bungalows. I like the sound of that."

"I like it too," Hope said. "I was afraid if we called them jungle bungalows, it would bring to mind lots of bugs, snakes, and bats. Not the image I'm trying to portray! They're going to be really nice. Upscale without being stuffy."

"Guess I'd better get busy comin' up with a new drink, then."

Hope laughed. "You've got a reputation to uphold now. But you have plenty of time, since you're skipping the mixology contest this year. Robert and I are having lunch. Can you run our orders to the kitchen?"

After giving Clark their selections, Robert and Hope sat at a shady table under the thatch roof.

"Alex was hurt that you wanted to have lunch with me instead of him."

"I'm sure he can live without me for a few hours."

"Not so sure." Robert grinned. "He said you were gonna pay tonight."

A pink blush graced Hope's cheeks. "He better watch it. He might get what he asked for."

"Why did you want to see me?"

"I'd like to hire you to take new photos of the resort. We need new pictures with the remodeling going on. I'd like to showcase more images of the resort. I'll still use the underwater and island scenes too, but I want to mix in pictures of the pier and the bungalows. The website will also have to be updated."

"I'd love to. Let me know when you want me to start."

"The project will need several sessions. We'll need exterior shots of the resort—the beach, pier, pool, and the lobby, as well as the new bungalows. And another shoot when the big building is finished."

Robert panned his gaze around the scene to the distant noise of construction on the new rainforest bungalows. "A lot has changed around here."

"And you've been pivotal to many of them."

He scoffed. "Hardly. You're the one who's helped me."

"I simply recognized your talent. But the photos I'd like first are for a special project Alex and I have been working on. Have you seen the new path being built next to the access road?"

He smiled. "Yes, but it's hard to see. I've been wonderin' where it goes."

"It's not obvious on purpose. Much of the resort property is across the highway to the east. There's an amazing freshwater rock pool and large cave that I'd like to offer as a private excursion to our guests. I'm calling it Half Moon Grotto."

Robert sat back in his chair. "Really? All that is hidden in the bush?"

"Yes. Cruz and I discovered it hiking one day. But I need photographs of it—stunning photographs. When would be a good time?"

He tapped his chin, thinking. "You said it's freshwater? Is the water clear?"

She nodded. "It's an amazing crystal blue."

"Then I'll need to shoot it midday with the sun shining straight into it. I'm workin' here the day after tomorrow, and there's no afternoon dive scheduled. How would that be?"

"Perfect! That way, Alex and I could both show it to you. Sara says Jack wants to see it too, so we'll make it an afternoon adventure!"

He grinned. "Sounds like fun. Besides, the pictures will be better if I have people in the pool—that will give it scale. Too bad Heather has to work..."

Hope's smile faded. "I would have given her that day off instead of today if I'd known. But there will be more chances. The pool's not going anywhere."

"I'll bring several lenses, and I can photograph the resort exteriors at the same time. When I'm workin' in the mornin', I'll shoot some panoramics from the dive boat as we head back in."

"They'll be wonderful. I can't wait to see them! Make sure you use your watermark, so people know who took them."

"I will. Thanks—this is a great opportunity for the exposure alone. I'm happy to do it for no charge."

Hope's eyes flared, and she pressed a hand into the tabletop. "No! Absolutely not. I will not let you give away your time or talent. How many times do I have to tell you that?"

Robert held both hands up, laughing. "Ok, ok! But you're getting the family rate, and don't try to talk me out of it."

"That I can live with." She gave him an enigmatic smile. "I've got big plans in the works, Robert. And you're instrumental to their success."

THE NEXT EVENING, Heather spent several hours of her shift preparing the new bar. They had repurposed one of two rarely used private dining rooms, and the new area was located at the edge of the restaurant next to the open-air patio. The location was lovely. Guests had a full view of the sunset from teak-wood tables placed inside, near the bar itself, or outside on the brick patio. Hope and Patti hosted a manager's reception every week, and the new bar would be much more convenient. They could do away with the portable coolers filled with ice now.

Heather ran her hand across the smooth bar top. Made of pure white quartz, small clear crystals glittered in the overhead lights, and several veins of bright blue ran through it. She was stacking bottles on the shelves when her text tone went off. It was Robert, and after a surreptitious glance to make sure she was alone, she picked up her phone. Hope and Patti didn't mind if employees kept their phones nearby, as long as they were circumspect in using them. Heather made a point to avoid hers during work hours, but at the moment, no guests were nearby.

Robert: I'm going through the cat pictures and I'm lonely. You want to come over after work and help me?

Heather grinned. *I'd love to see how he puts the finishing touches on his photographs!*

Heather: That would be great. But it will be after nine when I get there. It could be pretty late when we finish.
Robert: I'm not Cinderella. I won't turn into a pumpkin at midnight.

She laughed out loud.

Heather: Fine. I'll let you be Prince Charming then.

SHE SLID the phone back in her pocket, an anticipatory flutter running through her. Robert made her feel *seen* in a way she had never experienced. He wasn't just handsome and fit—he was kind, and that was a huge turn-on. Her mind turned to their first goodbye kiss, when she'd pulled away, and she snickered. *Don't think I'll pull back next time.*

Heather stopped for a moment to admire the view. A nearly full moon sat high in the starry sky, and its light glittered on the ocean. White LED rope lights illuminated the walkway of the pier, ending in spirals wrapped around the four supports of the palapa. Returning to the bar with renewed enthusiasm, Heather went back to work. Maybe life was finally turning around.

Chapter Seventeen

AFTER A WARM, lingering hello kiss, Robert ushered Heather into his home office. It was neater tonight, with photos piled into neat stacks instead of scattered about the surface of his desk. She smiled inwardly. *Looks like he cleaned up for me.*

Another difference was a second comfortable office chair sitting in front of the double terminal. As they took their seats, he asked, "You're sure you don't want anythin' to eat?"

"No, the resort gives us dinner. You know that, silly."

"Yeah, but that was hours ago. How about a beer?"

She noted the full glass of water at his elbow. "No, I'm fine right now."

He saw where her gaze had traveled. "I don't drink anythin' alcoholic while I'm workin'. But that doesn't mean you can't."

"Maybe after we're done. If you'll join me."

His brown eyes smoldered at that. "You've got yourself a deal."

Then he took a long sip of water and turned to his computer, all business. Several taps on his keyboard brought up a gigantic tile of images, and Heather felt her eyes go round.

"Wow. How do you even start?"

He laughed softly. "I can tell at a glance if they're any good or not. I just delete the ones that aren't."

Double clicking on an image, he brought up a full-screen photo of Snickers and immediately hit the delete key. His index finger rested on the right arrow key, and he moved forward, quickly deleting images that looked beautiful to Heather. Then he stopped at the fifth one, removing his hands from the keyboard. "This one's got promise." The tortoise-shell calico sat alertly on her bed, the accent light causing her coat to shimmer.

"I really like that one."

He nodded. "But there's a slight glare on the black cloth behind her. See?" It was hardly visible, and Heather said so. "I can take it out easily." A few clicks later, the glare was gone, and Robert had increased the contrast so Snickers was even more vivid. Then he dragged it to a separate folder titled Cat Keepers.

They proceeded through three more cats. Several times, Robert rejected images Heather thought were perfect, only to find ones much better. And once he selected an image of a black and white cat she thought was hopelessly underexposed. But after a few minutes, the cat was clearly visible against the black drape and meowing at the camera, its pink tongue sticking out adorably.

Heather laughed, clapping her hands together. "That's so great. I would have deleted that one right away."

"I can fix most any image with software as long as the camera settings were correct. With these, I'm lookin' at how the cat is posin', and how *alive* the photo will be when I'm done."

When they got to the first basket of kittens, both burst into laughter. "Let me just cycle through some of these to find the best one." Several lightning-fast clicks later, they both grinned at a full-screen image of four kittens. One was climbing up the side of the cat bed, one was jumping on a ball of blue yarn, and the crowning touch was the fourth kitten, which sat meowing unhappily while its litter mate bit its ear. The second batch of kittens contained a similar image, except two were pouncing on their brother's tail.

Heather wiped her eyes as they leaned together, their laughter finally winding down. "You'll have to send me a copy of that one. I love it."

They spent the next half hour cropping the images to isolate each kitten, so individual photos could be posted. Finally, Robert dragged the last kitten photo to the Keeper file and sat back with a sigh. Heather looked at her watch and her brows shot up. "It's almost midnight! I can't believe we've been at this for two hours."

He brushed a strand of hair away from her face. "It's a lot more fun when you're here to help me. How about that drink now?"

They moved to his kitchen, where he opened a bottle of red wine and removed two glasses from a cabinet. Next, he lifted a blanket from the back of a couch and folded it over his arm. "Let's go outside." A small patio set was arranged on the concrete patio, but Robert bypassed this, instead taking Heather's hand before leading her onto the grass and around the side of the house. "We'll go to the side yard. There's a hedge for privacy and a great view of town."

Robert handed her the bottle and glasses, then spread out an old patchwork quilt. A tall, thorny hedge separated his property from the neighbor's, and a large meadow was across the street, making the side yard remarkably private. They settled onto the homey quilt, and he poured out two glasses. "Here's to new starts."

With a smile, Heather touched her glass to his and drank. It was a nice sipping wine, full-bodied without being heavy. Stretching her legs out before her, she leaned against Robert's shoulder and watched Frederiksted's lights twinkle in the distance. The moon was edging lower now, but still provided plenty of illumination. She took a deep breath of the clean, grassy scent.

Returning her gaze to the quilt they sat on, she ran a hand over the large squares of fabric. It was mostly blue, with some patterned yellows and greens thrown in. Stitches were visible even in the moonlight. "This quilt looks like it has been around awhile."

"Yeah, my grandma made it. She gave it to me when I was a teenager." He paused, watching his wine as he swirled it. "I didn't appreciate it enough then."

"It's hard to appreciate your roots as a teenager."

"What was your life like as a teen?" he asked.

"Isolated. And privileged. I went to a private school, of course. But I never felt like I belonged. Some girls were so... superior and condescending. I didn't make close friends until I went to college and my parents let me do things my way."

"And what was your way?"

"Living in a dorm like a normal person. I took a part-time job as a bartender as soon as I was old enough. There were people in my dorm who didn't even know who I was, and that was so freeing. What was your childhood like?"

He hesitated, clearly thinking. "Happy. My mom was always around to look after my brother and me. Eddie and I hung out with a bunch of kids from the neighborhood. We spent a lot of time down at the marina and jumpin' off the docks. That's where I first became fascinated with what was underneath the surface."

"I can see how that would do it. Sounds wonderful."

"I fell in love with divin' from the start. Couldn't think of a better way to make a livin'. Except the pay is lousy," he added with a laugh. "When I was in high school, I took a photography class. When the teacher told me I had talent, I thought he was only humorin' me. So it was my secret passion for a long time." His smile remained as he shook his head. "It was actually Galendo that opened my eyes. I had been postin' pictures of my family and friends—normal stuff. But when I uploaded some underwater photos I'd taken, people *loved* them. They asked for more, so I uploaded some landscapes—beaches and waterfalls. And that was the start of it."

She brushed a finger down his cheek, her digit luminously pale against his dark skin. It was a beautiful contrast. "We had a connection even then."

His eyes were liquid in the moonlight, shining as he stared at her. "What about the connection we have now?"

Heather moved toward him, stopping an inch from his lips. "Let me answer that for you." Closing the distance, their mouths melted together, and the wine tasted even better now. He kissed his way along her jawline to her ear, then swiped his tongue into it. Heather shuddered, a groan escaping as she pushed him down on his back. His wineglass tipped over in the grass, the thick, heady scent enveloping them.

His shirt was untucked, and she slipped her hand under it. Robert was a wiry man, full of lean muscle. As she fanned her fingers out and drew them slowly across his stomach, his abdominal muscles quivered under her touch. He slid both hands under her shirt to unhook her bra and slowly traced one hand around to cup her breast. Heather gasped, shocked at how sensitive she was.

How badly she wanted him.

She sat up and quickly pulled her shirt off as Robert rose from the quilt. He slowly ran his tongue over his lower lip before drawing her breast into his mouth. He stroked her other breast with his hand, and she tipped her head back. The night sky glittered with stars, and she closed her eyes, nearly panting.

Heather ripped his shirt off, once again pushing him back

down onto the quilt as she moved his head back to her mouth. They stretched out side by side, their warm torsos pressed hard together. She ground her breasts against him, every jolt going straight to the middle of her. She wore a loose skirt that hung past her knees, and now he moved the material aside, slowly brushing his fingers up the outside of her thigh.

Her skin caught on fire everywhere he touched, and she lifted her knee. Sliding his hand around to her inner thigh, Robert lightened his touch to a whisper even as he devoured her mouth with his tongue. He brushed his hand up her thigh so slowly she wanted to scream, but at last he stroked two fingers between her legs. He did this with agonizing slowness, tracing his way over the fabric of her panties.

Heather groaned, partly in arousal and partly in frustration. "I want you. Make love with me, Robert."

His hand stopped, and he rose onto one elbow. "Are you sure about this?"

A slow smile crept across her face as she pressed into his hand. "You can't tell?"

"Yes, I can most definitely tell. That's not what I'm askin', and you know it." He gave her a quick peck on the end of her nose.

They stared at each other, and her smile fell. "I want you inside me. Now."

"Let me go in the house. I have a condom in my bedroom." He started to rise when she brushed a finger over his bicep.

"Wait. That's not necessary... I take birth control pills to moderate my cycles, and I'm safe. So we're ok unless there's a reason you need to..."

He smiled and stretched back out. "I don't need to." Then he stilled, just staring at her. "God, you're so beautiful. I want you so bad."

"I'm all yours, Robert."

She stroked a hand over the dome of his shaved head and pulled him to her mouth. Their kiss was wet and loud in the still air as Robert danced his fingers down her stomach and back to her inner thigh. Again, he slowed his touch, moving delicately up and down her thigh. He probed his tongue into her mouth and simultaneously moved his hand between her legs, keeping the same light touch that only ignited her more.

Heather bucked against his hand, pressing hard against him, and in an instant, his hand was under the fabric. He resumed stroking her, firmer now, and she cried out, breaking their kiss to wrap him tightly to her. Burying her face in his neck, she pushed hard against the pressure as she inhaled his scent. He circled his fingers faster, then faster, and the wave overpowered her.

Her entire body twitched, and she was shocked by how quickly her climax swept over her. Kissing him, Heather pressed him down onto the quilt and quickly unzipped his shorts. Dispensing with the teasing, she slid her hand under the fabric and gripped him firmly. His breath caught as she stroked up and down. He thrust his hips forward, pinning her moving hand between them.

Gathering a handful of hair, he pulled her head away and smiled. "You'd better stop that now."

Heather couldn't help laughing in return, but dutifully removed her hand. They shed the rest of their clothes and at last lay fully naked. Heather was still exquisitely sensitive—every nerve where their skin touched from head to toe was alive. She rolled onto her back and parted her legs as Robert moved in unison with her. Reaching between them, she guided him slowly inside her.

He took his time, closing his eyes and resting his cheek against hers as they moved together. A fine layer of sweat appeared on his back, and she slid her hands around on his skin, wrapping her legs around his waist. He moved faster, breathing against her ear. "Oh God... Heather. This feels incredible."

She opened her eyes to the eternal sky above. A million stars shone as she pulled Robert more tightly to her. Closing them again, she opened her legs wider, urging him on, and he called her name over and over.

Chapter Eighteen

A WISPY CLOUD raced across the moon, and Robert pulled a portion of the quilt over them. Heather snuggled tighter against Robert's shoulder, sated and completely relaxed. It wasn't really cool outside, but the sensation of being cocooned was heavenly.

"You warm enough?" he asked.

"Yes," she said, pressing a kiss against his damp skin. "I'm not sure I ever want to move. It's so beautiful out here." She closed her eyes as he stroked his fingers down her back, amazed at how quickly she had come to trust this man. Which inevitably brought thoughts of Grant. Robert was patient enough not to push her for explanations, but she owed him the truth. Especially now.

The whole thing was Grant's doing, not mine.

She breathed a deep sigh, and Robert poked her in the shoulder. "You ok? That was a pretty gigantic sigh."

"I'm more than ok. I was comparing how I feel now to a few months ago. You've never pushed me to talk about what happened, but I want to tell you."

He laced his fingers through hers, once again their skin

tones strikingly different in the pale light. "You can talk to me, Heather."

"I told you I left San Francisco to make it on my own, but I glossed over the reason. When I was a junior in college, I got a job as a salesperson at a major art gallery in San Francisco. I'm sure it was because of who I was, though I pretended otherwise. Over the next few years, I worked my way up and was recently promoted to manager. I was thrilled—it was what I've always wanted."

He rubbed his thumb back and forth over her hand, but didn't interrupt.

"When I was a senior in college, I met Grant Carrington. His family was also from Silicon Valley—his father was a venture capitalist. We became the *It* couple of high society, but there were fissures. He wasn't thrilled that I wanted to continue working after graduation, and I wasn't happy with the cocktail party scene. Except for galas at the art gallery—I could do those all year long."

She hesitated, swallowing thickly, then continued. "He asked me to marry him a year ago, and our wedding quickly grew into the Event of the Season. I loved him very much, and if playing society wife was the price to pay to be with him, I was willing to pay it. I see now how naïve I was—he wanted an accessory, not a wife with her own mind. I insisted on staying at the gallery but ignored that he wasn't happy about it."

She tugged at the quilt covering their bodies, re-settling herself and working up to the tough part. "I was like any bride, having the time of my life planning the wedding and growing more excited as the day grew near. And then it was my wedding day. I woke up that morning on top of the world. My text tone went off, and I saw it was Grant's name. I rushed to answer it— couldn't wait to read it. All it said was, *I can't do this. I'm sorry.*"

Robert gasped. "The son of a bitch *texted* you? He didn't even call?"

Heather blew a small, unamused laugh. "You got it. I called him back immediately and tried to work out the problem, but he wouldn't be moved. I'd noticed him pulling back over the previous few weeks, and just assumed it was normal jitters. It wasn't. He told me I wasn't his vision of the wife he wanted. Honestly, I was more in love with the idea of getting married than being married."

She paused as a cloud swept before the moon, making the hairs on her arms rise. "The bottom line is Grant left me at the altar. Not literally, but about as close as you can get. I yelled for my parents, and they started contacting the guests, but they only reached a small percentage. My father went to the church to make the announcement. There were over five hundred people there."

Robert kissed the top of her head. "I'm so sorry. That's awful."

"Oh, I'm not done yet. It gets worse. I had stayed the night in my old bedroom. There was a case of chilled champagne there for when my friends and I got ready for the ceremony. I started drinking immediately, shut away in my bedroom, and only emerged to eat a truly awful, morose dinner while my parents tried to console me. But I went straight to my room afterward.

"By morning, I must have drunk three or four bottles in total and was in pretty appalling shape. I decided since I wasn't married, I might as well go to work. So that's what I did. I drove there too—it's a miracle I didn't hurt someone or myself. The owner of the gallery was filling in for me when I walked in. He was giving a private showing to an exclusive group, and I teetered in, blind drunk, wearing dirty gray sweats topped off with bunny slippers. I ranted and raved, but the specifics are too fuzzy to remember. That's a blessing, I think."

She exhaled a long sigh, and Robert kissed her forehead, squeezing her shoulder gently. "The gallery owner fired me on the spot, of course, and in no uncertain terms. So I stumbled outside, and it had started raining. I stood there getting drenched and called my dad to come pick me up. He did, and we returned to their house and threw away all the champagne— I still can't drink the stuff.

"By the next morning, I had decided to leave. There wasn't really any choice. If being left at the altar hadn't been scandal enough, the spectacle at the gallery certainly would have. I wanted to move somewhere warm. There's a damp coolness to the Bay Area that seeps into your bones. So I chose the Caribbean." She turned to look into Robert's concerned eyes. "You want to know how I picked St. Croix?"

"How?" he asked softly.

"I printed out a map, closed my eyes, and put my finger down randomly. And now I'm here." She took a deep breath, turned her face into the hollow of Robert's neck, and started crying.

He enfolded her in his arms, entwining his legs around hers, and held her. "I'm so sorry. What an awful experience."

"I've been fired from two jobs in less than six months. I almost ran off again after Wayne let me go. People make mistakes all the time and have bad experiences—they don't have the luxury of just running away. If others can make it through, so can I. And I have. I love working at Half Moon Bay, and I've found you. Well, if I haven't scared you off, of course. I understand if you don't want to be with me."

Robert pulled back, starlight reflecting in his eyes. "Why would I want that? You went through somethin' terrible and made a mistake. That doesn't make you a bad person, Heather. It makes you human."

She was shivering now, but it was due more to catharsis than cold, and a single tear spilled down her cheek. Robert wiped it away. "Let's go inside, sweetness. I'll hold you all night long and you can cry as much as you need to."

DESPITE THE LATE NIGHT, Robert woke up before his watch alarm went off at 6 a.m. Quietly, he slipped on a Half Moon Bay shirt and shorts before making a pot of coffee. He watched the dark liquid drip into the carafe absently, his mind on Heather. As soon as they'd come in from outside, he'd brought her into his bedroom, where she'd fallen into a deep, drained sleep.

He was touched that she worried her revelation might push him away. If anything, it had done the opposite, strengthening his feelings even more. His eyes drifted toward the bedroom. *That's one resilient woman in there. Her fiancé was an idiot.*

By the time Robert had finished his coffee and eaten breakfast, Heather still hadn't woken. But he wasn't about to leave for work without saying goodbye. After brushing his teeth, he eased into the bedroom and sat on the edge of the bed. Heather faced him, asleep on her side with her long hair fanned out over the covers. Despite several months of living in the tropics, she was still pale but for a smattering of freckles across her nose. Her face was perfection, and he couldn't tear his eyes from her.

But he couldn't sit there all day. And if she happened to wake up, finding him staring at her would no doubt be creepier than hell. Robert gently brushed his hand over her hair, and she fluttered her eyes open. "Mornin', beautiful."

She smiled at him. There was a new shyness about it. "Good morning to you too."

"I've got a full day at Half Moon Bay, and it's almost time to leave. After the morning dive trip, Hope wants me to take some pictures around the resort. So I'm sure we'll run into each other at some point."

"Good."

She stretched and rolled onto her back. He leaned close and traced a finger over the side of her face. "You couldn't scare me off if you tried. Understand?"

"Thank you. I'm afraid I wasn't very good company after we came in here. I crashed pretty fast."

"You needed the rest." Then a smile rose on his face. "Maybe I'll let you make it up to me later."

She laughed and dragged a hand through her hair. "That's what I like to hear. Let me use the restroom and I'll meet you in the kitchen."

While Heather was getting up, he poured a cup of coffee and set out milk and sugar. She appeared a short while later, dressed in the same clothes as the previous night, but with her hair pulled neatly into a long ponytail. She fixed her coffee and took a long sip with her eyes closed. "Oh, that hits the spot. Thanks."

He nodded and checked the clock. "I'd better head out."

"Don't want Alex yelling at you?"

Robert laughed. "It must be the military thing." He stopped in front of her. "Stay here as long as you want. Just lock the front door when you leave."

"Thanks, but I'll head out soon. I want to upload all those cat pictures. There are a bunch of kitties depending on us." Then she sobered. "Thank you for listening—that was the first time I've told the whole awful story to anyone. Last night meant a lot to me. All of it."

Her lips were soft and warm as he brushed a kiss over them. "Me too. *You* mean a lot to me."

Chapter Nineteen

ROBERT STOOD ON THE PIER, photographing the palapa when Alex closed the door to the dive shop behind him and stepped into the sunshine.

"You ready to head out?" the tall man asked.

Nodding, Robert lowered the camera with a satisfied sigh. The water was the perfect shade of turquoise behind the large thatch structure, and the sky a bright blue above it.

Beautiful!

He slid the camera over his shoulder, adding it to the two already hanging there, including an underwater model. "Let's do this."

They had just finished with the morning trip, and April was taking the afternoon dive. As the two men walked up the pier, they were joined by Sara. "Jack has today off, but he's been dying to see the grotto, so he's meeting us here."

"The more the merrier," Alex said. "We've got quite the gathering."

As they stepped across the beach, Robert craned his head to see into the darkened pool bar, but there was no sign of Heather. It was still too early for her to be there, but he couldn't help the small pang in his stomach that she wasn't able to join this little party. Only half a day had passed since he left her at his house, but he couldn't wait to see her again.

Then Hope appeared, shuffling from the kitchen as she struggled to carry a large backpack. Cruz padded by her side. Alex quickly trotted toward her, and Hope's look of fierce concentration transformed to sheer relief at spotting her husband. "Oh, there you are! This is definitely a job for you."

After a quick kiss, Alex easily lifted the backpack with one arm and swung it onto his back, looping his other arm through the remaining strap. "Jeez, what do you have in here? Rocks?"

"Much better than that. Lunch! I knew you and Robert would be starving, so I had Gerold prepare a picnic for all of us. Jack is waiting in front of the lobby."

"Hey, I work too," Sara added.

"And I would never forget you. Don't worry. But these guys burn a lot of calories every morning."

Sara still wore a frown. "I'd like to see them stand on their feet for eight hours a day and see how they like it."

Alex arched a brow. He was opening his mouth when Hope dug her elbow into his abdomen, muttering, "Just don't. That won't help and you know it. Come on, guys. Let's go meet Jack."

As Sara moved to follow, she smiled sweetly at Alex, a triumphant gleam in her eye. He narrowed his eyes but remained silent, hurrying to catch up to Hope. Bringing up the rear, Robert was free to break into a wide smile. He'd noticed Alex and Sara's brother-sister antics before, with poor Hope stuck in the middle. And Alex could be extremely intimidating when he chose to—Robert had been on the receiving end of some of those encounters. Hope had joined his group once and Alex hadn't been shy about letting Robert know he better keep her safe. It was enjoyable seeing their leader one-upped occasionally.

They rounded the lobby building and Jack stood under a flame tree, also wearing a backpack. Sara ran toward him and tossed her arms around him, giving him a kiss that made him step back several steps. "How was your morning?"

"Good. I got that squeaky board on the back deck replaced and tightened the railing."

Robert laughed. "You're supposed to relax on your day off, not spend the whole time doin' repairs."

Sara arched a brow. "Don't let him fool you. He loves every minute."

Jack fell in with them as they continued over the grassy lawn, then across the parking lot. "I discovered I kind of miss construction." Then he laughed. "Being able to pick and choose my projects probably has something to do with that."

There was a sharp demarcation between the sand parking lot and the thick foliage. The asphalt access road was to their left, and to their right ran the unpaved sandy track that led to Hope and Alex's house. Directly ahead was a six-foot-wide dirt pathway. A sign had been pounded into the ground which read: *Half Moon Grotto lies just over one mile ahead. Follow the path across the highway to our secluded oasis, reserved for exclusive use by Half Moon Bay Resort guests. Please take only pictures and leave only footprints, so this private haven can be enjoyed for years to come.*

"You guys sure are bein' cloak-and-dagger about this," Robert said.

"We don't want a bunch of kids going out there to party," Alex mentioned as he stepped onto the path. Cruz bounded ahead to join him.

"Well, can't anyone follow the path and get there?" Robert asked, stepping onto the path and raising a camera to his eye. Once they stepped under the jungle canopy, the temperature cooled significantly, though the humidity increased.

"Nope," Alex said. "We fenced it in. I'll explain more when we get there."

Robert glanced around. Even though the road was close, it wasn't visible through the thick screen of vegetation. The track was remarkably secluded.

Robert took several photographs as they progressed down the path, meandering up and down hills and valleys. The sunlight filtered through the canopy, creating moving beams as it met the steam rising from the ground. The group remained silent, enjoying the birdsong that accompanied them. They crossed the highway, and the path continued, angling away so it was nearly hidden from the road.

Then Robert was stopped by the fence, and he craned his head up. The eight-foot fence was topped by three strands of barbed wire that angled out toward them. A padlocked gate lay directly in their path. "Are you guys tryin' to keep out an army, or somethin'? Barbed wire?"

"Alex likes to be thorough." Hope shot him a tiny smile before turning to her husband. "The key?"

Alex approached, digging in a pocket. "I keep the key inside my workbench in the gear room." He unlocked the gate and ushered them through before closing it again.

Robert smirked. "If it's locked, how are guests goin' to get in?"

"Oh, we'll issue them a key," Hope said.

"Right. What about the snipers hidin' in the guard towers?" Robert asked with a grin.

"They're under strict orders from me not to fire on guests," Alex said with a completely straight face.

Robert stared hard as he passed by, but relaxed when Alex broke into a grin. *Good, he's kidding.*

The path continued for another quarter mile before the vegetation thinned. "We're almost there!" Hope said. "Hold on for a second, Robert. I want Jack to go to the front with you. He hasn't seen it yet, either."

Jack moved up and the two men led the small assemblage, walking side by side. "They sure are excited about this," Robert murmured out the side of his mouth. "Is this thing an oasis or Fort Knox?"

Jack smiled, but his eyes were serious. "They have their reasons for wanting to keep it secure."

"Seems like a lot of work and expense for a tourist attraction."

They walked forward and the tree line cut off. Ahead was a small grassy meadow, but Robert's eye was drawn to a sandy beach which led directly into a stunning cobalt-blue pool. Black boulders surrounded the water. His jaw dropped as he stopped on the small beach and swept his gaze over the area. Jack gave a low whistle beside him.

The serene blue pool was surprisingly large, and so clear the dark boulders were visible as they continued underwater into a sheer cliff. To his left, the land rose sharply into a vertical stone cliff. There was a deeper black at the base of the cliff. Robert narrowed his eyes, finally making out that the feature wasn't a structure—it was the lack of one. He was staring at a large opening. "Is that a *cave*?"

Hope turned to Robert, a stunned smile rising on her face. "Yes. I still can't believe it sometimes. It's much bigger than it looks from here."

His head spinning, Robert turned his attention back to the pool. Small colorful birds swooped over it and tall trees surrounded it, dappled sunlight rippling over the blue water. "Holy shit! This is incredible."

He turned back to Hope. "You and Cruz found this?"

"It was mostly Cruz. There was a very faint animal track, and he led me straight here."

"Wow," Jack breathed as he stepped beside Robert. "You didn't do this justice when you told me about it, darlin'."

"I'm goin' to assume that comment was directed at Sara, not me."

Sara moved to Jack's side, encircling his waist. "Robert, if he starts calling you darlin', we're going to have a problem. It's beautiful, isn't it?"

Jack grinned and kissed her forehead. "Very."

"I've never even heard of this place. Now I'm startin' to understand why you guys want to keep this quiet," Robert said, though a part of him wondered. Neither Alex nor Hope was the kind of person who believed in exclusivity, yet they did where this grotto was concerned.

The Monroes had moved to the small grassy area, and Alex shrugged out of the large backpack. He started withdrawing Gerold's picnic lunch as Hope spread a blanket on the ground. He glanced at Robert. "Wanting to preserve the natural beauty of this place is part of it, but there's another reason for the security. Come over and I'll tell you about it while we eat."

Gerold's lunch contained a choice of homemade sandwiches, Caribbean potato salad, cut-up fruit and a giant bag of chips. Hope handed Cruz a fresh soup bone, and he lay down near the pool, gnawing on it. Jack unslung his backpack as they settled on the blanket. "Ok, I brought a six-pack of beer plus several bottles of water."

He held up a metal Half Moon Bay Resort water bottle with a flourish and Alex laughed. Turning back to Robert, Alex pointed toward the pool with his chin. "The main reason we've been so hush-hush is because there's two underwater passages. One is in the rock pool and the other is inside that cave. I've never investigated the tunnel in the pool, but Hope and I have followed the one in the cave." He set his sandwich on the blanket and looked Robert in the eye. "That dive could be deadly to an inexperienced diver. Or even a not so inexperienced one..."

A look passed between him and Hope, then Alex continued. "With this being a dive resort, we were concerned people—guests or locals—might try to dive those passages on their own and get killed. So, I had metal grates placed over them both. Now no one can enter either without the key, and Hope and I have the only copies."

Robert couldn't argue with his logic, and it meshed with his earlier thoughts that there was more to the story. "I imagine flooded passages would be quite a liability for the resort."

"Our attorney was quite insistent about securing the site," Hope added.

Then Robert remembered the hike. "You'd have to be a pretty serious cave diver to get scuba equipment all the way out here. Wait—didn't you say you and Hope dove one of the passages? How did you get your gear all the way out here?"

A proud smile rose on Hope's face. "He wasn't a SEAL for nothing, you know. He hiked it out here."

"Damn, Alex," Robert said, but the tall man just shrugged and took another bite.

Conversation paused while they finished the meal, then Hope gathered up the remnants into the backpack.

"Ok, Boss Lady," Alex said. "What's the plan here?"

Hope raised both brows. "Oh, I thought I'd leave the specifics to Robert. I just want some pictures of the grotto that show how beautiful it is. What do you think?" She directed her last question to the photographer.

"I can take some landscapes of the pool and cave, but I don't have enough light for the cave interior. I'd like to get some of you guys swimmin'. Nothin' shows scale better than people in the shot, and that pool is *big*." He looked at the bright blue water and sighed. "It's too bad we didn't bring masks and fins. I brought my underwater camera, so I'll try to take some shots with it."

"I've got free diving equipment stored in a small cave nearby," Alex said. He was leaning back on his elbows and lifted a foot to caress his wife's. "Hope and I come out here from time to time, so I keep that stuff here."

Robert bolted up, excitement thrumming through him. "You've got two sets? That's perfect. I can photograph you free divin', Alex!" They were both experienced free divers, and Robert could already see the pictures he wanted to take.

"Sounds good to me," Alex said. "Just don't take any pictures of the gates over the passage, ok? Don't even talk about them outside this group, except for Heather. Please."

Robert nodded. He still thought Alex was overreacting a bit, but as he looked around the peaceful scene, a strong desire to bring Heather there built inside him.

To be there with her *alone*.

Two hours later, Robert was packing his camera back into his backpack, very pleased with his shots. Landscape photos of the grotto had been easy—the pool was incredibly photogenic. And when the two couples had gone for a swim, he'd taken many more. As he had climbed over boulders, hunkering down to get the best angles, Robert had captured some beautiful moments between the two pairs.

Sara and Jack had been near the edge of the pool standing on a submerged boulder, and Robert had caught a tender smile from Sara as Jack pulled her tightly toward him. Hope and Alex were in the middle of the cobalt pool, her legs wrapped around his waist as he treaded water. When she leaned in and whispered something in his ear, Alex tipped his head back and laughed, then gave her a lingering kiss.

Robert loved capturing images like these. There was nothing like genuine interactions between two people in love, and he looked forward to sharing the photographs with them. But many of the moments he had captured had been private and not meant for public display. He would email the best images to each couple, and he'd also captured plenty of more playful moments that would be perfect for Hope's advertisements.

Robert couldn't wait to see the pictures he'd taken of Alex while they were both free diving. Alex had moved gracefully through the water with his hands clasped in front, his body highlighted against the black rock. While photographing him, Robert had paused, lowering the camera. The barest hint of an idea danced around the edges of his mind. He couldn't form it yet, but it would come to him.

As they started back, Alex whistled through his teeth for Cruz, who had been working on his bone the entire time. Perking up his floppy ears, the dog picked up his treasure and carried it in his mouth all the way home.

WHEN THEY RETURNED to the resort, the two couples left for home. Cruz followed the Monroes, still carrying his bone. Robert made a beeline for the pool bar. The sun was low on the horizon and a golden light lit the beach. He couldn't resist snapping a few pictures, then hurried on.

Heather first, then more photos...

Robert continued to the bar, and this time Heather stood behind the counter. The sight of her immediately brought him back to the previous night, and his strong desire to repeat it.

She was scrubbing the sink and heard him sit on a bar stool. "Afternoon. What can I get—" She looked up and recognized him, breaking into a wide grin. "Hi there, gorgeous. I wondered if you were still around. Done taking pictures?"

Robert shook his head and tried not to think about how delicious her mouth tasted. "I've got some sunset shots to take, then I'll be finished. Want some company tonight?"

She leaned on her forearms, her eyes becoming smoky. "Your place is more secluded, but for a shared house, ours is private enough. And I'd love some company. I'll text you when I get off."

He nodded, then sat back as Clark appeared, holding a case of soda. He and Robert exchanged hellos, then Clark placed the cans on ice.

"You two mind if I get some shots of you? It would serve as photographic proof that you actually do somethin', Clark, instead of standin' around all the time daydreamin' about new drinks."

Clark nodded sagely. "That's a good point. Never hurts to have proof."

With a grin, Robert moved to the back of the bar and took pictures from several angles. Mostly highlighting Heather, of course. "Ok, that should do it. I'm movin' on to the pier. I'll see you later." He directed the last sentence at Heather, who gave him a smile and a wink.

Chapter Twenty

AUGUST…

HEATHER WAS BUTTERING toast when Cindy walked into the kitchen, stretching her arms over her head. "Mornin'." She headed straight for the coffeepot, then looked around blearily. "Robert leave already?"

"No, he's taking a shower," Heather replied. When Robert had spent the night for the first time, she'd been somewhat nervous the following morning. But he and Cindy had been completely nonchalant about it, merely exchanging hellos and acting like it was any other day. *And would I have acted any differently if Cindy's boyfriend had appeared one morning? Of course not.*

Her nerves had disappeared, and a new routine was established. Now Heather heard the water shut off and poured a cup of black coffee. Minutes later, Robert bounced into the kitchen, alert and wearing fresh clothes he'd brought over the previous evening. He took the offered coffee after giving her a kiss. "Thanks, sweetness."

Cindy smirked over her mug. "You're sure ready to go. Big plans this mornin'?"

"I'm headed over to Half Moon Bay. Hope looked through the images I sent her but wants my help pickin' out the final selections. She's updatin' the listing with the Tourism Board, so she wants the best images for those."

"I'm sure there are plenty of great ones to pick from," Heather said, which brought a laugh from Cindy.

"Hope and I ran together the other day, and she told me you gave her an impossible number of images to comb through, Robert. She said there was no way to sort through the best ones."

He shrugged, but pride gleamed in his eyes. "I can pick them out. Shouldn't be too hard. You headed to the shelter today?" he asked Heather.

"Yes. It figures—I wake up early on my day off. I'll relax for a bit, then head over."

After Robert left, Heather refilled her mug and sat outside on her private patio, which faced east. Warm morning sunshine lifted her spirits even further as a flock of bright-yellow birds flitted through the small yard, twittering. Their house was in a quiet neighborhood, and the only other sound was the laughter of a couple of kids on their way to school. Heather's phone rang, and she picked it up, swiping eagerly. "Hi, Mom! You're up early."

"Yes, I have an appointment with my personal trainer in an hour. I remodeled our home gym with all new equipment, so I figured I might as well hire someone to make me use it."

Heather laughed, happy to hear her mother's voice. Like her husband, Laura Galen hadn't been born with untold riches. She enjoyed their wealth but kept her strong practical roots.

"How are things in Palo Alto?" Heather asked.

"Good. I'm organizing a charity ball, and it never fails to

astonish me how stingy rich people can be. But that's not why I'm calling. I have some exciting news—at least I hope you'll think it's exciting."

Heather leaned forward. "Don't keep me in suspense."

"Dad and I are coming for a visit. It won't be for a few more days—he's tied up with some rigmarole regarding a congressional oversight panel. Is that all right, darling? Do you mind?"

"That's great! I can't wait to see you." This was true, though a little more warning would have been nice. "But I'm not sure I can get time off. Do you have a place to stay?"

"Oh, you don't need to rearrange your life for us. We'll arrange our schedule around yours. And yes, I'm booking a place now. Let's see... what was it called?" There was a sound of shuffling papers through the phone. "Here it is! The Stephenson Villa. The brochure says it's set on the expansive grounds of a former sugar plantation just west of Christiansted."

"Sounds nice to me."

"Yes, doesn't it? How are things with you? Is your new job working out better?"

"Everything's going great. I'm really happy. Actually... I'm seeing someone."

"Oh, I'm so happy to hear that, darling! Tell me about him."

"His name's Robert and he was born and raised on St. Croix —his family has been here forever. He's the most incredible photographer, and getting his own business going. He's charming, and sweet, and makes me feel wonderful. Oh, and he's Black, just so you know."

"Yes," Laura replied drily. "I gathered that when you said he was a local and his family had been there forever. As long as he treats you like you deserve, his skin color doesn't matter to me."

"I know. He's so different from Grant—in every possible way."

Looking back now, Heather clearly saw the sides of Grant

she had refused to acknowledge. How condescending he was, especially to those he considered his 'inferiors', like employees or his household staff. He'd been a handsome prince who had swept her off her feet, then taught her a terrible lesson about it being better to keep both feet on the ground.

"That's certainly a good sign. I hope we'll get to meet him."

"Definitely. He's very easy to get along with. You'll love him. What do you want to do while you're here?"

"Relax. Hopefully, I can convince your father to take it easy for at least a full day. This hearing thing has him wound up in knots. I was hoping we could go diving, since you're back into it. If diving is involved, Tim will have to disengage from his damn phone for a few hours. Do you know any sites well enough to take us on a dive?"

Heather burst into laughter. "Not really. I've only been diving twice since I've been here. But it just so happens I know the perfect person to take us all."

<hr>

As HEATHER WALKED from her car to the entrance of Pet Paradise, her feet hardly touched the ground. Her frame of mind was so much better than when she'd left California—she couldn't wait to see her parents again. And to relieve some of their worry about her. After explaining that Robert was also a divemaster, her mother had been even more excited about their upcoming trip.

Donna was on the phone when she entered and gave her a distracted wave as she talked to someone about adopting a cat. One of the basket-of-kittens pictures was now Pet Paradise's signature image and several adult cats had been adopted as well as most of the kittens. Heather pushed through the door into the Dog House, enjoying the cacophony that erupted as she entered. As usual, she casually glanced in each kennel as she walked by, and made it halfway down the aisle before she stopped cold, gasping.

Am I seeing things?

Lucky sat at the front of his kennel, just behind the chain-link door. He wasn't barking, but he thumped his tail eagerly at the sight of her. Still dazed, Heather hunkered down in front of him. "What are you doing here?" Then tears filled her eyes as she realized. "Someone brought you back? You're the sweetest dog ever!"

The door burst open from the reception room, and Donna waved an arm frantically. "Oh, damn. I'm too late. I was hoping to stop you before you came in here, but I was on the phone."

Heartbroken, Heather rose and turned to her. "What happened?"

Donna joined her, and Lucky increased the tempo of his tail. "He was returned yesterday. He just didn't get along with their kids. Even though they're older, he was still skittish and snapped once at them. The father refused to take the risk of keeping him."

Heather closed her eyes. "No one's going to want a shelter dog who's already been adopted, then returned. What now?"

"I know." Donna heaved a deep sigh. "It's my fault. I shouldn't have pushed that family to take him, no matter how badly I needed the adoption fee. You and Robert have made such a difference, but the adoption fees I've taken in have only paid off my past-due bills. Lucky will find the right home—don't you worry. And I won't rush any more adoptions. It's too hard on everyone if it doesn't work out."

"I feel terrible."

Donna wrapped an arm around her. "Don't. It's my fault and no one else's. I can't imagine this place without you now.

Everything will work out. Maybe you could ask Robert to take another round of pictures? That would help."

"Yes, of course. He'd love to."

With a last squeeze of her shoulder, Donna plodded back to her desk. Heather turned back to Lucky. "All right. Let me get a leash and we'll go for a walk, ok?"

At the word *walk*, Lucky rose and scratched the gate of his kennel, woofing softly and bringing a smile to her face.

Chapter Twenty-One

AFTER FINISHING dinner in the restaurant kitchen, Heather still had time to enjoy her break, so she headed down to the pier. The sun wasn't quite touching the horizon yet, but a golden light filtered over the ocean. Several days had passed since the conversation with her mother, but there had been no further updates on their visit. She was walking through the tunnel when Laura called. Smiling, Heather answered. "Are your ears burning? I was just thinking about you."

"I'm sorry this has been so haphazard," her mother replied. "But the good news is we're on the plane now and headed your way!"

Heather stumbled, then hurried to the swing under the palapa. She needed to sit for this news. "You're coming here? As in—right now?"

"Yes. Joshua says we should land in less than two hours." Joshua was their personal pilot. "I finally dragged your father out of the office. He desperately needs a few days of R and R, and he's promised to put away his phone for an entire day."

"Mom, I'm at work right now. And the next few days too! I can't meet you at the airport or anything."

"Oh, darling. Don't worry about it. We'll work around your schedule. We got that house all set up, and it comes with transportation. But I really do hope we can go diving. If you have the morning off, you should be able to join us, right?"

"I'll see what I can do. We'll touch base tomorrow, ok? Text me when you land."

Heather ended the call with a deep sigh, staring at the dive boat. Tanks were in their holders with BCDs attached, which was unexpected this late.

Hearing footsteps, she turned as Alex walked by with a regulator in each hand. "Hi there. Enjoying the sunset?" he asked.

"Trying to. I've got a few minutes before I need to get back. Are you taking the boat out?"

"Yeah, Jack and I are working a night dive. What's wrong with the sunset?"

She smiled. "It's spectacular, as usual. The problem is that my parents just called. They're on their way for a visit."

Alex set the regulators on the side bench of the boat, then joined her on the swing. "I take it that's not good news?"

Her smile turned into a laugh. "I can see how you'd interpret it that way. No—I can't wait to see them. But Mom gave me no notice whatsoever, and I have to work the next several days. Plus, they want to go diving with me and Robert."

"I'm sure we can find someone to cover the bar for a couple of days. Don't worry about it. I'll talk to Hope—she'll find a way. She always does."

"Thanks. I hate to be a bother."

"It's not. Hope and I both lost our parents, so enjoy them while you can. And I might be able to help with the diving. I was just checking the schedule. Robert is working the day after tomorrow. I can ask Tommy to switch days off and take Robert's group myself. That way, he can lead you and your folks on a private dive. Boat dives might be easier for your parents."

"That sounds fantastic! I was hoping to dive Cane Bay Wall again, but I'm sure other sites would be fine."

Alex's eyes were alight. "We've got a full-day three tank trip scheduled. That would be perfect! We can dive Cane Bay on those longer trips. Maybe hit Horseshoe Key for the second dive and have a picnic there." A faraway look came into his eyes, a small smile forming. Then he snapped out of it. "Let me call Hope."

As he stood, guilt stabbed her. "Are you sure? This is so much trouble."

The tall man grinned at her. "Instead of a day of drudgery driving the boat, I'll get to lead three fantastic dives. Trust me, it's no bother. In addition, your parents will have a great time."

***

THE NEXT MORNING, Heather lay stretched out on a pool lounger next to one of the most opulent pools she'd ever seen. The 'house' her mother had booked was actually an expansive, modern villa with eight bedrooms and enormous grounds. It perched on a hillside overlooking the north shore and had a path down to its own private beach.

After Heather had returned to the bar the previous evening, Hope had come by saying Charlotte could cover Heather's shift the day they had planned for diving. Then Hope had offered to work the following day, but Heather wouldn't hear of it. She wasn't about to make the resort owner work just because her parents planned their visit last minute.

"How long can you stay this morning?" Laura asked. Lying on the lounger next to Heather, she wore a flattering one-piece swimsuit. Her figure was still trim and curvy at fifty-four.

Heather had inherited her hair color from her mother, though Laura wore hers much shorter, in a long A-line cut.

Heather glanced at her watch. "A bit longer. But we'll have all day tomorrow."

Tim Galen sat on Heather's other side, tossing his phone on a small round table after taking a quick call. His brown hair was liberally sprinkled with gray now, but he had kept his boyish features throughout life. "That's it. No more work. Don't want my only daughter thinking she's not important." He drew her close and kissed her cheek.

"I know better, Dad. But I'm glad to see you taking a real vacation."

"So am I. Half the senators I've been talking to think I should do more to foster freedom of expression on Galendo, and the other half want me to censor the site. It's maddening."

"Tim..." Laura said mildly.

He rubbed his face with both hands. "You're right. I'm looking forward to meeting Robert tomorrow."

"I can't wait for the two of you to meet him," Heather said. She'd exchanged a few quick texts, letting Robert know her parents had arrived and confirming he was ok with the dive trip. But he'd had a dawn photo shoot this morning, so they hadn't spoken. "You'll like him. He's very down to earth and easygoing."

"That's promising. Glad you're not dating another snotty, stuck-up prick like Grant Carrington."

Heather burst out laughing. "Tell us how you really feel, Dad."

Tim's face was grim, his eyes hard. "The whole Carrington family is aware they've made an enemy of me. What Grant did to you was unforgivable. But I must admit, it has some bright sides." A smile rose on his face that wasn't at all humorous. "Marcus Carrington was inches away from closing a merger with a tech startup he'd been after for two years, and I stole it away at the last second. I would have loved to see his face when he found out."

"Tim, you're doing it again," Laura said.

Heather stepped in quickly. "Do you guys have anything planned this afternoon?"

"Yes," Laura said. "We're going for an island tour and spending some time in Christiansted. What a beautiful town—I can't wait."

Heather thought about their upcoming dive adventure. "Do you guys want a short refresher before you dive tomorrow? Robert gave me one before my first dive here and it really helped."

"I'd love one," Laura said while Tim shrugged. Neither had dived in several years, but her father was half-fish, and never minded a long layoff.

"I'd better get a move on," Heather said, gathering her things and replacing her cover-up. "Why don't you two show up at 7:30? That will give Robert enough time. The full-day trip leaves an hour earlier, at eight instead of nine."

After saying goodbye, Heather headed home to change for work. Driving past Serenity, she gave the luxurious white apartment complex the finger. "You never would have worked with me so I could see my parents. Thank God for Half Moon Bay, and especially Robert."

AT 7 A.M. THE next morning, Robert gathered an armload of wetsuits and headed toward the boat. He exhaled forcefully, trying to breathe out his nerves. Tommy, Alex, and Jack were all busy preparing for the long day ahead. He stepped aboard *Surface Interval* and set out a wetsuit by each diver's tank.

Jack glanced over, brows raised. "You nervous about this?"

Robert shrugged a shoulder, but now Tommy and Alex were paying attention too. "A little, I guess. But I'd rather meet Heather's parents like this. At least here I'm in comfortable surroundings."

"They're not stayin' here at the resort?" Tommy asked.

"We're booked solid," Alex said.

Robert smirked. "They rented the Stephenson Villa."

Tommy froze, blowing a long whistle. "I can't believe you're not nervous, man. I heard that place goes for twenty grand a night."

"Jeez, Tommy," Jack said. "Lay off the poor guy. Sara read up on them—" He shot Alex a long side-eye as the instructor snorted, "—and she said they have the reputation of being pretty normal people."

Robert laughed. "Well, I'm glad Sara did all my snoopin' for me."

Jack shot another look at Alex, who now held up both arms, grinning. "Hey, I didn't say a word."

They were interrupted by the sound of wheels rolling toward them. Hope strode down the pier, leading a wheeled cooler with each hand. As she neared the boat, she spotted Alex and called out, "Honey, would you and Tommy give me a hand?" Both men jumped to do her bidding, rolling the coolers under the canopy as Hope joined Robert and Jack.

"I brought an extra special lunch today. Gerold came early to prepare a cold Caribbean fried chicken lunch for everyone. This is the first time we've had this level of VIPs on board, and I want to make sure they enjoy themselves. I also have a freshly baked mango coffee cake to eat on the way out, and a big thermos of coffee."

"Take it easy, Hope," Alex said gently. "We're not going to treat them any differently than the other guests. Well, Robert might." Then he frowned. "You're not planning on advertising this, are you?"

"No, of course not. But word of mouth is our best possible advertisement. And I wouldn't be surprised if their visit does become known. If they had a fantastic time diving with Half Moon Bay Resort, what could it hurt?"

"Are you comin' with us?" Tommy asked.

"No, I'm meeting with the Tourism Board this morning to go over our new ad." She gave Alex a deadpan look. "Assuming it's all right with you if I advertise with the Tourism Board."

He just looked straight back at her, expressionless, until Hope burst into laughter. "I'll let you all get back to work. I strongly believe we have the best dive staff on the island, and I'm just excited to show you off."

Alex's expression softened, and he took Hope in his arms, planting a kiss on top of her head. "And we thank you. It'll be a great day—the forecast is perfect. Now go enjoy your board meeting." He swatted her on the butt, then she was off the boat and walking away.

Alex moved to Robert's side. "I put your group's stuff here at the stern. We'll plan on putting you in the water first. I'm sure Tim Galen will be recognized, but if we make it obvious you guys are a separate group, hopefully he won't be bothered."

"Sounds good," he replied. "I'm goin' to do a quick refresher as soon as they get here."

Robert looked up the pier, where three people were walking toward them. Heather was in the middle, flanked by her parents. As he welcomed them aboard, Tim Galen shook his hand firmly, not trying to prove anything. Robert couldn't help but smile when introduced to Laura, who was a somewhat older version of Heather.

Tim laughed. "Yes. Fortunately, Heather gets her looks from my wife, not me."

Robert smiled and bowed. "I'm enchanted. The only problem will be tellin' you two ladies apart all day." Heather smiled and winked at him as Laura blushed exactly the way her daughter did.

"Well," Robert said, "Shall we get to it?"

Chapter Twenty-Two

THE SETTING SUN threw long shadows across the lawn. Robert ran a hand over his smooth head, more out of nerves than making sure he hadn't missed a spot shaving. Several shrubs had been groomed into animal topiaries, and the fading light made them appear to move, further unsettling him. Gripping his large flower bouquet tighter, he approached the mammoth front door of the Stephenson Villa, a carved mahogany monolith displaying tropical birds and foliage.

He'd come from thirty paralyzing minutes in a wine shop, his first-ever attempt at a hostess gift. But his lack of knowledge on the subject, coupled with the fact that Tim Galen probably threw away wine that cost more than Robert made in a year, rushed him out of the store in a cold sweat. Fortunately, a fresh flower stall enticed from next door, and he'd bought a bouquet of tropical flowers, which was probably more suitable anyway.

Their morning had gone exceedingly well. Heather's parents had taken Robert's quick scuba refresher with no signs of impatience or boredom. Laura had been a bit nervous, but he'd quickly calmed her down. And Alex had chosen three fantastic sites—Cane Bay Wall, Horseshoe Key, and The

Chapel. Robert had warmed to both Tim and Laura immediately, and had gotten the impression they liked him too. Over lunch on Horsehoe Key, Laura had invited him to dinner at their villa. He'd happily accepted, as Heather gave him a wink. By the end of the trip, he could almost forget he was with one of the richest couples in the United States, if not the world.

But that fact was once again obvious as he reached out to ring the bell. After much consideration, he'd dressed in a white long-sleeved shirt, black slacks, and a gray suit coat. The door was answered by a man younger than Robert, and a slightly awkward moment ensued. "How you doin', Theo?" Robert had gone to school with Theo's older brother and had known him nearly his whole life.

Theo was dressed in a formal white shirt with tan ankle pants and smiled slightly. "I'm well, Robert. Good to see you. The Galens are on the back patio. I'll take you back." He followed the butler through an endless hallway with multiple giant rooms on either side, including a music room with a grand piano and a library lined with shelves. They turned down another seemingly random hallway and continued. "You ever get lost in here?"

Theo smirked, and some of his natural personality flickered through his polished manner. "Not for a while now. I did at first, though... So, you know the Galens?" He asked this casually, but it was clear he was wondering why on earth Robert had been invited to dinner.

"Their daughter lives on St. Croix. We're dating," he said as neutrally as possible. Theo's face registered surprise for a moment before he covered his expression, and Robert suppressed a grimace as the fluttering in his stomach increased even more. They emerged into a living room that was bigger than his house. A seating area took up much of one end, and several billiards tables were placed in a row down the other side of the room.

Opening a huge sliding glass door, Theo ushered Robert out ahead of him, and announced, "Mr. Davis has arrived."

"Robert!" Laura exclaimed, hurrying over. "We're so glad you could make it!" He handed her the flowers, and she made a big fuss over them, eventually handing them to Theo. "Can you find a vase for these?"

"Of course. I'll place them in the dining room."

Theo's training and demeanor impressed Robert. You'd never guess that he'd once been a kid who liked to pull the legs off spiders. The butler turned back to Robert and indicated an open ice chest on the patio. "There is an assortment of beverages on ice, or I can get you a glass of wine if you prefer."

"No thanks. I'll rummage through the ice chest."

Theo responded with a nod, then bowed to Laura and retreated inside. Heather came to Robert's side and looped her arm through the crook of his elbow. "We didn't rush you too much, did we?"

"No, not at all."

When the boat crew heard he'd been invited to dinner, they had pushed him off *Surface Interval* as soon as the Galens left, so he had plenty of time to get ready. Heather led him to the ice chest where he was relieved to find several bottles of Leatherback and opened one.

He raised his brows to Heather, who shook her head. "I've got a glass of white wine over there. Let's join Mom and Dad."

Tim and Laura stood next to a resort-style pool, which was gigantic, like everything else at the villa. That morning, the Galens had insisted he call them by their first names right off the bat.

"My dad is Mr. Galen, so don't call me that unless you want me to feel eighty years old." Tim had said this with a grin, and Robert had to admit the man was easy to get along with. Now he held up a matching beer to Robert's in a toast as Heather retrieved her wine. "Here's to a great day. Thank you, Robert."

"Yes! All three dives were incredible! And so different," Laura said, then lifted a hand to her breast. "Oh, that beach where we had lunch! What an amazing place. I just loved the whole day."

"You sure know the sites like the back of your hand," Tim added.

"Been doin' this for a long time. Close to fifteen years."

"I wish we could stay longer," Laura said. "But Tim has to get back, so it's wheels up first thing tomorrow morning."

"At least you were able to come down for a couple of days," Heather said. "It's so good to see you two."

Tim's face turned to mush. "For us too, baby."

Laura squeezed Heather's hand before turning her attention to Robert. "Heather told us you're a photographer too. I noticed the glass prints hanging in the dive shop and saw your name in the corner. You took those?"

"Yes," Heather said, clasping his hand in hers. "His pictures are all over the resort. He sells them regularly to guests."

"We'll have to check out your website," Laura said. "I'd love to buy one."

"Thank you. That's very kind," Robert said.

Laura turned to Heather. "You *have* to see the flowers in this place. Absolutely amazing!" Grabbing her hand, the two women marched off through an opening in the hedge.

"Laura seems to be enjoyin' herself."

"We both are," Tim said. "And we've missed Heather terribly. But it looks like this was a good move for her." He straightened, and Robert could feel the conversation turning. "She told us your family has deep roots on the island."

"Been here a very long time. The family business is fishin', and has been for generations. My father owns two boats."

Tim nodded. "Very hard work, that. I tip my hat to your father. But fishing isn't the business for you?"

"No. I've loved divin' since the first time I tried it, and I've been able to make a livin' as a photographer for the last couple of years."

"I can understand. My dad was a high school teacher—PE and football coach. He couldn't figure out why his nerdy son was so obsessed with computers. He wanted me to play football and try for a scholarship. But I ended up with one anyway, academic, and he was still every bit as proud. Family is important to me, Robert."

He met Tim's stare head-on, instinctively knowing that showing weakness would be a grave mistake. "Your daughter is important to me."

Tim's eyes softened. "I'm glad to hear that. Because the last piece of shit she was with damn-near destroyed her. I'm working on doing the same to him and his family. Robert, I'm a fair man. I couldn't care less where you came from, what you do, or what color you are. All I'm interested in is you making Heather happy. As long as you do that, I'm the best friend you could ask for." He didn't need to present the opposite case. He'd already stated that pretty clearly.

"Sounds like you and I want the same things," Robert said evenly, and his gaze wandered to where the women had disappeared. "I haven't known your daughter long, Tim. But she knocked me senseless from the first moment I laid eyes on her."

Tim surprised him by breaking into a wide grin. "Yep, she's definitely her mother's daughter. Laura did the same thing to me."

. . .

THE GALENS and Robert were nearly lost as they clustered at the end of a table that seated twenty. Dinner was steak and Caribbean lobster, and judging from Robert's prior experience, Theo was definitely *not* the chef. But the young butler was fully present, and the divemaster was even more grateful he decided against the store-bought wine when Theo presented a bottle covered in dust to Tim. He poured out a dark-red tasting sample, which Heather's father approved. When his glass was poured, Robert tried to read the label, but it was in French and faded from age. The sense of unreality he'd been experiencing since he entered the villa doubled.

Laura gave him a warm smile. "This is such a beautiful island! I've spent hours just walking around the grounds here. The sugar mill is so picturesque sitting on the bluff like that. Beautiful."

Robert tried to cover his expression but couldn't help flinching.

Heather saw it. "What's wrong?"

"Nothin'. It's just..." He was conflicted. Laura's comment had been innocent and unthinking, which was exactly the problem. *If race is an issue, better to find out now...* He met Laura's concerned gaze. "It was your comment about the sugar mill. It's not quite so picturesque when your ancestors were enslaved to feed sugar cane into it."

Laura's eyes became round as an expression of horror overtook her face. "I didn't think of that—how completely thoughtless. Please forgive me."

Robert smiled, a pang ringing through him. "No forgiveness needed. I didn't mean to make a big issue of it. Our history is a complex issue, but if no one talks about it, nothing will ever change."

Tim stared at him evenly. "Thanks for bringing it up. You're absolutely right. What might be a fun adventure for us has completely different connotations for someone in your shoes. It never hurts to think a little harder about the impact you leave, especially when you're in our position."

Robert nodded. "The Tourism Board is doin' more to show both sides of the island's history to visitors and acknowledge there were some pretty dark times here."

Heather grasped his hand under the table and turned those green eyes toward him. He was held by the pride he saw in them and squeezed back, exhaling a silent, relieved breath.

Robert was cutting another piece of his perfectly cooked steak when a young man dressed in an expensive-looking blue suit hurried into the dining room and leaned over Tim's shoulder. "I'm terribly sorry to disturb you, but Senator Armstrong called my phone and insists on speaking with you."

Tim scowled, glancing around the table as he set his fork down. "So much for putting my phone away. I apologize, but it's not a good idea to keep the head of the Senate Judiciary Committee waiting." He followed Blue Suit out of the room.

Heather leaned forward, concern creasing her brow. "Judiciary? Is Dad in trouble?"

Laura waved carelessly and took another sip of wine. "No, it's nothing different. Congress likes to squawk now and again about Galendo getting too big."

The unreality increased further, making Robert slightly dizzy, and he took a drink of water. *Senate Judiciary Committee? He knows senators?* While Robert was one-on-one with the Galens, it was easy to forget who they were. He was just getting to know his girlfriend's parents, like any other man. On the dive boat, they had seemed so average.

But they weren't.

Within a few minutes, Tim returned, sending everyone an apologetic smile. "Sorry about that. Bill Armstrong is one of the most impatient people on the planet and does not like being ignored. I glanced at my phone and had six missed calls and ten texts from him."

Great. He calls the Senator by his nickname.

Heather studied her father carefully. "Is anything going on I should know about, Dad?"

Tim reached over and squeezed her hand before taking a large drink of wine. "No, baby. It's the same old, same old. Some of the senators on the committee got their feathers ruffled by the Photosweep takeover. They think Galendo's too similar. The word *monopoly* is being thrown around, and they're murmuring about a Justice Department investigation. Bill wanted to update me and let me know he should be able to work it out. Tempest in a teapot."

"Good," Heather said. "I hate it when you're in the news."

Robert reached over and squeezed her hand. She gave him a grateful smile and kept hold of it.

"It's not exactly our favorite thing either," Laura added.

With the senator placated, they returned to their steak and lobster. Robert stared at his plate, but his appetite had decreased substantially.

LATER THAT NIGHT, Robert's head was still spinning as he sat alone on his patio, staring at the stars. After diving with Tim and Laura, he'd almost convinced himself they were two ordinary people, who happened to be the parents of the woman he was falling in love with. There was no point in denying that.

But dinner had brought it all home in no uncertain terms. Tim and Laura hadn't acted any differently. They were simply in their familiar environment. One which couldn't be more opposite to Robert's. He'd been so busy worrying about his parent's acceptance of Heather, maybe he hadn't thought enough about how he would fit into her world.

I lost one woman who didn't think I was good enough. How can I make this work?

He sighed, crossing his legs at the ankles before him. "By continuin' the same way you've been all along, Robert. Be yourself—if that's not enough for Heather, then this relationship wasn't meant to be."

Having said the words out loud, he expected to feel despondent. But another emotion rose instead—certainty. He'd looked deep into Heather's eyes when she'd bared her soul that first night under this same sky.

He was enough.

Chapter Twenty-Three

HEATHER STOOD in the shower with Robert, kissing him languidly and letting her pounding heart return to normal as the water sprayed over them. One leg was wrapped around his waist, and she slowly slid it to the shower floor. After a final brushing of lips, Heather pulled back. "There's an advantage to being nearly the same height, I guess. Makes some positions easier."

He laughed softly, his teeth flashing against his dark skin. "Better not plan on wearin' super high heels, or you'll tower above me."

"I don't wear heels, period. You're safe on that front." She reached behind him and gave one cheek a healthy squeeze. "Come on. Let's go out to the kitchen."

Heather had stayed at her parents' villa late, catching up as much as possible before they departed. She and Robert hadn't seen each other again until the previous evening, where they'd been occupied by thoughts besides her parents. But the senior Galens were on Heather's mind now as she pushed a cup of black coffee toward Robert. "My parents really liked you, and they loved diving with you. Are you doing ok after meeting them?"

He had been lifting the mug to his mouth and paused midway. "Ok? Is there some reason I shouldn't be?"

"My family isn't exactly normal. The lifestyle is a lot to take in, even for people who grew up in Silicon Valley. I wouldn't be surprised if you're a little shellshocked."

Robert inclined his head. "It was kind of surreal, I have to admit. On the boat, everythin' was so normal. But dinner was... different. Your dad can't even go a day without people houndin' him."

"I know. It's one reason I had to get away from there. Everything you do is under a microscope. Mom and Dad are used to it and consider it the price of success. But I don't want to pay that much."

He watched her closely. "You're givin' up a lot."

"I know—I'm not in denial about it. But I like that everything I've accomplished here has been on my own merits. And I'm not trying to distance myself from Mom and Dad, just the chaos that always surrounds them. I don't need a private jet or fancy car." She took a deep breath and met his gaze. "I need you."

His brown eyes softened as he kissed the end of her nose. "You've got me."

"You impressed them a lot. Dad hates it when people try to schmooze him, and there was none of that with you. And he really liked that you corrected my mother's misstep about the sugar mill."

"I was worried there might be a price on my head after that."

Heather laughed. "My father started Galendo as a way to bring people together. He's ok with gentle reminders when he or my mother makes a blunder. Your reaction was just right."

She reached out and stroked a finger across his chin. "This is kind of new to me. Thanks for speaking up. Keep doing that, ok? Especially when I say something I shouldn't."

A smile rose on Robert's face. "Deal. As long as you correct me if I screw up when I'm talkin' about hostile takeovers and stock options."

They both laughed, and Heather topped off their coffee mugs. "So, when am I going to meet your family?"

Robert hesitated before replying, "I'm workin' on it. Mother loves to host family dinners once a month or so, so I'll invite you to the next one. Just don't expect surf and turf in a private villa, ok? We're from pretty different worlds, Heather."

"Does that have to be a problem?"

"No... but my folks are traditional. They have kind of old-fashioned values."

She cocked her head. "What are you trying to say? Are they going to object to me being white?"

He sighed and set his mug on the counter. "This is hard to explain. The problem isn't about race—it's about bein' from *away*. Bein' different, and not havin' the same upbringin' to understand our local culture and history. It makes them... unsure."

"Cindy said something similar to me once."

Robert nodded. "It's not unusual on the islands. You might have to be a little patient."

She slid both arms around his waist and whisked her lips over his. "I can do that. You're worth waiting for."

Robert kissed her hard, clutching her tightly against him before whispering against her mouth, "You mean a lot to me. Don't doubt that."

But as Heather drove home to get ready for work, his last words reverberated inside her head.

I haven't doubted his feelings for me. But discussing his

family made him think I might. Maybe meeting the Davises won't be the simple process I was expecting. Any more than meeting my parents was simple for Robert...

———

AMBER SUNBEAMS GLINTED into the pool bar, lighting up dust motes as they danced in the air. Heather scattered a final scoop of ice over the six beers inside a steel bucket and slid it toward the diver. She was well used to the rhythms of the resort now, one of them being the late-afternoon return of the final dive trip.

A group of thirsty divers immediately thronged the pool bar, requesting drinks to enjoy back in their bungalows before dinner. She and Clark were both busy until 6 p.m., when the restaurant opened. Then one would work the new bar, leaving the other to cover the now-quiet pool bar.

As she returned from delivering two mojitos to a table in the sand, Sara sat at the bar.

"Chardonnay?" Heather asked.

"Not after today. I need something icy and sweet. Can you make me a Dream?"

"Comin' right up." Heather began mixing the drink, using a pinch from the top-secret, unlabeled jar of ground cloves. "Rough day?"

Sara rubbed her temples. "Busy, with lots of juggling. I can't *wait* for the new spa to open."

"How much longer?"

"Several months yet. There's been a delay on a feature wall we ordered, so the crew is concentrating on other areas of construction." Heather set the Half Moon Dream in front of Sara, and she took a long sip from the bamboo straw, closing her brown eyes in ecstasy. "I love this drink. Wonder what Clark will come up with next?"

"He's always experimenting when he's got a free moment. Some experiments are more successful than others."

Sara grinned. "Well, he gets them dialed in eventually, that's for sure. As soon as I'm done, I'm headed up to the new spa to check the progress. That always cheers me up."

"It looks like quite the project. You'll have to give me a full report."

Sara cocked her head. "It's after five. Aren't you due for your dinner break?"

"Yeah. Charlotte should be here any moment to cover me. Why?"

"Come tour the spa with me! I love to show it off. It will be incredible when everything is all done."

TEN MINUTES LATER, Heather and Sara were walking north along the shore. Sara wore a long black and green dress with a swirling pattern and carried her sandals in one hand. Silver earrings dangled almost to her shoulders.

"How's life on your private beach?" Heather asked.

"It's been a bit of an adjustment, but we haven't had any major issues. As long as Jack stays willing to kill the creepie-crawlies for me, we're golden."

Heather laughed. "That's the big test, huh?"

Sara arched a brow. "You should see some of the spiders that have found their way inside. Horrible things. Cruz ate several when he was with us. If we ever got a dog, we probably wouldn't even need to feed it!"

"Well, if you decide you want a dog, let me know. I can hook you up."

"Maybe someday. I'm not sure I want all that extra work. If it were up to Jack, we'd be buried in dogs."

A long white building rose before them. Enclosed alcoves

with open rectangular doorways at the far end were spaced at even intervals facing the beach. They entered through the last in the row, turning around on the covered cement patio to face the serene ocean. The only sound was the waves softly washing onto the sand.

"There will be eight massage rooms—four like this facing the ocean and four more on the other side. Each guest can decide between an ocean or rainforest view." Sara laughed. "Hope insists we call it rainforest and not jungle. And after my experience with the spiders, I'm inclined to agree with her."

"Rainforest does sound more genteel."

They continued through the empty doorway into a ten-foot-wide hallway that bisected both sides. The floor was unusual. A four-foot empty channel meandered down the unfinished surface, twisting from one wall to the other.

"What's with the floor?" Heather asked.

Sara beamed as she stepped into the depression, twirling in a circle. "This is going to be one of our crowning glories. The floor will be flattened river rock. We're going to run water through the channel, creating a river that ambles through the spa. Low wooden bridges will cover the river where people need to walk."

Heather stopped, imagining the finished structure. "That sounds amazing."

"It will be."

They continued to a central reception hall. "On the other side is the salon, with multiple hair and mani-pedi stations, as well as more treatment rooms for wraps." The dry canal wandered throughout the large room before continuing into the salon. The room they stood in towered to a twenty-foot ceiling, and a large opening faced the ocean. A smaller one mirrored it on the jungle side. Sara pointed to each. "These will be glass walls with entry doors. We'll make a small patio facing the ocean here and serve smoothies and infused water. Guests can watch the ocean as they enjoy them."

Heather turned around to a concrete-reinforced wall that dominated the space next to the main entry facing the jungle. "What's that?"

Sara sighed and her arms fell to her sides. "That's the holdup. You're looking at the feature wall I told you about, a twenty-foot-tall stacked-stone wall. But there's a delay with the stone, and it won't be delivered for several more months. We've had other hiccups too, but that's the major one. In front of the wall will be the reception counter, which will be turquoise-colored glass to match the ocean."

"Wow," Heather breathed, her eyes following the winding river-to-be. "Water is definitely the theme here."

"Exactly."

"Are you going to bring potted hibiscus trees in here to suggest the name?"

A slow smile rose on Sara's face as she shook her head. "This is a completely new vision, and it deserves its own name. You're standing in the middle of Aqua."

Heather whipped her head around, eyes going wide. "What an incredible name. I love it!"

"Thanks. This has been my dream my whole adult life, but it's maddening to be held up by construction delays. The foreman estimates the spa won't be finished until early next year."

"January will be here before you know it."

Sara shrugged one shoulder. "It might be February. But until then, I can live vicariously next door. That should be open sometime in December."

"There's more?"

"Yeah. Come on."

The women walked out of the opening on the beach side

and continued. The building was bigger than Heather had thought. Approximately thirty percent was a separate open room on the north end. They stepped up onto the concrete floor. Metal framing extended around three sides. The only solid wall was the common one separating the large area from the spa, but there was no framing for a door.

A flock of yellow warblers flew by along the tree line behind the building, their song filling the open room. Sara smiled at them before turning back to Heather. "These three sides are going to be one-way glass, so people have to enter to see what's inside."

"There's no door into the rest of the spa," Heather said. "Are they cutting that in later?"

Sara's gaze sharpened. "This isn't part of the spa. Didn't Hope tell you?"

"No, she talked mostly about the bungalows."

"I can believe that. She loves those." Then Sara broke into a giant smile, as if she possessed a secret she couldn't wait to tell. "When you came over to our place, I remember you saying that you love art."

Heather strolled around the empty area, imagining how stunning the room would be with three glass walls. *I could do so much with this space.* "Absolutely. And I can see this area becoming an actual piece of art."

"That's kind of the point. This is going to be an art gallery."

Heather's heart nearly stopped as she whirled around. *"What?"*

Chapter Twenty-Four

"GREAT DAY FOR A PHOTO SHOOT," April said as Robert held the camera to his eye. The pair stood alongside Tommy in the elevated wheelhouse of *Surface Interval* as they motored back to the resort.

"Yeah," Robert said, glancing at the azure sky without a cloud in sight. "Today is pretty perfect, so I wanted to retake the wide-angle resort pictures since they're so important." He took dozens of shots as they approached the resort and was especially pleased with the present view. There was almost no wind, and the sea was glassy. The beach and central complex buildings visible just behind the pier were the focal point of his shot.

After Tommy brushed the boat against the dock, April hopped off to secure them. Robert clapped Tommy on the shoulder. "Thanks for a great mornin'. April and I are headin' to the dive shop now to make sure the afternoon is covered."

When Robert entered the bright shop, Zach and Alex stood behind the counter, with Zach leafing through a scuba textbook. He straightened and smiled at Robert, who slowed his step for a moment in surprise. Zach had just graduated from high school and was working more in the dive shop. The small local boy had been a fixture there for the past year, but Robert had just realized he wasn't so small anymore. "Zach, how much have you grown?"

The kid broke into a wide smile. "Six inches! My mother says I'm a late bloomer." He was around Robert's height now.

April laughed. "Before you know it, you'll be as tall as Alex."

Zach shook his head. "Don't think that's in my genes."

Her eyes drifted back to the former SEAL, who was zipping up a blue pouch on the counter. Since Alex had gotten involved with Hope, April's presence had steadily declined. Robert felt bad for her. She hadn't exactly hidden her attraction to Alex, but he hadn't returned it, even before he'd met Hope. After, no other woman existed for him.

Robert pointed to the blue pouch. "Teachin' a scuba class?"

Alex nodded and pushed the bag toward Zach. "I'm dropping off the rescue course manual."

Robert and April both gave the boy big smiles. "Takin' rescue, huh?" Robert asked. "That's a great class."

Zach closed the manual and slid it into the pouch. "Eventually. Alex says I need more experience first."

Robert turned his attention back to the instructor, surprised once again. There weren't any minimum required number of dives for rescue diver class. "Never hurts to have more dives under your belt."

"It's more of a personal requirement of mine," Alex replied. "The situations in the rescue course, not to mention real emergencies, require you to react without thinking about your own situation. Which means you need to be a very confident diver before you attempt the course. Plus, I want to see if Hope and Sara want to take it with him. But for now, Zach will tag along on a lot of morning dives now."

The boy broke into an enormous smile. "It's a dirty job, but someone's got to do it."

Smiling, Alex turned back to Robert and April. "What brings you two in here?"

"We want to make sure no one else signed up for the afternoon trip," Robert replied. "Eddie wants to have lunch with me this afternoon, and I thought April might be able to take the group alone."

Alex moved over to the terminal and studied the screen. "Oh yeah. No problem—there's eight signed up. Take the afternoon off and say hi to Eddie for me."

When Robert passed by the pool bar, Heather was thronged by patrons, and the pair weren't able to say more than a quick hello to each other. After giving her a wink, he continued to his SUV. He had a couple of hours before meeting Eddie and drove back to his house. As Robert climbed into the foothills east of Frederiksted, his attention turned away from the resort and the photos he'd taken for Hope. His little brother would be a good sounding board and he needed to discuss his experience with the Galens.

"YOUR DINNER WAS INTERRUPTED BY A SENATOR?" Eddie gaped at Robert, then barked a laugh. "Man, you're sure movin' in different circles now."

Robert bristled, setting his fork on his plate. The two brothers were eating at Charlie's, a bar and grill in central St. Croix. They sat in a corner booth, dark wood looming around them. Eddie had showered and changed into a clean T-shirt and jeans, the smell of fish blissfully absent.

"No, I'm not!" Robert said. "Heather lives here, not in California."

"Did she act differently around her parents?"

"Not at all. They have a good relationship—you can tell. Though her father warned me not to hurt her."

Eddie had taken a bite of hamburger and now held up one finger while he swallowed it. "Hold on. He threatened you?"

Robert smiled, knowing that would get a reaction from his brother. "Not with life and limb. But he's a protective father, for sure."

"Robert, the man is on a first-name basis with senators. And richer than hell. You sure you know what you're doin'? What if he puts out a hit on you?"

"He's a computer nerd, not the Godfather."

"You must really like this girl."

"Not just like. I admire her. I respect her, and what she's tryin' to do. Turnin' her back on all that money and power."

Arching a brow, Eddie gave him a remarkably shrewd look. "But she's really not, is she? If things don't work out here, she can always run home to mommy and daddy. Sounds like they'd welcome her with open arms."

"That's true, but she's pretty committed to makin' it on her own. And I'll stand by her."

Eddie paused for another bite. "Mom and Pop know about her yet?"

"No, not yet."

"You can't hide her forever."

"I'm not hidin' her!" Robert pushed his plate away. "That's one reason I wanted to have lunch with you. She asked me about meetin' them, so I'm thinkin' about invitin' her over for a family dinner. Will you come?"

Eddie snorted. "I wouldn't miss it for the world. The entertainment value alone will be worth the price of admission."

Robert stared back steadily. "I'm countin' on you to back me up if things get tense. Her parents made me feel welcome. It was a bizarre day, but I liked them—and I'm pretty sure they liked me too. I'm just not sure Heather's goin' to have things as easy."

Eddie sobered. "Probably not. Especially with Mom."

"Yeah. Why don't you marry one of her suggestions and take the heat off me?"

"I did go out with Chantal. The date was super awkward, and she was as eager for it to end as I was."

Robert's phone buzzed on the table. The photo he had isolated of Heather on their first shelter photography session was now his home screen image, and it always made him smile. Even more so when she was the caller. "Hey, beautiful. What's up?"

"You won't believe what I found out today from Sara! Can you come over after I get off?"

"Sure. What's the big news?"

His phone practically vibrated from her exhilaration. "I'll tell you later. I'm on a break and need to get back to work. But it's exciting!"

"I gathered that already. Let me know when you're home tonight." After the call ended, Robert turned back to Eddie, who was finishing his beer.

"Somethin' big happen?"

"Not sure. A friend gave Heather some news she's excited about. I'll find out soon enough."

"So, when's the big, happy family dinner?"

"I'll call Mom and set somethin' up for a week or two from now. What should I say to her and Pop about Heather?"

Eddie leaned back, considering the question. "It's a lose-lose either way. If you give them too much information, it just gives them more ammunition to use against Heather. If you don't say much, they'll accuse you of ambushin' them because you knew they wouldn't approve."

"Thanks. That's very promisin'."

Eddie laughed again. "Hey, you asked. Though if you're vague about her, you could claim it never occurred to you to say more, bein' twenty-first century and all. And that your marriage to an Althea-approved local girl wasn't too successful."

"Think that will work?"

"Doubtful. What I want to know is what you plan on sayin' to Heather beforehand."

"I already warned her they might need some time to warm up." Robert finished his beer and sighed. "Maybe things won't be as bad as I'm expectin'."

HEATHER PACED AROUND the living room, trying to be quiet since Cindy was already asleep. She had been bursting since Sara's explanation about the gallery and couldn't wait to share the news, counting down the minutes until her shift ended. When a knock rapped on the front door, she ran to it and pulled Robert inside.

He laughed as she dragged him onto the couch. "What has you so stirred up?"

"It might be nothing. It might be everything." Heather explained about the new art gallery. "Did you know?"

He shook his head. "No, I thought that whole building was the spa. Interestin' concept though. I take it you want to work there?"

"More than anything! I need to talk to Hope about it. Of course, she has no idea I've got gallery experience. No one does. I hate to beat her door down and say, *hire me.* I need to introduce the subject somehow, though."

"Don't wait too long. If the place is goin' to open in a few months, she'll be hirin' before too long."

"That's true. If I got a job there, I wouldn't have to work evenings anymore. We'd have schedules that actually meshed."

He swept her hair off her face. "Don't go puttin' the horse before the cart. I'd hate for you to be disappointed if this didn't work out."

She shrugged. "I would be, but if the gallery becomes successful, they'll need to hire more staff. And I'll already be there, toiling away at the bar."

"There's one thing I'll say for Hope. When she sees talent in someone, she stops at nothin' to foster it. Clark and I are both examples of that. She even helped Alex to come into his own again. If there's a chance to make your dream happen, you're in the right place."

She swung her legs across his lap. "What have you been up to since I saw you?"

He had been brushing his hand up and down her thigh, but now he paused. "I had lunch with my brother Eddie."

"You two are close?"

"Yeah, we are." Robert resumed stroking her thigh. "I'm excited for you to meet him. That was one of the things we talked about tonight."

Excitement filled her at his words. "I'd like to meet him too."

"I'll try to set up a family dinner, so you can meet my parents too. My mother likes to have us over once a month or so. I'll shoot for a couple of weeks from now, so you can get the evenin' off work."

"I'm looking forward to it."

He paused, about to say something, then changed the subject. "I'm glad I got to meet your folks."

Robert had been a hit with them, especially her mother. Laura had been touched by his patient and skilled care while they were diving. Heather was shrewd enough to realize that Robert had been more at ease in an activity where he was the acknowledged expert. And he was smart enough not to act differently around them. Her father had honed the skill of reading people to a razor's edge over the years, and Robert had impressed him. Simply by *not* trying to impress him.

Their relationship was moving in a more serious direction, and she was still surprised how at ease she was about that, given her disaster with Grant.

It's because this feels right. With Grant, I was always swept along with the tide, never in control. He was the heir-apparent to his father's company, but I didn't respect him like I do Robert. And at this point, it's much more than respect.

Not only had Robert worked hard for everything he'd earned in life, but he was also generous, willing to help anyone who needed it. Which brought her back to the shelter. "We've got some new intakes at Pet Paradise. Could you take pictures soon?"

"Sure. I'm pretty booked up for the next week, but I'll come out after that. Lucky still there?" He stroked his hand slower and slower, lingering at the top of her thigh.

"Yes. He needs to go to someone older. We took outdoor shots of him last time. Let's try indoor ones during the next session. That might appeal more to people not looking for an active dog." Heather settled tighter against him as his hand slipped around to her inner thigh. The bulge in his pants was hard to miss.

"Tell me where to point the camera, and we'll get it done."

"Something tells me your mind isn't on photo shoots at the moment."

Robert leaned forward and kissed her, barely touching his lips to hers. Then he whisked his tongue over them. "Photography is usually the last thing on my mind when I'm around you."

A sensuous warmth spread through her midsection. "Is that an invitation?"

"This is your place. I'm waitin' for you to ask me."

He inhaled sharply as she slipped her hand down to squeeze him. "Consider yourself invited to my bedroom."

Chapter Twenty-Five

SEPTEMBER...

HEATHER SAT behind the desk at Pet Paradise, uploading Robert's latest pictures. She was currently working on Lucky's. His short black and brown coat shimmered against the black fabric, and his mouth hung open in a doggy smile. "We'll see if that brings anyone in, sweetie."

The front door opened to the sound of an excited young voice, which was quickly followed by an excited little girl. Her thick black hair was separated into three ponytails, each sporting a different, colorful ribbon. Her parents entered behind her, both slightly less thrilled.

The girl, who looked about ten, took a gigantic jump forward, landing on both feet in front of Heather's desk. "We're here for Tigger!"

"I can see that!" Heather laughed as the girl's parents winced slightly. "You must be Abigail." At the child's exaggerated nod, she rose and handed a file folder to Abigail's mother. "Here's all the records. I'll take you back."

"Is Tigger fixed?" Abigail's mother handed her husband a pet carrier and thumbed through the file.

"Yes, he's been neutered and had all his shots."

Heather led them through a door directly off reception, straight to the Cat Shack. They currently had two litters of kittens and she headed for the second one, stopping before a large cage. There was a fabric-covered tree in one corner and the enclosure was dominated by a soft oval bed. Half a dozen ten-week-old kittens curled up in a fluffy pile in the middle of the bed. At the sight of the family and Heather, several rose and began meowing as they reached through the wire.

"Which one is he?" Abigail stood in front, wiggling a finger at the kittens.

"Tigger is on the right," Heather said, pointing to an orange tabby with four socks and a white face. "He's wearing the green collar."

Five minutes later, the family walked out the door with one loudly mewing kitten inside the carrier, and one extremely happy daughter. Donna passed them as she entered. "They look happy. Thanks for filling in for me."

"No problem. I got the latest photos uploaded, so that's all done. I'll go walk a few dogs." As she came into the Dog House, she paused by Lucky's kennel, wiggling her fingers through the chain-link gate. He padded up and presented his head to be scratched. She was distracted by excited yipping from across the aisle and turned around. A white Jack Russell Terrier with brown spots was jumping up and down on all four legs.

Heather approached, stopping before the kennel. "You're the new guy. I need to figure out a name for you. Let's go to the dog park and get to know each other." She produced a leash from her back pocket and the yipping increased in volume, as did the jumping. After easing her way inside, she clipped the leash onto the dog's collar, his entire body wiggling like a long snake. She opened the kennel, and the dog tore out, gasping as he pulled on the leash. Heather pushed through the door and went through the reception area.

"Oh good! You're taking the new boy," Donna said. "He still needs a name. I was thinking about Freddy, after Frederiksted."

"That might work. We're off to the park."

The morning was sunny and a nearby frangipani tree was in bloom, bathing her in its heavenly fragrance as they crossed the lawn, the dog still tugging at his leash. Heather sped up so he wouldn't choke himself. When she opened the gate to the fenced area, he sat down and whined. "What? After all that, you don't want to go in?" She tugged lightly, and he obediently followed as she latched the gate behind them. Heather led him around the perimeter, so he would be familiar with the area before she let him off-leash.

After they turned the first corner, he suddenly backed up, twisting his head. Before Heather knew what had happened, he had wiggled out of his collar and took off galloping around the enclosure. He wore a huge smile and ran with abandon, having the time of his life. Heather couldn't help laughing. "Ok. Knock yourself out."

An assortment of dog toys lay in the enclosure's corner, and she picked up a ball, launching it to the other side. The Jack Russell ran after it, catching it on a bounce before bringing it back and holding it in his mouth. His stubby tail wagged back and forth. As she leaned down to take the ball, he took off again, throwing a sly glance at her. "Oh, you like to play that game, huh? Well, I can't throw it if you don't give it to me, Freddy." She frowned, not sure the name fit him.

Eventually, he let her throw the ball several times, and she tried out other names. "Spot? Scrappy?"

She still wasn't happy about the names as she refastened the collar and leash. Heather opened the gate and led him through.

They had walked five feet when the dog twisted out of his collar once again and took off across the grassy meadow toward the trees.

"No! You can't do that out here!"

Heart pounding, she ran after him, and he would let her get within a foot before taking off again. They weren't near the road, so at least she didn't need to worry about car traffic. Hopefully, it would stay that way.

After ten minutes of the mad chase, Heather was huffing and puffing and beyond irritated. The dog was still having a marvelous time, and thought it a wonderful game to *almost* let her catch him before running away again. Only now, he was easing his way toward the road.

"Easy... just let me... catch you, ok?" Breathing hard, she approached him with one arm out, talking in a soft voice even though she was ready to throttle him. The dog stood completely still except for his panting sides, his tail twitching. "Good boy," she said as she got closer... closer. Her idea was to grab the scruff of his neck—the collar and leash were in her back pocket. She figured the sight of them would send him on another happy dash.

When her hand was only inches away, the dog barked twice and took off again. He was undoubtedly smiling at her, and her frustration boiled over. "Oh, goddammit. I give up!"

Throwing her hands in the air, Heather collapsed onto her back in the warm grass. She was still breathing like a bellows and threw an arm over her eyes. Tears built as she pictured the dog running into traffic and getting hit. Two tears rolled down her cheeks. Just as she was getting ready to go after him yet again, a loud snuffling came from nearby. She lifted her arm, and the dog stood right above her. He licked the tears off her face, then sat down, panting. Heather rose to a sitting position, her legs straight in front, and the dog climbed into her lap and licked her chin.

She started laughing. "Oh, you are too smart for your own good, aren't you? You were only waiting for me to give up." He let her put his collar back on, and this time she made it much tighter. "You get a harness next time. No more collars for you, boy."

They returned to the shelter uneventfully. "You definitely need an active family with a fenced yard. But you're very sweet, aren't you?" He *huffed* in agreement.

When she came in the door, Donna sat behind the desk and greeted them with a smile. "Well, that was a nice, long session. Looks like you both got some exercise. How nice!"

Heather snorted and crossed the room, wiping the sweat from her brow. As she opened the door to the Dog House, she turned back. "Oh, by the way. His name is Houdini."

FINISHED DIVING FOR THE DAY, Robert stepped across the sand to the pool bar, smiling at two divers. Peering behind the bar, he was pleased to see only Heather. He sat down on a stool as she gave him a warm smile. "How was the afternoon dive?"

"Uneventful, which is a good thing. Not the most excitin' dive in the world, but some are like that."

"You want a beer?"

"Sure, I'm off work now."

She poured him a Leatherback, and he took a deep breath. "Could you get next Sunday evenin' off? I talked to my mother about us comin' over for dinner, and that works for them."

"I have Monday off, and I'm sure I could switch days with Clark."

He'd stopped off at his parents' house that morning, trying

to come up with a way to break the ice. His father had left hours previously, so Robert flat-out asked his mother about having a family dinner so they could meet the new woman in his life.

Althea's face had shone like a sunburst. "Oh, you're seein' someone! Is it Candace, June's daughter? I thought I saw you two makin' eyes at each other a while back."

Robert froze in place, nonplussed. "Huh? I haven't seen Candace in two years, Mom. And we've never been interested in each other. Heather works at Half Moon Bay as a bartender."

"Well, who's her family? I can't wait to meet her."

He met her eyes evenly. "She's not from the island. She recently moved here from California."

Althea's face went blank. "California?" Her tone of voice indicated Heather could have been from Inner Mongolia. "Well... I'm just surprised is all."

"Don't know why. Plenty of people date folks from the mainland."

Both corners of her mouth drew down. "I'm well aware. And that's part of the reason our culture and traditions are bein' lost."

He kept his voice soft and coaxing. "The world is gettin' smaller, Mother. People are minglin' more, and cultures are blendin' together. That's not such a bad thing."

Althea pressed her lips into a thin line, but didn't respond. Finally, she looked over at him. "How about six o'clock on Sunday?"

"That would be fine. And one more thing. It shouldn't matter, but she's white. Just so you know."

"I assumed that when you said she was all the way from California."

Robert forced his clenched hand to relax. "Mom, Heather is important to me. I need you to understand that."

She stared straight back. "I'll try. That's all I can promise."

Now Heather glanced at him, a worry line forming between her brows. "Robert, what do your parents know about me?"

He reached out and squeezed her hand, keeping his wrapped around hers. "They know you mean a lot to me, and that's what counts. It'll be fine, Heather. They aren't monsters."

She raised a corner of her mouth at that. "I'm sure they're not. I'm just curious... what you said to them."

"Yes, I told my mother all about you. I even mentioned the words white and California. She didn't shriek and run out of the house."

Heather laughed, the deep rich sound he loved. "Well, that's a good sign. I'm sure everything will be fine."

Chapter Twenty-Six

HEATHER GRIPPED the paper-wrapped bouquet tighter, frowning as the rich, tropical fragrance filled Robert's car, her mind full of second thoughts. "Are you sure we shouldn't have bought a bottle of wine too?"

"My folks don't drink wine. They don't even drink Leatherback. Kalik or Red Stripe is more their style."

She turned to stare at him as he drove through the congested streets of Frederiksted. "Maybe we should get a six-pack, then."

He reached across the console and gripped her hand. "Relax, sweetness. The flowers are gorgeous. Mom will love them."

But will she love me?

This was an unfamiliar experience for Heather. Growing up as one of the Silicon Valley elites, she had always been courted. But this evening, the last thing she planned to do was play up her privileged upbringing.

Robert parked behind a Nissan Altima in front of a small one-story house made of cement bricks. It had once been white, but was now the off white that spoke of seasons without a touchup, though the yard was neatly kept with a palm tree in the middle.

"Looks like Eddie is already here," he said, indicating the Altima.

They climbed onto a wide covered porch and stopped before a dark-blue front door. Robert entered without knocking, calling out, "We're here!"

Heather shut the door behind her with a nervous sigh, but the inhale afterward was full of the delicious scent of dinner cooking—mysterious spicy aromas. Taking in the living room around her, the carpet was a somewhat threadbare beige Berber, and the walls were white. A floral couch and loveseat took up much of the room, with an old tube-style television hulking on a table at one end. But a smile rose on her face at the family photo hanging on one wall. It showed the Davises as a younger couple with two boys sitting before them. Robert looked around ten, and his killer smile was in evidence even then.

A large man, younger than Robert, walked into the living room, breaking into a wide, welcoming smile as he made eye contact with her. Robert pressed a hand against the small of her back as he introduced them. "Heather, this is my little brother Eddie. He got the height, but I got the brains, so I still won."

Laughing, she shook Eddie's hand. "Pleased to meet you."

A man walked into the living room from another entry. He had mostly gray hair, and a thin, wiry build, and Heather immediately saw the echoes of Robert in him.

The man approached and shook her hand with a polite nod. "I'm Bennett. Welcome to our home."

"Good evening, sir. Thank you for inviting me."

Eddie rubbed his hands together. "Mom's finishin' up some conch fritters as an appetizer. You guys want to head into the kitchen?"

Robert turned to Heather, grinning broadly. "That's an automatic yes. Our mother's conch fritters are legendary."

"I can hardly wait!" With a smile that was hopefully less nervous looking than she felt, Heather followed Eddie through the doorway. Robert's hand was still on her lower back, giving solid support. They emerged into a kitchen with oak cabinets and black appliances. A substantial oak table and chairs for eight diners anchored the opposite side of the room.

Facing away from them, a matronly woman with her thick graying hair tied neatly at the nape of her neck placed round, flattened fritters onto a platter. Hearing the group enter, she turned around. Her expression was neutral, and her light brown eyes gave nothing away.

The same light brown eyes Robert possessed, who now joined Heather's side. "Mother, I'd like you to meet Heather."

"Welcome. You can call me Althea, if you'd like," she said rather formally.

"I'm very pleased to meet you. Thank you for the invitation." Heather presented Althea with the large bouquet of tropical flowers.

She accepted them with thanks before turning to her younger son. "Can you get a vase and put these in water?" Then she turned back to Heather, whose heart was pounding. Robert's mother stood stiffly, and her face remained impassive. "They're lovely, thank you. Would you like to sit at the table?"

Heather sat next to Robert, with Eddie across from him and Bennett at the head of the table near the two men. Althea set the platter of fritters in the center and returned to a large stockpot bubbling fragrantly on the stove. Robert served Heather first, and she quickly confirmed his opinion. The fritters were light and crispy, with a dipping sauce containing just the right amount of spice.

"The conch is nice and fresh," Robert said. "You guys catch it this mornin'?"

"Yeah," Bennett said and glanced at Eddie, who ducked his head. "Your brother set his nets in the wrong area and caught more conch than fish. Good thing it's in season. We kept a few for tonight and threw the rest back."

The criticism obviously stung Eddie, prompting Heather to speak up. "It was lucky for me. These are amazing." Robert's brother gave her a smile as Althea set the stockpot on the table. Heather quickly turned to her. "Can I help you with anything?"

"No, thank you. I would never ask a guest to help. But Robert, could you bring over the johnny cakes? I think we're ready."

Robert hopped up to retrieve the fried bread cakes while Heather tried not to flush. Althea was almost excessively polite, and her words left no doubt that she wanted Heather to know she wasn't family.

Althea sat at the other head of the table, near Heather, and gazed pointedly at Bennett.

"Let's say grace." Bennett recited a brief prayer after they all joined hands. Althea's palm was cool and dry in Heather's and gave her a sense of reassurance. *Maybe things will be ok after all.*

The older woman caught Heather's eye and indicated the large stockpot. "Have you heard of callaloo?"

Heather smiled bravely, her reassurance fleeing like rats from a ship. *Is that question a trap?* "No, I haven't."

Althea gave her a small, tight smile in return. "I thought not and wanted to make a traditional dinner tonight. Callaloo is a stew common on many Caribbean islands." She took Heather's bowl and filled it with a rich broth full of leafy vegetables, potatoes, tomatoes, and flaky meat. "I use whatever greens are in season—these are spinach, and I like to add other ingredients too. Bennett brought the wahoo home just a few hours ago."

"It smells heavenly. I can't wait to try it." Heather gave her another smile, feeling like the temperature in the room had risen ten degrees. Robert passed her a johnny cake, then squeezed her knee under the table.

The stew was rich and bursting with flavors unusual to Heather's palette, and the delicious fried bread was the perfect accompaniment.

When she said so, Bennett gave her a crooked grin and reached for a nearby bottle of antacids. "It is divine. Too bad it plays havoc with my stomach."

Robert frowned at him. "Are you gettin' an ulcer, Pop?"

Bennet shook his head and grunted. "Nothin' that fancy. Just heartburn, is all."

After a few minutes of silent eating, Eddie looked at Heather, his eyes crinkling as he smiled. "You moved from warm, sunny California to warm, sunny St. Croix?"

Heather laughed, relaxing slightly at his question. "The part of California I'm from isn't very warm or sunny. San Francisco is cool and temperate, with frequent fog."

"Oh, yeah," Eddie said, staring absently into the distance. "I've seen pictures of the Golden Gate Bridge in the fog."

"Are you just here temporarily?" Althea asked in a deceptively mild tone, and Robert raised his head sharply.

"No, Mother. She's not. I already told you she moved here."

"Don't get defensive, Robert. I was merely wonderin' what would cause a young woman to leave such a large... cosmopolitan city for a small island thousands of miles away."

Robert stared hard at his mother, and Heather patted his forearm. "It's ok. She's asking a legitimate question." She turned back to Althea, having worked this answer out ahead of time. "I was at a point where I needed a change. A job I'd been after for a long time didn't work out and my long-term relationship had recently ended. I've lived in the Bay Area my entire life and wanted a new perspective."

"You think there's somethin' wrong with stayin' in the same place all your life?"

Shit! I didn't see that one coming.

"Not at all. I can absolutely understand never wanting to leave here. This island is incredible."

"Do you miss your family?" Eddie asked. Robert shot him a narrow look, which he ignored.

"Yes, very much. They came here for a visit last month, and we had a wonderful time. They loved Robert."

"Where'd they stay on the island? Half Moon Bay?" Bennett asked, dipping his johnny cake into the stew.

Heather thought for a moment. "No... a place near Christiansted... something villa... Stephenson! That's it."

Althea and Bennett both called out simultaneously, "The *Stephenson* Villa?"

"I'll get the popcorn." Eddie grinned gleefully at Robert, who scowled back.

Heather's heart sunk even further. But it wasn't like she could hide the truth—or wanted to. "My father has been quite successful in the internet technology business."

Eddie snorted, then covered it with a cough. "I don't think Mom and Pop are too familiar with Galendo. It's more of a young person's thing."

"Galendo?" Bennett asked. "I've heard of it. Just never knew what it was."

"It's a photo and video sharin' app," Robert said. "I've used it for years."

It was important that they understood her father wasn't some mindless billionaire playboy. "My dad developed Galendo from the ground up—he wasn't born with money. He built it from a small app used by his friends to a necessity billions of people around the world use every day."

"Don't think Heather is flittin' around, livin' off her parents," Robert said, putting an arm around her shoulders. "She moved here completely on her own, and doesn't take any financial help from them. She earns her own way."

Althea set her spoon down. "Your father worked his entire life to build this company, and you have no interest in bein' part of it?"

As panic set in, Heather tried to keep her voice even. "No, it's not like that at all. I love my parents very much—I just want to stand on my own."

"I might not know much about Galendo," Althea said, her voice tight. "But I know what family loyalty is."

"Stop it!" Robert yelled, and all heads turned to him as his eyes blazed at his mother. "I won't have you talkin' to her like that, Mom. If you can't be civil, we'll just leave." He removed his arm from Heather's shoulders to take her trembling hand under the table. She gripped back, grateful for the reassurance and support.

Althea dotted her mouth with her napkin, then turned to Heather. "I apologize if I upset you. I'm only tryin' to understand. You obviously come from a very unique background, Heather."

"Don't leave," Bennett said, frowning at his wife. "Althea's just bein' protective. We don't want to make you uncomfortable. Let's change the subject."

With a guilty glance at Heather and Robert, Eddie went into a play-by-play of the local baseball team's game he'd attended a few days prior. The tension around the table dissipated, but it was several minutes before Heather realized she was squeezing Robert's hand like a vise and consciously relaxed it.

The rest of the dinner passed uneventfully, if somewhat stiffly. Heather's tension dissolved further when discussing how much she enjoyed working at Half Moon Bay and the pet shelter. Althea remained mostly quiet, except for a polite comment now and then. But the experience hadn't been the warm introduction Heather had hoped for, despite Robert's caution.

He wasn't kidding, but things seem to have settled down. Maybe Althea just needs a little more time to warm up to me. On another visit—I've had enough for tonight.

Finally, Robert placed his napkin on the table. "Thanks for dinner, but we should get goin'." Heather could have wept with relief when he stood and gathered his and Bennett's plates.

Robert's father snapped his fingers, widening his eyes. "Oh, before you go, son. Eddie and I found some beautiful glass floats the other day. I thought you'd want to have them. Come on."

"Oh, ok." Robert raised a brow at Heather, asking his question silently, and she answered with a tiny nod even as her heart rate went supersonic.

No! Don't leave me alone with her.

Heather stood, and with an apologetic shrug, Robert handed her the plates and followed his father out of the kitchen, with Eddie trailing just behind.

Straightening her spine, Heather smiled at Robert's mother. "I'll help you with the dishes."

"You really don't need to."

I know. I'm not family... "Oh, I insist."

"You can stack the dishes in the sink, and I'll get to them later. Thank you."

The two women were quiet as they cleared the table, the men's voices murmuring from the living room.

As Heather placed the last plate in the sink, Robert called distantly, "You ready to go?"

"Be right there." Turning to Althea, Heather's smile was

stiff, and her palms itched to get out of the house. "Thanks for dinner. I really enjoyed experiencing a traditional Cruzan meal."

"Thank you." Robert's mother stood like a cold marble statue before the sink, one hand on a dish sponge. Heather turned away and forced herself to move at a normal pace, despite her eagerness to flee the house.

When she was halfway across the kitchen, Althea called out to her. Heather's heart nearly stopped, and she paused, turning around as oily dread filled her stomach.

The older woman eyed her steadily. "You seem like a nice woman. But make no mistake—you're not what my son needs. He's better off without you."

And without another word, Robert's mother turned her back on Heather and ran the faucet.

Chapter Twenty-Seven

THE GLASS FISHING floats were beautiful, and Robert was sure he could use them in photo shoots. In one hand, he held a light-green float the size of a cantaloupe with netted rope covering the lower half. Six others of varying sizes and colors rested inside the canvas grocery bag Pop had handed him, and Robert added this one, trying not to worry about Heather. She had indicated she was coming right out of the kitchen, and he didn't want to think about what might have held her up.

It's only been a minute. Take it easy—dinner went fairly well once I put my foot down, and Mother at least stayed quiet.

Robert smiled at his father. "Thanks. These will work great in beach photos."

He was swinging the bag over one shoulder when Heather rushed out of the kitchen. Her head was down, and both hands were clenched as she stared hard at the floor. Her pressed lips and tight face were the expression of someone doing everything possible not to cry. Then she opened the door and closed it behind her with a loud thump, without even saying goodbye. Robert's heart stopped for a moment, then resumed at a gallop as a red cloud descended in front of his eyes.

"Uh-oh," Eddie breathed. "That didn't look good."

"Mom!" Robert stormed to the kitchen entrance, where Althea stood rinsing dishes and placing them in the dishwasher. "What did you say to her?" His voice was hard and tight, and he couldn't care less whether he sounded respectful.

His mother paused but didn't turn around, merely turning her head so the long profile of her nose could be seen. "Only the truth. That can be hard to swallow sometimes."

Needing to go after Heather, Robert threw a frustrated glance at the front door, then pointed at Althea. "We're not done here, Mother. Not by a long shot."

When he stomped by Pops and Eddie, his brother's jaw was hanging open while Bennet stared toward the kitchen, his posture tense. "I'll see you later," Robert said. "I need to clean up Mom's mess."

He descended the porch steps and hurried to his SUV. Heather sat in the passenger seat. Her heaving shoulders were clearly visible in the glow of a streetlight, her face covered with both hands. "Oh my God, Mom. What have you done?"

Robert opened the driver's side door to the sound of crying, and a blade twisted in his gut. Sliding in, he placed one hand on the back of Heather's headrest and the other on her leg. "Talk to me, Heather. What did my mother say to you?"

She whipped her head back and forth and kept her face covered. "Just take me home."

With a final, furious glare at his parents' house, Robert pulled away. It was a fifteen-minute drive to the house she shared with Cindy, and Heather stopped crying about halfway, lowering her hands to her lap and leaving her tear-stained face bare. He gripped her hand tightly.

"I'm so sorry. Whatever she said, it isn't true."

Heather grunted tiredly at that. "This seems to be a pattern for me. That I'm not what my man needs."

"That's what she said?" Robert whipped a glance at her tear-streaked face, his knuckles pale against the wheel. "You're not what I need?"

"And that you're better off without me."

"You know that's not true, Heather. You're the best thing that's happened to me in a really long time."

She didn't respond, only stared blankly out the windshield as they drove down her street.

Robert's heart thundered in his chest, and his mouth was parched. "We can get past this. My parents aren't as important to me as you are."

"It's not that simple. You can't disown your whole family."

"Mom just needs some time to get used to you."

He pulled to a stop under a streetlight in front of her house, and she rolled her head toward him, the light emphasizing the tears on her face. "I'm not sure about that, Robert."

Panic was rolling in a long wave through his gut. He couldn't leave things like this. "Can I come in?"

She shifted in the seat, preparing to exit. "No. I need to be alone right now. I only want to go to sleep."

He squeezed the hand he still held. "We have to talk about this, Heather."

"I know. But not tonight."

With a last, devastated look at him, Heather left his car and trudged up to her front door.

FIFTEEN MINUTES LATER, Robert flew into his parents' house, slamming the door behind him. Surprisingly, Eddie was still here. *Maybe he'll back me up now, since he was only interested in enjoyin' the show at dinner.* Pop and Mom sat side by side on the couch as they all watched a game show. Three heads turned to him in unison as he halted in front of them.

"Who do you think you are, Mother?" Chest heaving, Robert did everything possible to keep from yelling his words.

With a deep sigh, she reached for the remote control and turned off the television. "She'll only break your heart, Robert. I'm tryin' to help you."

"By tellin' her she's no good and I'm better off without her? That's *helpin'*?"

Bennett swiped a hand over his forehead. "Althea, did you really say that?"

Eddie gave Robert a sympathetic wince as Mom responded, "Yes! It's the truth. Robert, do you really think a woman like that will stay here and continue working as a bartender? The moment things get rough, she'll run back home. You mark my words."

"Things have already been rough—you have no idea," Robert said. "Yet she's still here. And you have no right to interfere. I'm thirty-three years old, for God's sake!"

Althea's eyes flashed. "Watch your language! You might be a grown man, but you're still my son. I'll continue watchin' out for you until the day I die."

Robert continued in a lower voice. "All I'm sayin' is that I've earned the right to make my own decisions—and mistakes. And at least I'm not makin' the same mistake twice, am I?"

"You gotta admit," Eddie said, "The local girl you were so in favor of didn't work out so well. Did she, Mother?"

Althea glared at her younger son. "Leticia has nothin' to do with this."

"Yes, Mom, she does," Robert said, staring hard at her. "Leticia is proof that upbringin' isn't nearly as important as someone's character."

Bennett leaned forward and clasped his hands. "But Heather's upbringin' might as well have been on a different planet from yours, son. I think you've got an uphill battle here."

"Maybe. But it's my battle to fight, not yours." Robert whirled around and left, slamming the door behind him.

FEELING like her arm weighed a thousand pounds, Heather pushed the front door open and plodded inside. Her eyes widened at seeing Cindy on the couch, reading a paperback. "You're still awake, huh?" She glanced at the wall clock, astonished it was only eight o'clock. "Wow. It seems much later to me."

Cindy put the book down and patted the cushion next to her, a deep line forming between her brows. "Come sit down. I wanted to see how dinner went. Judging from your expression, it wasn't real successful."

Heather flopped down next to her like a sack of potatoes. "No, it wasn't."

"There's a bottle of wine in the kitchen. You want me to open it?"

"No. That's not the answer. I've already learned that lesson."

Cindy scooched closer and put her arm around Heather's shoulders. "Want to talk about it?"

When Heather had relived the dinner in the car with Robert—and especially Althea's parting words—discussing the evening was the last thing she'd wanted. But Cindy's quiet, supportive presence comforted her, and soon Heather had explained everything. "She told me I'm not what Robert needs."

"Oh, wow. That's pretty harsh. I'm sorry you had to go through that."

Then something occurred to Heather. "You tried to warn me about this, didn't you? When I first started dating Robert."

She had slumped against Cindy's shoulder, and now Cindy

lifted it in a shrug. "It can happen, especially in families where the parents expect children to follow in their footsteps."

"I also got the sense of what you meant about it not being a race issue."

"No. If you were exactly the same but your skin was Black, I doubt her reaction would have been much different. I've never met Robert's mother, so I'm makin' an assumption here, but the situation isn't unheard of."

"I knew we'd face racial issues. When we were on our lunch date at Cane Bay, we passed a couple who looked at us like we were dirt. I expected that, but this is different."

"And the racial prejudice is hard enough."

"That's right—you've dated white men, so you understand. More than I do, certainly."

"It's gettin' better. People are more open-minded than ten years ago, but you run into it regularly." She gave Heather's hand a squeeze. "Was it tense with Robert when you left?"

"A little. He wanted to talk things out, but I couldn't. He can't abandon his family for me—I wouldn't want him to do that. But his mother was just so... *cold.*"

"Hopefully there's a middle ground he can find with his folks. If his relationship with you is important enough, you two will work it out."

"He was really pissed at Althea, and he defended me at the table, which made me feel a little better. God, this is complicated." Heather yawned hugely and patted Cindy's knee. "Thanks for being here for me—you're a big help. But what I need most is a good night's sleep. Maybe morning will bring a new perspective."

As she lay in bed, Heather tried to wipe her troubled mind clean and allow sleep to overtake her. Several times, she started to drift off when those final words came back, *"Make no mistake. He's better off without you."*

Chapter Twenty-Eight

HEATHER RAISED the coffee cup to her lips, wincing at its cold contents, but didn't feel like returning to the house to reheat it. Setting it back down, she closed her eyes and drew in a long breath. The morning sun caressed her face and birdsong filled the air, but she had spent more of the last hour on her patio staring into space than waking up. Cindy had been gone when she'd woken up, and she soaked in the solitude. On the table, her phone buzzed, and she picked it up to reveal a text from Robert.

Robert: I didn't want to call in case you're still asleep. Can we get together to talk tonight? I'm worried about you.

As she read his words, a smile rose on Heather's face. Althea might not think much of her, but Robert clearly wanted to work out their problems. And so did she. One of her realizations during the restless night was that Althea's words had stung so much because Heather cared deeply for Robert. She texted back.

Heather: Thanks, I'm ok. Of course we can talk tonight.

Robert: Mom was way out of line. Last night, I went back and told her that.

Heather arched a brow, impressed. "Wonder how that went over?"

Another text came in.

Robert: I want to make this work. Us.

With a smile, she answered.

Heather: We will. I'll let you know when I get off.

Robert: Thanks. I'm sorry this happened.

With a deep sigh, she tossed her phone back on the table. "That makes two of us."

AT 6 P.M., Heather left the pool bar and headed toward the restaurant. Tonight, it was her turn to set up for the weekly manager's reception. Stepping onto the beach, she automatically glanced to the right at the extensive building to the north. The exterior was nearly finished, and the tall glass walls of the gallery were installed.

As she was filling the new bar's fridge with bottled Leatherback beers, Hope appeared, dressed in a pale, yellow sundress that fit her like a glove. Her long silver earrings caught the last of the sun's rays. "I thought I'd come help you set up tonight."

"Thanks," Heather said, and pointed with her chin at the cardboard box on the counter. "I was about to refrigerate the white wine."

Hope opened the box and pulled out two bottles before moving to the refrigerator. "How's it going?"

Heather's mind immediately returned to the previous night's dinner, but she pushed that away. "It's been a good day."

"Now that you've been here a few months, are you still liking it?"

Heather had been thinking of a way to bring up the art

gallery and being alone with Hope was the best opportunity she could wish for. "It's great. I really enjoy interacting with the guests. Though I'm not sure if it's what I'd like to do long term."

Hope shut the refrigerator door and looked up. "Oh? What else interests you?"

Here we go...

"I toured Aqua recently with Sara. That place is going to be amazing."

"That's what we're hoping, and my sister knows what she's doing. Are you interested in a position in the spa?"

Heather leaned against the bar and faced Hope squarely. "No, that's not it. When Sara gave me the tour, she also showed me the art gallery next door."

Hope beamed. "If Aqua is Sara's dream project, the gallery might be mine. One of them, anyway. Since the spa has a water theme, I went with fire for the gallery. It's going to be called Ember."

"Great concept! Have you hired anyone yet to work it?"

"No, I've written the ad, but haven't posted it. That's on my to-do list for this week. Are you interested?"

A thrill raced down Heather's spine. "Yes, very much."

"Do you have any experience?"

She hesitated, but Hope had given her a chance when others might have shut the door in her face. Heather owed her the full truth. "Yes, I managed one of the most prestigious art galleries in San Francisco. I have a degree in art history from Stanford."

Hope's eyes became huge. Then she laughed. "I think you may be overqualified! The first person working will be more of a salesperson than a manager." She cocked her head. "How did you go from art gallery manager in San Francisco to bartender in St. Croix?"

Ten minutes later, Hope gaped at her. At least Heather

managed to get through the whole awful story without crying. "Needless to say, not many people are aware of this. Only you and Robert. I'm not proud of it. But I want you to know the entire truth—that I've been fired from my last two jobs. I didn't deserve what happened at Serenity, but San Francisco was another story. I made a terrible decision to go to work, and I deserved to be terminated."

"I'm not sure deserved is the right word," Hope said quietly. "Everyone makes mistakes, and I certainly don't blame you for reacting the way you did. I can't promise you the position, but I'd really like you to apply for it."

Heather smiled as tears sprung to her eyes, and she turned back to the counter to cover them. "I'll do that. Thanks, Hope."

"Don't mention it. I take it things are going well with Robert?"

Heather almost dropped the glass she held. "Yes. Mostly. There's a bit of family conflict."

Hope gave her a sympathetic flinch. "You two come from different worlds. I can imagine how that would create waves."

"His parents weren't too fond of me, and the situation seems really complicated now. I left California because things were so rough. In a different way, the same thing is happening now. Robert is incredible, and I know he feels strongly for me too. I want to work this out, but what if we're not meant to be?"

Hope touched Heather's wrist, but gave her a very shrewd look. "Things got complicated in California, so you moved. Now things are getting complicated here. Do you think breaking up with Robert will fix that?"

"Some of it, perhaps. I'm not sure."

Hope's eyes softened. "And maybe the next time, there will be different problems. Heather, the situation is complicated because *life* is complicated. You can't run away from that—it will just catch up to you. I should know. I ran or hid from my problems for years before Alex helped me to finally face them. The right person can make all the difference in the world. Don't give up too easily."

An hour later, Heather circulated around the packed patio with a wine bottle in each hand, topping off guests' glasses. The conversation with Hope had left her feeling uplifted—the relief of unburdening the shame of why she'd left California, and not finding herself judged. *I've been so mortified and hesitant to tell anyone here, and neither Robert nor Hope recoiled. What if I've been scared over nothing?*

Robert's handsome, concerned face entered her mind, and she couldn't wait to see him after work.

Maybe it's time to find my courage.

Chapter Twenty-Nine

ROBERT'S HEART rose into his mouth as he approached Heather's house. After transferring the wrapped bouquet of roses to his other arm, he knocked on the front door. *This flower thing is becoming a habit, along with the nerves.* He hadn't spoken with his parents since the previous night, not trusting himself to be civil. All he could think about was making things right with Heather. Her willingness to meet gave him some reassurance that they could work out the disaster.

We have to figure this out. She means too much to me to let my damn parents drive a wedge between us.

During the eternal sleepless night before, Robert had imagined life without her, and a hollow chasm opened inside his heart. He needed to make sure Heather knew how he felt.

She answered the door dressed in a navy-blue tank top and white shorts, and swept back the long copper sheet of her hair as she smiled at him. "Hi." Then she dropped her eyes to the flowers he held, and they widened.

He presented the wrapped bouquet. "I brought these for you. I'm really sorry, Heather. Can I come in?"

"Of course."

After closing the door behind him, Robert pressed the flowers into her arms. She placed a hand on his cheek, giving him a long, leisurely kiss, and he reached his hand in a mirror image to her cheek.

Finally, she broke away and rested her forehead against his. "I missed you today."

The anxious knot in his stomach began to untangle. "I missed you too. You can't imagine how much. I'll keep sayin' I'm sorry until you believe me."

Heather settled the flowers in one arm and led him by the hand to the kitchen. "You don't need to apologize. You did nothing wrong. In fact, you defended me, and I'm sure that wasn't easy." She removed a vase from a cabinet and placed the roses in it one by one. "Thank you. They're wonderful."

The rose scent wafted through the room. "You're welcome." He glanced around. "Is Cindy here?"

"No. She's out tonight."

Good. We're alone. "I haven't talked to my parents since last night, and I meant what I said. I won't let them come between us."

"I don't want you to cut them out of your life, Robert. They mean too much to you."

"They do, but so do you."

Finished arranging the flowers, she headed back to the living room, indicating for him to follow. After placing the bouquet on a table near the door, she sat on the couch. He dropped next to her, sliding close. "Mother couldn't have been more wrong, you know. I can't imagine my life without you. I love you."

Her eyes became round, and her pink mouth opened before snapping shut again. A pulse throbbed in her neck, and he smiled, reaching for her hand. "Relax, sweetness. You don't have to panic. Given how your last relationship ended, I can understand how hearin' those words might upset you. You don't need to say it back."

Heather's expression had changed during his explanation, and she stared at him intently, a tiny smile playing at the corners of her mouth. "I had an interesting conversation with Hope today. About how I keep expecting life to be easy and can't handle it when it's not. She helped me realize I need to stop being so afraid of everything going wrong. You're right—being in love is scary to me. But I love you too. We'll make this work." Then she smirked. "Though you might need to keep me away from your mother."

He closed his eyes and snorted. "For a little while, at least. But she's gonna have to get used to us, whether she likes it or not."

"But what if she can't get used to us? What then?"

He took her hand and placed it against his larger one, dark skin against light. "I don't think that's somethin' we need to worry about tonight, is it?"

"Not tonight." She leaned in to kiss him, but her eyes were troubled before she closed them.

Instead of kissing her, Robert grasped her face in both hands. "Don't give up on us, Heather."

When she opened her eyes this time, they were no longer clouded. "I have no intention of giving up, on us or anything else. Robert, I can *tell* how important I am to you. You stood up for me at dinner last night, and you're here—now—making sure we're ok. That means everything to me."

He smiled and tucked a lock of red hair behind her ear. "Ah, I'm just a local boy tryin' to win over a girl who's way out of my league."

There was no humor in her eyes. "No, I'm not. And a local boy is exactly what I need. Do you understand that?"

"Yes." He squeezed his eyes shut before staring at her

straight-on. "My marriage ended because I wasn't what Leticia wanted. I tried to be, but came to realize that was wrong. Ever since we met, I've been myself, even though there were times it scared me to death. Thinkin' about all the things I'd never be able to give you. But maybe I can give you somethin' more important—the man I've been tryin' to be my whole life."

She placed her fingers against his chest, his heart pounding against them. "That's all I want. You'll always be enough." Heather stood and held out her hand. "Come on. Let me show you."

As he shut her bedroom door, Robert took his time drawing her close. He cupped both hands behind her head, running the soft silky strands of hair over his fingers before pulling her head to his lips. She ran her hands under his shirt and up his back, caressing him slowly. Opening his mouth, he brushed his tongue across hers and she met him just as softly. There was no rush— he wanted to make love tonight, not rip her clothes off in a frenzy.

He slowly pulled her tank top off, revealing a light-pink lacy bra that nearly glowed in the room's dimness. After opening it, he hooked a finger under one shoulder strap and eased it off, following every inch of warm skin with his mouth.

After he tossed her bra aside, she pulled off his shirt with more urgency, now pushing her breasts against his chest. Smiling, he said against her lips, "Take it easy. We've got all the time in the world."

She unzipped his shorts and palmed him, running her hand up and down as his shorts fell to the floor. Robert groaned and ground hard against her hand, causing her to laugh lightly into his ear. "Now who's getting all hot and bothered?"

"Oh, I'm not denyin' that. Merely pointin' out that good things come to those who wait." He opened her shorts and slid his hand inside. "Besides, I'm not the only one, am I?"

They quickly removed the rest of their clothes and tumbled into Heather's bed. Her skin felt molten as he pressed the length of his naked body against hers and rolled her onto her back, tracing wet circles with his tongue down her neck until he reached one beautiful, full breast. He used his mouth and both hands, his fingers barely touching her skin, until her breath deepened in the silent room.

Moving down further, Robert slowed, teasing and tantalizing her. After tracing a row of kisses across her inner thigh, he tasted her at last. Heather arched her back and cried out, placing both palms flat against the sheet. After several months together, he knew her well, and exactly how much pressure to use. It didn't take long before both her hands gathered up the sheet and she pressed her legs together against his head, her cries loud in the still air.

As he began climbing back up, she growled and pushed him over onto his back. He tensed, trying to stop her. "No... you don't—"

"Yes." She whispered the word in a hard exhale. It wasn't a request, and he twitched, moving onto his back with a grin. But the smile faded when she wrapped her mouth around him. He looked down at her fiery hair spread out over his lap, and he almost lost it.

"Oh my God, sweetness. I can't take any more of that tonight."

She stopped her ministrations to glance up at him. "I don't mind. As you well know."

"Not tonight. Please—I need to be inside you."

Holding him with her eyes, she sat upright and guided him inside her, massaging his chest with both hands as she moved above him. Her pale body was silhouetted against the darkness.

"Come here." He wrapped his arms around her back and

turned them onto their sides. She threw her leg over his hip, opening wide, and he thrust into her.

Heather gasped and pressed her forehead into his shoulder, gripping his ass tightly with one hand and urging him on. He didn't need any encouragement, and their earlier tenderness disappeared. She moved back to his mouth, raking her teeth over his. His climax rolled in a long wave over him, ebbing and flowing in an eternal rhythm.

Afterwards, Robert was hardly capable of movement. He shifted slightly, and his chest slid easily over her breasts, their skin slick with sweat. But Heather's back was soft and dry as he brushed two fingers down her spine, smiling as she shuddered. He opened his eyes to find her staring straight at him.

"Thank you."

He gave her a crooked smile. "You don't need to thank me for that."

She didn't smile back, and he understood she was completely serious. "That's not what I mean. Thank you for showing me that I *matter*."

Robert closed his eyes and leaned his forehead to hers, his heart twisting. "I'll do my best to make sure you never worry about that. Because you've shown me the same thing."

Chapter Thirty

THE DINING ROOM became silent as the Davises started eating. Robert took a healthy serving of chicken from the platter, trying not to be cynical. Now that Heather wasn't at dinner, Althea was back to cooking roasted chicken served with peas and carrots. Tonight, it was just the three of them since Eddie was at a baseball game. This was the first time Robert had seen his parents since the dinner disaster a week before.

"What is Heather up to?" his mother asked with practiced casualness.

"She works most evenings. She made special arrangements to come the other night." Heather had pushed him to accept his mother's invitation tonight, and Robert understood he needed to play both sides in order to find middle ground. But that was tough when his blood boiled every time he looked at his mother. He looked Althea in the eye. "Sorry to disappoint you, Mom, but we're still goin' strong."

"Robert," Bennett said, snapping his head up. "Don't speak to your mother like that."

Oh, but she can talk however she wants? But voicing that

thought out loud would *not* be a good idea, so he just ate another mouthful.

Althea set her fork down. "Son, please don't be upset with me. I've watched several friends' children leave the island because of a love interest. I don't want this woman to take you away from us. This is difficult—I'm tryin' to wrap my head around it."

Well, try harder. But at least that was a glimmer of hope, and he regretted his thoughts. "I know, Mom. Dinner's fantastic. Thanks."

"Of course. Have some more potatoes."

Bennet handed him the bowl. "Geordie is out with the flu. I could use another hand tomorrow. Can you help?"

"Sorry, I'm workin' at Half Moon Bay."

"Can't you tell them you're not able to make it?" Althea asked, a deep line forming between her brows.

"No, they're dependin' on me. I can't stand them up because you're short a hand, Pop." *If I did, you'd be on me even more.* "I'm sure you can find somebody on the dock who needs work."

"Robert," Althea said. "Your father has worked his whole life to build this business. We depend on you too. He asks you for one small favor and you can't say yes? Are we that much of a burden to you?"

Exasperation warred with guilt inside Robert. Althea was an expert at pushing the right buttons, but she wasn't wrong, either. "Of course not. You know better, Mom. I'm proud to be your son, but you also raised me to honor my obligations." He paused, then met Bennett's gaze. "If Geordie's not back the day after tomorrow, I'll help you out. Does that work?"

Pop stirred his mashed potatoes. "Guess it will have to. I'll let you know if I need a hand."

THE NEXT MORNING, Robert turned to check on his six divers. One had to be low on air, so he pointed to the man and tapped his own palm, asking how much air the diver had left. The man held up six fingers—600 psi. Robert nodded, then pointed at the boat overhead, gesturing for the man and his wife to head toward the surface for their safety stop. Ten minutes remained of this last dive of the morning and the rest of the group still had plenty of air, so he wanted to make sure the majority got their full allotment of time.

After watching them ascend, he spun around and led the rest of his group through a sandy channel. His expert eye spotted a dark shape underneath a shallow overhang, and he breathed out, descending. *Ha! Just what I thought. Nurse shark.* After making sure everyone got a close look at the brown, eight-foot shark, he swam on, emerging out of the channel to see the other pack of divers.

He and Alex nodded to each other. The former SEAL's group was more spread out than Robert's, but they were also more experienced, and Alex didn't like to babysit divers. A short distance away, Hope peered into a dark hole with her buddy, an older man whose wife didn't dive. Turning around, she spotted Robert and gave him the signal for lobster.

Robert nodded and led his group over. As soon as he peeked into the ledge, he was glad he did. Half a dozen large lobsters were lined up facing out of the narrow cave, their long antennae twitching in the water. He beckoned his divers over, satisfaction filling him at their round, excited eyes when they spotted the large crustaceans.

The next time he checked the dive time, they were at fifty-eight minutes, and he signaled to begin their safety stop. *Another mornin' in the bag.*

. . .

As Tommy motored back, the guests spread out on the main deck. A storm lay low on the horizon, but the sky above them was sunny with fat, puffy clouds overhead. Robert sat next to Alex in the elevated wheelhouse. Hope stood next to Tommy, frowning at the divers stretched out on the fiberglass bow, and enjoying the sunshine. "I really should go mingle with them."

Alex sprang up, wrapped both arms around her waist from behind, and pulled her back with him and onto his lap. "Don't you dare. I hardly ever see you during the day, and I'm not about to let you get away now."

Smiling, Hope settled and draped an arm over his shoulders. "Ok, you talked me into it."

Robert laughed and moved over a little to give them more room.

"Yeah," Tommy said to him with a grin. "Don't get too close. It might be catchin'."

Hope arched a brow at the captain. "I'm sure if Heather was here, they'd be all snuggled up too. You're just jealous, Tommy."

"I can do plenty of snugglin' at home. Don't need to subject my co-workers to it."

"Well, if it bothers you so much, you probably shouldn't have married us," Alex replied with a grin.

Tommy couldn't help a laugh. "Don't remind me."

But Hope's comment made Robert wish Heather were there instead of at the pool bar.

Alex stroked his thumb over Hope's butterfly tattoo on her shoulder, then glanced at Robert. "A diver asked me about doing a Nitrox class tomorrow morning. Are you available to work, by any chance?"

And that brought the family complications roaring back. "I'm not sure, but don't count on it. Pop has a hand out sick and asked me to cover if he's still out tomorrow. I should know by late afternoon."

"Don't worry about it," Alex said. "We can do the class in the afternoon if necessary. No big deal."

Hope reached out and gave Robert's forearm a gentle squeeze. "Have things improved any with your parents and Heather?"

"It's still a work in progress." Robert smiled at her. "She told me you two talked the day after my mother upset her. You helped—thank you."

"I'm glad. Sometimes relationships take a while to work out. You two are great together, so I'm sure they'll come around."

"Thanks, Hope."

Tommy glanced over his shoulder and shared a long look with Robert. The divemaster gave him a small shrug. Tommy knew all about traditional families.

"Oh!" Hope said. "In other news, Half Moon Grotto is officially slated to open November first. We're doing teasers on our social media pages now with your images, Robert."

He grinned at Alex. "Those pics of you free diving turned out great."

Alex responded, but Robert's attention faded. When he'd taken photos at Half Moon Grotto, an idea had flitted around his brain and now it was tickling him again. He kept getting flickers having to do with pictures in the grotto, but he couldn't nail the thought down.

He returned to the conversation as Hope poked Alex in the shoulder. "Can I borrow Robert for a little while after lunch? I promise I'll have him back before the afternoon dive leaves."

Alex heaved a long, theatrical sigh. "I swear. You're always pulling Tommy or Robert away. What about me?"

She tipped her head. "You have other uses."

They all broke into laughter, and Alex winced. "Guess I asked for that."

"You sure have been in a good mood," Robert said to him.

Alex burst into laughter. "Oh, yeah—you'll appreciate this, since you received the brunt of my displeasure about it. My good friend Cody got fired and left the island. Apparently, the scuba agency thought he was attempting programs that—" Alex held up both hands in air quotes, "—weren't consistent with their brand standards. And I never said a word to them, which means he was trying to shovel shit at other people too."

"I can see you're pretty broken up about it," Robert said.

Hope frowned, resettling on Alex's lap. "Will not having a regional rep affect the dive operation?"

Alex shook his head. "I can get what I need through the Miami office. Good riddance to Cody. God, I love it when people get what's coming to them."

As the resort came into view, Robert stared at the distant pool bar. *And when Heather and I get what's comin' to us, will it be good or bad?*

HALF AN HOUR LATER, Robert walked north with Hope across the beach. As they passed the four northern bungalows, the sound of saws and hammers echoed around the area. "They're still doin' heavy construction?"

"We're almost done! What you're hearing is work on the outdoor shower on Orchid Bungalow. The rainforest rooms are nearly ready for occupancy, but I want all the loud remodeling finished before I open them. After that, we'll move construction to the south end."

Robert still wasn't sure why Hope wanted to see him, but he was plenty happy to walk along the beach instead of prepping the boat for the afternoon dive. Being able to rub it in Alex's face when he returned was an added bonus, and he grinned broadly. They passed by the new spa, its treatment rooms now hidden behind one-way glass.

"That's smart," Robert said. "That way, the guest can enjoy the view without worryin' about people starin' at them."

"Exactly, and it keeps them—and the staff—cool too. But we're setting up three thatch-covered pavilions on the beach for clients who want the full beach and ocean experience."

They continued, and the white building ended suddenly, transforming into a sheer wall of smoked glass. Jagged streaks of dark orange and red ran through the glass, making for a stunning exterior. "Wow. Is this the art gallery? Heather told me about it."

Hope smiled and inclined her head. "Welcome to Ember. This is what I wanted to show you." She opened one smoked-glass door and waved Robert through before her, and once again he was immersed in the sounds of hammers and saws.

Robert gaped at what lay before him.

Ember's interior was brilliantly bright, and the glass was still dark on this side, showing only a hint of what lay outside. The chocolate-colored glass continued in a seamless wall on three sides of the gallery, twenty feet high. The common wall it shared with Aqua was pure white, and more red and orange streaks accented it.

But the floor was extraordinary. Made of blond hardwood, the color theme continued. Dark-red and orange veins criss-crossed over the floor, some narrow and some wide. All were made of colored glass, causing the floor to resemble a lava field. Robert snapped his jaw shut. "My God, Hope. You're gonna make a fortune with this place."

She gave him a light laugh. "Well, we'll see, but that's not my primary aim with it. The gallery will be a charity venue. All profits will be split evenly between the displaying artists and local charities."

He wrapped an arm around her shoulders with a friendly squeeze. "That sounds incredible. I'm sure you'll have artists beatin' your door down to exhibit here."

"That would be terrific, but I'm being selective. Especially for the gala grand opening, which should be in December. I only want the best."

"Definitely." Robert bent over to inspect one of the red glass lava runnels. He ran a finger over the smooth surface. It blended almost seamlessly with the blonde wood, making the floor easy to walk on. "You want me to put out the word? I know plenty of people who'd give anything to have their work exhibited here."

I can't even imagine... This could change someone's entire business. Their whole life.

There was no reply, and he looked up. Hope stood with both hands parked on her hips, frowning at him. "Seriously, Robert? That wasn't obvious enough? I want *you* for the opening!"

"What?" He rocketed to his feet, heart pounding out of his chest.

"Unless you're not interested..."

He barked out an incredulous laugh. "Not interested! Hope, this could make my entire career."

"Well, don't go that far. I don't want that much pressure. But the workers are going to build several display areas around the interior and more prints can be hung on the walls since they're dark. Heather will work out all the displays—she's the expert. I wanted to give you plenty of advance notice, so you'd have time to plan what you'd like to exhibit. And sell."

He stared vacantly around the busy interior, blood roaring in his ears. "Yeah... I'll need to put some thought into this."

I can't wait to share this with Heather!

Then the image exploded inside his head, like lightning out of the clear blue sky. The idea that had been hiding around the edges of his mind for months burst forth, stunning him in its sheer beauty. He became dizzy at the force of it and raised a hand to his temple.

Hope placed a steadying grip on his bicep. "Are you ok, Robert?"

"Oh my God. I'm more than ok." He crushed her in a bear hug, making her yelp. "Thank you! I just had the most amazin' idea for what I want to exhibit." He glanced around the building, teeming with excitement now. "Since you've got a fire and water theme goin' on with the gallery and spa, I'll play on that. Especially since I'm an underwater photographer."

"That sounds perfect! Tell me about it."

He whipped around to her, breaking into a grin. "Oh, no. It's gonna be a secret. Until I bring the prints in here, no one's goin' to know."

Except the person I need to help me, anyway...

ROBERT STEPPED aboard *Surface Interval* at 1:50 and gave Alex a broad smile. "See? Here I am, with ten minutes to spare. Guess you'll have to find somethin' else to bother Hope about."

Tommy snorted from the console. "That shouldn't be a problem."

Robert laughed, maybe a bit too giddily, but he didn't care. But it made Alex arch a brow. "Nice to know my wife makes you so happy. Anything I should be concerned about?"

He shook his head, but the elation remained, joined by a warmth spreading through him. "Alex, your wife is one of the most amazin' people I've ever met. I can't believe what she just asked me."

Tommy had turned around, quizzical, but Alex smiled, his

eyes softening. "She finally asked you about the opening at Ember, huh? I figured that's what it had to be."

Robert straightened, his jaw dropping yet again. "You knew about this?"

"Yeah. For a while now. You're the only person Hope even considered for the opening. Sara will have some of her paintings displayed, but not during the premiere."

Tommy guffawed from the bridge. "Who knew you could keep a secret like that? Congratulations Robert."

Coiling a regulator in his hands, Alex shrugged. "Believe it or not, I'm actually pretty good at keeping secrets."

"Yeah, I know you are," the divemaster said.

Shaking his head, Robert turned to the orderly row of scuba tanks, making sure everything was ready. Laughing divers came aboard as a bright Caribbean sun warmed his shoulders, giving its own blessing.

Chapter Thirty-One

LATE-MORNING SUNLIGHT FILTERED through the thick, steamy canopy, and Heather could have been lost in the Amazon somewhere, instead of hiking down a discreet but clear path just east of Half Moon Bay Resort. Though hiking might be too strong a word—they were walking, and slowly. Moderating her step further, she glanced at Robert, who closed a chain-link gate in an eight-foot fence and resumed moving stiffly beside her.

"You sure you want to do this today?" she asked. "I don't want you keeling over on me."

He grinned and shook his head. "I've already put this adventure off so I could help Pop on the boat. No more. I've been lookin' forward to it too much."

"You're a good son, you know, helping your dad out for three days while his hand was sick."

Robert stretched his back and winced. "Sure am payin' for it now."

He'd been very secretive about their purpose that morning. All Heather knew was they were going to the mysterious grotto, and he wanted to photograph her underwater. But he was only carrying camera equipment—there was no sign of scuba gear.

Heather sidled up to him, brushing a soft kiss across his lips. *Oh, you wonderful, loyal man.* She took one of his chapped hands and lifted it, studying the abraded, roughened surface. "So, did your nautical adventures make you wish you'd been a fisherman after all?" She laughed at his shudder.

"I don't know how Eddie does it."

"What about your dad? He's been at it a lot longer."

Robert shrugged. "It's always been a part of him. He makes it look so easy. I never thought about the job bein' hard on him. But you're probably right—he must feel it as he gets older."

Heather hadn't had any further interactions with Robert's parents. But he'd mentioned Althea was trying to get used to the idea of them as a couple. Maybe a good relationship with them wasn't so unrealistic after all.

A curly growth of black hair covered most of Robert's head, except the top, and he ran a hand over it. "I haven't even shaved my head in a week."

"Why do you do that, anyway?"

He darted a glance at her before looking down the trail again. "Leticia wanted me to do it. I started losin' my hair pretty young. You've probably noticed I take after my father. She wasn't real fond of the recedin' hairline and asked me to shave it all off."

Heather stumbled to a stop, gaping at him. "Are you freaking kidding me? What an absolute, class-A bitch! Robert, I never want you to feel like something about you isn't good enough. If you want to grow your hair out, do it. Please."

He strolled back to her and kissed the bridge of her nose. "Thank you. That's only one of the many reasons I love you. Leticia did make me feel like I wasn't good enough. You never have." He took her hand, opening her clenched fist, and they continued for a few steps before he burst into laughter. "But I have to admit, I look a hell of a lot better with a shaved head. Even after we got divorced, I kept it. Don't have plans to change that."

"Well, I think you're gorgeous, no matter what. Just so you know."

"That goes double for you, sweetness."

"So you brought me all the way out here, without another soul anywhere near. Do you have designs other than photographs this afternoon?"

His sweet smile became a supernova, blinding in its brilliance. "If I told you, that would spoil the surprise. Be a good girl and wait."

"Maybe I don't want to wait. Or be a good girl."

The pair came together in another kiss, this one decidedly more heated. They were becoming as hot and steamy as the jungle around them. Robert pulled away with a soft groan. "Keep your mind on business, missy."

"You might want to follow your own advice."

"I'm tryin'. You don't make it easy, you know."

Heather laughed as they continued, tightening her hand in his. His fingers were noticeably more ragged after his fishing misadventures. She couldn't wait to see this mysterious grotto, and her steps increased when they emerged from the heavy vegetation into a large clearing. Her arms flopped to her sides as she stared at the picture-perfect scene before them. The water was a bright cobalt blue, shimmering against the black rocks behind. She turned to Robert, who was placing his camera in an underwater housing. "Wow—you weren't joking about this place. I can't wait to explore it! So, are we going to be diving?"

"Sort of. Free divin', but nothin' too advanced."

She unslung her backpack and unzipped it before pulling out a white sundress with tiny blue flowers. "Ok, this was the best dress I could come up with, given your very specific requirements."

He brightened and set the camera down. "Does it have a long, loose skirt? That's the most important part."

"Yeah, and it falls to mid-shin. The dress is fairly modest, though. If you want to take racy pictures, this might not work." She waggled her eyebrows, but he shook his head.

"Nothin' racy about this." Robert rose and ran a hand over the cotton fabric. "This is perfect. You want to get changed? And make sure you let your hair down."

She'd had the mass contained in a large clip and now whipped her head to him, horror-struck. "Wear it down! I'll boil over. Though I'll be more than ready for the underwater part after that." She wore a one-piece swimsuit under a tank top and board shorts.

He gave her an enigmatic smile. "I promise you won't get overheated. Just the opposite. I want you to free dive with the dress on."

"Not the swimsuit?"

"Let's sit on that boulder over there and I'll explain every-thing to you." They sat, and Robert took her hand in his. "This photo shoot is for the gallery openin'."

Her heart tried to pound out of her chest. "Are you kidding? I'm sweaty and my hair is a mess. You don't want pictures of me like this. Why would you want me to wear a dress *in* the water?"

"I want to photograph you in movement underwater, swim-ming in front of the black boulders. With your long, red hair and that white dress, it'll be an incredible image."

The picture came together in her mind. "Oh—I see what you're getting at. What a great idea!"

"It's been nudging me for months now, ever since I first saw the Grotto. And when Hope asked me to be the premiere artist, the idea burst into my brain. And having the session here will be easier for you than if we were in the ocean. You don't need to worry about the salt water stingin' your eyes. I don't want you all squinty and frowny on me." He rummaged in his backpack and withdrew a spherical, green fishing float. It was made of clear glass and half of it was encased in netting. He passed it to her, and she needed both hands to carry it securely. "I'd like you to stretch out and hold this between your hands. I'm going to put a weight belt on you so you can stay submerged. But it will only be four pounds, so it won't prevent you from surfacing easily to breathe."

She smirked. "That would be beneficial. Thank you."

HALF AN HOUR LATER, Heather stood barefoot in the white sundress with her sweaty hair hanging halfway down her back. The dress had short sleeves and a fitted bodice, and though it wasn't provocative, she was more than slightly self-conscious. She looked to a nearby boulder where Robert was completing the final checks on his camera. "I'm completely naked under here."

He broke into that wide smile she loved. "I noticed—thanks for remindin' me. I'm tryin' to keep my mind on work here. Per your suggestion."

She sighed, biting back a smirk. "White doesn't exactly hide things, you know. I don't want a bunch of strangers seeing all my, uh... assets."

"I'm not too keen on others seein' them, either." Then his smiled faded. "I promise. I'll airbrush out anythin' that shouldn't be there. You don't need to worry."

"Ok, then. Let's get to this." She glanced around the area. It was remarkably peaceful, once again reminding her they were there all alone. "The sooner we finish, the sooner we can get to other things."

Robert tossed her another suggestive smile as they walked to the small beach. He had fitted the weight belt under her dress, around her hips so it couldn't be seen. He'd warned her the water was almost ten degrees colder than the ocean, and she felt it immediately upon submerging. They swam to the other side of the pool, where a wide vertical wall of black rocks descended into the water. Robert wore a dive mask and long fins, with a weight belt around his waist, and carried a camera enclosed in a large, clear plastic housing.

"You'll cool off fast, so we'll work quickly," he said. "Start slowly swimmin' horizontally with your eyes open and a neutral expression. Hold on tight to the glass float—it will want to bob up to the surface."

With a nod, she took a breath and submerged. He was right—her heated ardor fled in the cool water, but that only helped her to concentrate on the job at hand. When she opened her eyes, the water felt strange against them. There was pressure, but no stinging. Heather stretched out horizontally and held the float out. It immediately started rising, and she arched her back, trying to keep the glass orb immersed, but it took her to the surface. Robert rose beside her. "I'm sorry. The float is hard to keep down."

"No. That was perfect! The arch in your back was beautiful." Unexpectedly, he moved forward and gave her a kiss. His lips were wonderfully warm after the cool water. "You're beautiful."

The second time, she had a better handle on what was needed and remained submerged longer. She alternated looking at the float with gazing straight at the camera. As she got accustomed to the cool water, the sensual nature of her movements took over, and she stared straight at the lens, confident in Robert's love for her.

He was graceful and effortless under water, diving much

further down to shoot upward. Upon rising after the fifth pass, Robert declared he had the shots he required. "I just have one more pose I'd like. Can you dive a little deeper, so I can photograph you from above? Roll onto your side and then your back."

Heather nodded and dove deep enough that she had to clear her ears, tucking the float under one arm while she pinched her nose and blew to equalize the pressure. Next, she stretched out again, slowly rolling until she swam on her back, performing a slow dolphin kick that sent a rolling wave along her entire body. Robert was silhouetted against the sun, beams dancing around his head. The image was one of the most beautiful things she'd ever seen.

But beauty was no match for needing to breathe, so she hurried toward the surface. The sound of the camera's shutter came through clearly in the water as Robert continued taking pictures. After the third round, her teeth were chattering when she surfaced. "I need to warm up a little. Can we take a break?"

"Of course. Let's get out."

Heather let the float bob on the surface, slapping it forward with a hand as they moved toward shore. "You're not cold?"

"I'm ok. I moved around a lot more than you did. Plus, I was watchin' you the whole time. That kept me plenty warm."

She tipped her head back to laugh, and soon they were back on the sandy beach. Robert set his camera on the large rock and withdrew a towel from his backpack, wrapping her tightly in it before pulling her to him. "Come here. Let's get you warmed up."

Shivering, Heather smiled as she burrowed her face into his neck, her arms swaddled within the towel. "Oh, this is much better. I can't believe I'm going to be featured in the exhibits of a gallery opening! It's kind of surreal."

Robert rubbed his hands up and down her back over the towel. "I took some good photos of Alex free diving when I was here the first time, but these images of you will be out of this world." He tipped her chin up, meeting her gaze. "How could they not be, with you as the model?"

Their eyes locked together, and Heather forgot all about being cold. "Thank you. You have the most incredible way of making me feel *seen*. And loved."

All traces of his normal good humor were absent. "I never want you to feel any other way. We might have a few bumps along the way, but nothin' worth havin' is ever easy, is it?"

A corner of her mouth lifted. "No, and I need to stop expecting that. You're worth fighting for, Robert—never doubt that. I won't give up on us, but I really hope your parents will come around." *And I wonder if I'll be able to find the courage to stand up to your mother if it comes to that.*

"So do I. Though I can't help thinkin' about what your father would say if we got more serious. How acceptin' he'd be of me then."

She laughed. "Let's deal with one parental problem at a time." But it was a good point. Despite Grant's wealth, her father had insisted on an extensive prenuptial agreement. A sense of warm unreality washed over her that she was even thinking about this subject. *We're not quite at that point yet—we can save future problems for the future.*

Robert grinned, then pulled her tighter, resuming his brushing movements over Heather's back. He kissed across the soft curve over her shoulder.

She gave a long, happy sigh. "After a few more minutes of this, we can go back in the pool if you need more pictures. But for right now, I don't even want to move."

He traced a finger over her jaw. "No, the photo session is over. I've got somethin' else in mind now."

Heather twitched a smile. "Oh? And what might that be?"

"Well, this incredible place won't be a secret much longer. I think we should take advantage of that fact, and I am acutely aware you're naked under that dress."

She pressed her lips to his, which were cooler now after being submerged, then opened her mouth and deepened the kiss. A rumble emanated from in Robert's chest, and she drew back with a laugh. "There's a nice grassy area by the boulders. What do you say we continue this conversation over there?"

Dropping the towel, Heather pulled the sopping dress over her head. Robert watched every movement, his eyes languidly traveling from her head to her feet. They stopped at her breasts for a long beat before he met her gaze again. The sun immediately had a warming effect on her naked body, but not as much as Robert's intense stare did.

She took his hand, and they sank into the fragrant, warm grass together. His body did far more to remove the effects of the cool water than the sun. Her shivering became a distant memory as they moved toward each other.

Chapter Thirty-Two

OCTOBER...

A small, bright-yellow lizard dashed across the meadow, long tail whipping from side to side, and Houdini bolted after it. He was promptly yanked to a halt by the leash firmly clipped to his harness, and sat down, waiting for Heather to catch up. Meanwhile, the lizard scrabbled up the trunk of a nearby tree, venturing onto a branch to stare at the dog. Houdini barked once, then whined at Heather, who reached down to scratch behind his ears.

"Yeah, I feel you, boy. That lizard is totally taunting you, but let's keep going." Once she started walking again, the Jack Russell happily trotted at her side. The harness had worked like a charm, and Houdini might need another name. But that would be up to his new family to decide. Heather gazed fondly at him. "This is the last time I'll get to walk you. You're headed to your new home this afternoon. You might have given me a few gray hairs, but I'll miss you, little guy."

When she entered the reception area, Donna was pushing a

handcart with several large bags of dog food across the room. A cacophony of barking could be heard even from where they stood, and Houdini whined, straining on his leash. "Oh, good!" Heather said. "You're here to save the day with breakfast. I can feed everyone before I take off."

"Oh, thank you! I needed to wait for a deposit to clear before I went shopping for food. I feel so bad the dogs had to wait." She shook her head. "I can't believe how expensive pet food is getting."

"Let me put Houdini back and I'll take over for you. I don't want you straining anything with those heavy bags." As Heather returned the dog back to his kennel, guilt niggled at her heart once again. *I'm trying to avoid asking Mom and Dad for money. There's got to be another option. Keep thinking, Heather...*

After crossing the room, she looked into Lucky's kennel. Instead of sitting behind his door, tail wagging, he was curled up asleep in the back. He had been less active the past week, and she was concerned he was becoming depressed. After returning Houdini, she approached the black and brown dog's door. Lucky rose with a yawn and padded to the front of the kennel, happy to have his head scratched. "I'll write another Facebook post about you. All our adopters have been families lately, and that's not your ideal situation, is it, sweetie?"

After closing the gate, she hurried to the door and the food beyond, her mind working on solutions as the barks of hungry dogs followed her out into reception.

THE MORNING'S sunshine had given way to a steady rain by the time Heather started work. *Surface Interval* could barely be seen through the mist, tied up at the end of the dock. A couple of tables at the pool bar were occupied under the thatch roof, but the pool was empty, raindrops pattering on its surface. The next time she looked up, Sara and Jack were approaching, huddled together under an umbrella Jack carried. Heather couldn't help smiling at seeing Jack's drenched shoulder while he made sure Sara stayed dry. He positively doted on her.

When they reached the covered bar, Jack deposited the umbrella in the sand, and they stood before the bar. As usual, Sara looked beautiful, her curvy figure encased in a colorful full-length dress and her hair perfectly styled.

"Good afternoon, you two. I see Jack sacrificed his comfort to make sure you stayed dry, Sara."

The stylist broke into a wide smile and slung an arm around Jack's shoulders. "He takes excellent care of me."

Jack shrugged, but his smile betrayed how much he liked the praise. "I spend all day getting wet. Sara's the one with the image to protect, and she looks out for me just as much." Then he laughed and glanced up as the downpour intensified, pounding on the thatch above. "Though with this rain, I have a feeling I'll be taking care of her most of the night."

Sara's eyes widened before she snorted, holding a hand to her mouth. "Oh—you're talking about the creepie-crawlies coming in to escape the rain. I thought you meant something else there for a moment."

He pulled her closer. "Maybe I did."

"All right, you two," Heather said, trying not to laugh. "This is a family resort. Are you ordering something?"

"We're on our way to lunch," Sara replied. "And came by to say hello."

"After this morning, I wouldn't mind something stronger," Jack said. "Too bad we have an afternoon trip."

"What happened?" Heather asked.

"Strong currents on both dives—it was a lot of work keeping

everyone together. Alex actually had to chase someone down who didn't listen and rescue him."

Heather's jaw dropped. "Is the diver ok?"

Jack burst into laughter. "Yeah, he's fine. Alex gave him a stern talking-to about following directions and he became meek as a lamb. I have a feeling he'll be a model diver now."

Sara stared at him, concern lining her brow. "Should you cancel the afternoon trip?"

He waved a hand absently. "Nah, we'll be near slack by then. Just part of a day's work."

"If you say so. I'm glad I work inside." Sara shook her head before turning her attention to Heather. "You still on for girls' night out tomorrow?"

"Absolutely."

"We're not making you postpone a hot date with Robert or anything?"

Heather laughed. "No. He's holed up in his office, working on his photos for the Ember opening." He had sworn her to secrecy about their grotto trip, and even she wasn't allowed to see the images ahead of time.

"Heard anything about the gallery job?" Jack asked.

"No, not since I interviewed last week. Hopefully soon, though." After Heather had talked with Hope about the position, the resort owner had emailed her the application link, which Heather quickly filled out. Her interview had been informal, but encouraging. Hope had asked several questions about art and been impressed at Heather's knowledge.

She thought about asking if Sara had any information, since she was known for her love of gossip. But the answers would come in time. And if Sara was staying quiet because Heather didn't get the job, she'd rather hear the bad news from Hope.

"We'd better head to the kitchen for lunch." Jack held out

the crook of his elbow to Sara. "Come on, darlin'. Your umbrella awaits."

After they left, Heather's gaze was drawn toward Ember. Hope had given her a tour during her interview, and she had been stunned at the progress since last visiting the gallery with Sara. That floor with the orange and red glass was a work of art in itself. When Hope had asked how she'd arrange the displays, Heather had almost exploded with excitement. The vision was clear in her mind as she described where to put the temporary displays and which of the exterior walls could best be used to display different formats of art.

Heather was distracted from the distant building as she caught sight of Hope trotting along the path from the lobby. She hadn't bothered with an umbrella, simply holding a folded newspaper over her head. Cruz loped at her side, his ears flattened against his head as the rain beat down. Breathing an enormous sigh as she stepped under cover, Hope tossed the paper in the trash before stepping up to the bar. "Wow. When I went into the office, it was sunny and beautiful. Not much going on in here, huh?"

Heather shook her head. "Pretty dead right now—the divers are all eating so they can be ready for the afternoon. Must still be a lot of divers for the next trip, despite the morning's excitement."

"What do you mean?"

"Jack and Sara were just here. He mentioned strong currents, and that Alex had to rescue someone. He didn't tell you about it?"

Hope snorted. "Only a text saying that there was some current, but at least the boat didn't sink."

Heather had heard the story of their first boat's demise and the strong current pulling Alex and the survivors away from shore before being rescued, but she still thought his response was odd. Her confusion must have shown on her face, because Hope continued with a glint of pride in her eye. "It takes a bit more excitement to get Alex stirred up than you or me—or any other normal person." Then she slapped her palm twice on the wooden counter. "But that isn't why I'm here."

"What can I do for you?"

"I'm here to formally offer you the position as Ember director, though I still want to point out it will be more salesperson than director to start. Are you interested?"

The entire world narrowed down to the woman before Heather. "Oh, yes. I absolutely accept!"

"And I want you to know you were clearly the most qualified of anyone I interviewed. I always prefer to hire from within, but not if there's someone better suited who's an outside candidate. You won this job on your own merits, Heather."

Goosebumps rose all over her body. "Thank you, Hope. I can't tell you what it means to me."

The resort owner gave her a small smile. "I think I do. I know a thing or two about having a dream fulfilled. So plan on celebrating when we go out tomorrow!"

A long roll of thunder boomed overhead, and both women flinched. Cruz ducked behind Hope's legs. "Did you get to enjoy the morning before this storm came in?"

"Yes. I spent several hours at the pet shelter. I really enjoy it." Lightning lit up the sky and thunder exploded all around them. Cruz gave a large yowl and crawled around to lie on top of Hope's feet, tail tucked. "But I don't think Cruz enjoys thunder much."

"No, he doesn't. He went through a rough patch before we found each other, and he gets scared sometimes." She reached down to scratch his raised rough, and he thumped his tail tentatively. "You'll be ok, baby."

Smiling, Heather watched Hope lower to her knees, comforting the yellow dog.

The idea came in a flash and her breath caught.

She moved her gaze to Ember in the distance, barely visible through the rain. "Hope, can I ask you something?"

She straightened. "Sure."

"You mentioned proceeds from the gallery would go to local charities. Pet Paradise is barely hanging on. Could they be one of the first charities we support?"

Hope's face became guarded as she hesitated. "I've planned for the first two charities to be the domestic violence shelter and veteran's support center. Those are very important to Alex and me. Let me think about it, ok?"

"Of course. Thanks." With Alex's history, the veterans outreach service was an obvious choice, but Heather was curious about the other one. Did Hope have or know someone with a history of domestic violence?

The rain let up and patches of blue sky peeked through the heavy clouds. Hope looked down at her dog. "What do you say, Cruz? Shall we make a dash back to the lobby while the coast is clear?" After he sat up and barked, Hope turned to Heather with a laugh. "I think that's a yes. See you later."

Heather and Cindy arrived at Marimba together, and the rest of their group was clustered around a picnic table in the sand. The previous day's storm had given way to calm, sunny skies, though the ocean was still rough.

Cindy draped an arm over Heather's shoulder. "I drove so she can celebrate as much as she wants to."

A round of applause sounded as Sara poured a glass of sparkling wine for Heather and handed it to her. "Congrats on your new position. But now I really have to ask if we're making you postpone something with Robert."

Heather took a taste, the bubbles tickling her nose, and shook her head. "Robert and I celebrated last night."

"And I am extremely grateful our house has master suites on opposite ends," Cindy said, accepting her glass from Sara as laughter erupted around the table. Hope and April were already enjoying their drinks.

"Speaking of celebrations," Hope said with a faraway, wistful cast to her eyes. "Alex and I are taking *Surface Interval* out tomorrow for our own private sunset cruise. It's our one-year anniversary."

A round of toasts sounded at that, and Sara set her flute down with a thump. "How can it be a year already?"

"I know. It's hard to believe." Hope turned to April. "I've been meaning to tell you! Alex and I ran into a friend of yours when we were honeymooning in the Keys. It's such a small world. Maia... I never learned her last name."

April laughed. "Maia Markham. We were in the same divemaster class, and her family owns a resort on Calypso Key. Did you stay there?"

"Yes. Very nice place, but there were a few bumps. She got sick and Alex had to lead dives for a couple of days, but he actually enjoyed that. Alex isn't a very good follower."

"Oh?" Heather asked, grinning. "Doesn't like to be told what to do?"

Hope grinned slyly behind her flute. "Depends on the situation. Sometimes he's more than fine with it."

"I need to call Maia," April said, smiling fondly. "We haven't actually talked in a while—just Facebook posts and texts. I miss her."

Sara raised her glass to Heather. "You and Robert are another item we have to celebrate. And I'm taking credit for getting you two together when I engineered that meetup at our cozy little love shack."

"Your matchmaking skills have improved since your last attempt," April said, then grinned.

Everyone around the table laughed, but Heather was in the dark. "What was that about?"

"Hope likes to say I'm a busybody, but I prefer to think of it as giving Cupid a little nudge," Sara said. "Though I admit last time I might have nudged too hard. He lost his aim and shot me instead."

April came to her rescue, explaining, "Sara originally thought Jack and I would make a great couple. Until she finally figured out she liked him instead."

"My sister is incapable of not meddling," Hope said. "Unfortunately for you guys, since I'm married, now she has more opportunities."

Sara pressed her lips tightly together and held up a finger. "Examine the evidence, ladies. Three women with successful relationships are sitting around this table. And all were beneficiaries of my expert influence."

"Sounds like another toast is due, then," Heather said, grinning. "To Sara—master matchmaker!"

"Oh, I'm celebrating too!" Hope said. "The updated Half Moon Bay listing is finally live on the Tourism Board website. I've been fighting with them for months about it—Robert gave me the photos ages ago. Apparently, they have some big island-wide tourism push they've been planning, so I got completely ghosted. But they came through at last. And if they get more traffic to their website as a result of their promo, our listing will be up to date. Well, except for Aqua and Ember."

"When's the big opening?" April asked.

"December," Hope replied. "I've already got an ad running for another bartender, so Heather can start planning the gala."

"Ooh," Cindy said, her eyes becoming round. "That sounds fancy."

"That's the idea," Heather said. "Hope and I will work on it together, but we're planning a big formal bash to launch Ember."

"And I have one other piece of news," Hope said to Heather, her eyes sparkling. "I've thought about your request to make Pet Paradise a beneficiary. How about this: the proceeds from the opening will be donated to them, and we'll start with the other two charities after that?"

The gala would likely take in more revenue than the first several weeks combined, so Heather was thrilled. "That sounds perfect! Everybody wins."

Sara wrapped an arm around Hope's shoulder and pulled her close. "My big sister is very good at finding solutions that benefit everyone involved."

Cindy poured more sparkling wine for Heather, who drank up, elated at the change in her fortune in just twenty-four hours.

I got the job, and Pet Paradise will get some money. Everything's finally turning up roses!

Chapter Thirty-Three

ROBERT CUT into the flaky fish, wrapped in its golden fried coating. A week had passed since Heather's promotion, and once again, he was having dinner with his parents. Without her. "You guys run into a school of mahi-mahi?"

"Big one," Eddie replied, spearing another piece of fish.

"Mahi's always been my favorite," Althea added.

Bennett stared evenly at Robert. "Missed you on the boat the past few days."

Eddie grinned at Robert. "Not sure big brother feels the same way, Pop."

"I was sore for days after that." Robert rolled his shoulders, grateful the achiness was finally gone.

Bennett scowled. "Too much soft livin'. I was hopin' bein' on the boat would make for a nice change."

The last thing Robert wanted was to spend any more time on either fishing boat. "It was a change, all right. But it didn't alter the fact that Eddie is the natural fisherman between us, Pop." Desperate for a new subject before his father got any more stubborn, Robert looked at his mother. "I have some good news. I've been selected as the premiere artist at an art gallery openin' at Half Moon Bay Resort."

Althea smiled, but her eyes were perplexed. "That sounds nice."

"It's more than nice, Mom," Eddie said after a glance at Robert. They had talked before dinner, and Eddie wanted to offer his support. "It's a major career move."

"The first night will be dedicated only to my work. I might sell a *lot* of pieces."

Bennett placed his fork on his plate. "You're workin' in an art gallery?"

"Not workin', no. I'll have my photos displayed for sale. But Heather will be employed there. She just got a job as director of the gallery. There's goin' to be a big party the first night, and you're all invited."

"You want us to go to an art gallery?" Bennett asked, like Robert had suggested they travel to the outer reaches of space.

Eddie laughed. "Don't worry Pop. I doubt they'll make us buy anythin'."

Althea frowned at her plate, but spoke carefully. "I thought your girlfriend was a bartender."

"Her name is Heather, Mother," Robert chided softly. "She has a degree in art history and worked in a gallery before movin' here. This is the perfect opportunity for her." He took a deep breath and plunged in with the issue that had been haunting him. "You keep sayin' you're gettin' used to the idea of her, but you haven't mentioned wantin' to get together again."

"Robert, I'm just afraid this woman is pullin' you even further away from us. You refuse to help your poor father, and now she's got you workin' in her gallery."

Robert's blood pressure rose, but he kept his voice even. "Exhibiting," he said, emphasizing the word. "Not workin'. Mom, I love her. Nothin' you do or say will change that."

Althea whipped her head toward him. "Is that supposed to be a threat?"

"Of course not. It's simply a statement of fact. And I'm happy to help Pop out when he needs it."

Bennett watched his wife carefully. "Well, I'm grateful for that. You're always welcome." Then he flinched, rubbing a hand over his stomach, and Robert's brows lowered.

"Pop, you could stand to turn more of the business over to Eddie, anyway. Before you burn a hole in your stomach. There's absolutely no reason it has to be me just because I was born first."

"That's how it's always been."

"Doesn't make it right. Eddie's better at this than me and you know it."

Bennett crunched two antacids and picked his fork up. "If anythin' gives me an ulcer, it'll be you boys, not the fishin'. So I'm fine, ok? The good Lord provided this meal for us, so let's eat it."

"Now that's somethin' I can get behind!" Eddie said with a grin.

Althea passed the rice to him and shook her head. "We love you boys to death and you both know that. We just prefer our traditions. Now finish this up. I don't want any leftovers."

Robert couldn't help smiling at his mother as he accepted the plate of plantains, but he also noted she had deflected the conversation away from Heather when things became tense. In the name of family harmony, he bit his tongue and returned to dinner.

***

ROBERT WOKE up entwined with Heather, her head nestled in the hollow of his shoulder, and an incredible sense of peace washed through him. Not wanting to open his eyes and end the moment, he tightened his arms around her, breathing a contented sigh.

"Are you awake?" Heather whispered.

Smiling, he gave up and opened his eyes. The morning had to start sometime. "I am. How did you sleep?"

"Lousy." She laughed. "I didn't keep you awake, did I?"

"Nah. I was beat last night. An earthquake wouldn't have woken me up."

Heather shivered in his arms. "Don't say that to a girl from San Francisco!"

"Sorry. Didn't think about that. What kept you awake? Good or bad things?"

"Wonderful things. I can't wait to work in the gallery. You're going to have to show me your pictures at some point, you know. I have to figure out where to display them."

"I know, but not until they're printed, framed and ready to go." Robert grinned at the ceiling. He'd spent most of the past two days processing the pictures, but had refused to say anything specific about them to Heather. He was enjoying his secret immensely.

She sighed. "Fine. Be that way." Then she laughed. "Can you believe this? Would either of us have thought in the spring that I'd be managing the gallery where you were having your first feature? Things are really coming together."

"It's pretty incredible." But his smile faded. Some items were coming together, but not everything. His mother had shown no signs of wanting to mend matters with Heather. Though Heather had been patient, she had to be speculating if the situation would ever smooth out with his family. He couldn't help wondering the same thing.

But I can save that lovely thought for another time.

He glanced at the clock. "I need to get a move on. I have a photo shoot this mornin'."

"Tourists?"

"No, this is a local couple. I'm shootin' engagement pictures for them."

"You want to have lunch afterwards?"

"I'll be done by noon, so that should work." He swung out of bed. "I'll text you when I'm finished."

HEATHER DROVE to lunch as Robert directed her from the passenger seat to a quaint café in Christiansted, tucked away in a side alley. As they ate, his thoughts returned to his mother, though he didn't voice them out loud, not wanting to ruin the mood.

When Heather had asked him about his recent family dinner, Robert emphasized that he'd told his mother their relationship was going strong. Then he'd expressed his frustration over his parents' reluctance about him not wanting to continue the family business. His despondency must have been obvious because she dropped the hot-potato subject. Neither of them wanted a repeat of the last time Heather had interacted with the senior Davises.

But his unhappiness was in the past now and they spent their lunch talking about the upcoming gallery opening. Before being picked up by Heather, he'd met with the picture framer Hope had used for years, who was excited to prepare his pieces for the premiere. And he couldn't resist teasing Heather with hints of what the final images would look like.

After leaving the restaurant, they were almost at Frederiksted when Robert's phone vibrated. He picked it up and flinched, seeing his mother's name on the screen. He considered not answering, but respect for her was too ingrained. Althea might be exasperating, but she was still his mother, and he loved her. Heather had turned off Main Street toward her house when he answered. "Hey, Mom. What's goin' on?"

Althea's distressed, panicky voice made him grip his phone like a vise. "Oh, Robert. Come quick. Your father's had a heart attack!"

Robert vaulted upright in the passenger seat, gasping as he braced himself against the dash with one arm. "What?"

"He collapsed at the dock after they got back from fishin'. Eddie called an ambulance, and they took him straight to the emergency room. That's where we are now. Hurry!"

Robert's head filled with roaring, and he waved frantically at Heather to pull over. "Hang on, Mother. We'll be right there."

Heather yanked the wheel and screeched to a stop on the side of the road. "What's wrong?"

"Turn around! We have to return to Christiansted. Pop's had a heart attack!"

"Oh my God!"

Heather spun the wheel and peeled out in a U-Turn, speeding back the other way. She drove fast, weaving around cars. They were at the hospital in less than fifteen minutes, and she let Robert off at the door so she could park the car. He ran through the automatic double doors and found Althea and Eddie huddled in a corner of the nearly deserted waiting room. Wet trails streaked down both their faces. Upon seeing Robert, Althea rose from the plastic chair and collapsed in his arms, sobbing.

Oh, no! Am I too late?

"What's happenin', Mom?"

"We don't know anythin' yet. He's still in the emergency room bein' evaluated."

The lead ball anchoring his gut diminished a little as he held his mother tighter and nodded to Eddie. "I'm sure glad you were there. Thanks, man."

Eddie gave a slow nod back, his eyes wide and stunned.

Then Heather rushed through the doors, panic etched on her face. He caught her eye and answered her silent question. "He's still back with the doctors. No updates yet."

As relief filled Heather's face, Althea pulled away, confusion lining her brow at who Robert was addressing. She turned her head to follow his gaze and saw Heather. His mother's wet eyes became enormous as she stumbled backward, then she whipped her head back to him, fury turning her broad face into a rictus. "You brought her *here?*"

Heather responded, her voice calm. "I'm very sorry, Mrs. Davis. I was driving and got us here as soon as I could."

Althea ignored her, focused completely on her son. Robert was unable to look away even as bile filled his stomach at her expression.

"How could you bring her here? Now—of all times?"

No, no! Not now.

Robert's heart hammered so hard he was surprised no one else heard it. "Mom. Take it easy. She wants to hel—"

Althea snapped her head back to Heather, taking a large step forward. She clenched both hands into fists and held them tightly to her sides. "Get OUT! You don't belong." She was shrieking, wet streaks running down her dark face. "We don't want you here. Remove yourself from our sight this instant!"

Robert froze in place, completely unable to move or even close his gaping mouth as he watched this stranger before him. He was barely aware of Eddie's matching expression.

But Heather straightened, grinding her teeth together as she marched toward Althea, and spoke in a low, steely voice. "Fine. I'll leave because your sons don't need any distractions right now. Just know that I came here to offer comfort and help, even though you have never once done the same for me. I hope Mr. Davis is ok, and I'll be thinking of him."

Spinning on her heel, Heather strode toward the door. She was halfway across the room when utter panic filled Robert, and he called out, "Heather! Please..." He was incapable of more words, and a fine sheet of sweat broke out over his body.

She stopped and turned around. Althea wailed behind him as Eddie made soft, shushing noises, but Robert couldn't look away from those moss-green eyes. They were filled with pain, but something else too. Sympathy. "Stay here, Robert. Your family needs you. Keep me informed, ok?"

He jerked a nod, and she mouthed, "I love you," before turning and walking through the glass doors.

A knife had entered his heart when he'd heard about Pop. Now it twisted fully.

Chapter Thirty-Four

HEATHER PLODDED through the front door and tossed her keys on the nearby side table, too stunned and demolished to even cry. She'd been so worried about Bennett, she hadn't even considered Althea's reaction to her. It had been devastating... seeing that furious, tormented expression in a pair of eyes that were so like Robert's. But the clear desperation in his eyes when Heather had left was a blade slicing into her gut. She wouldn't force him to choose—especially during a family crisis.

As Heather flopped on the couch and threw an arm over her eyes, a buzzing came from her phone.

Robert: They just took him back to cath lab. They're putting in three stents.

He was still typing, but she answered back.

Heather: Thanks for the update.

Robert: I'm so sorry Mom spoke to you like that. I was too stunned to say anything.

Heather: Thanks. Not like you could berate her at a time like that. At least now I know how she really feels about me.

Robert: She was just stressed.

Heather didn't know how to respond to that, so she didn't.

Robert: Please talk to me.

Heather: You need to concentrate on your dad right now. Not me. I love you—that's all that counts right now, and we can figure out the rest later.

Robert: I love you too. I'll keep you updated.

Heather tossed her phone on the end table and rested her head on the back of the couch, eyes closed. The front door opened, and Cindy walked in, but she remained motionless.

Cindy could be heard setting her things on the table near the door, then silence. "You ok, Heather?"

"Not really. Robert's father had a heart attack." She gave Cindy a summary in a dull monotone voice, and her roommate rushed over to the couch, pulling Heather into the hollow of her shoulder.

"I'm sure Robert's dad is goin' to be ok."

"I hope so."

"Don't worry too much about what his mom said."

Heather raised her head to stare at Cindy. "Are you serious?"

Cindy gave a weak laugh. "I know it's difficult, but yes. Haven't you ever said or done somethin' you regretted during a really stressful moment?"

Heather groaned and flopped over sideways on the couch. "Oh, God. Cindy, you should have gone into counseling, not physical therapy. In one sentence, you just made me change my entire outlook on the disaster, and actually feel sympathy for Althea."

Cindy's laugh was more genuine this time. "Hers was a bigger blunder than most, but we've all said things we wish we hadn't."

"You have no idea. My blunder was much worse than Althea's, so maybe I shouldn't judge her too harshly." She lifted her head and peered at Cindy. "You want to hear a real doozy?"

Ten minutes later, Heather's head was back on Cindy's shoulder. "Sounds like you're better off without that guy, at least," Cindy said.

"No doubt there, but I'm not sure Althea and I can put the pieces back together again. Or if she even wants to try. She might have meant every awful word she said to me."

"Give it some time, at least until you know what's goin' to happen with Robert's father. Look at it this way—you made a mistake and left San Francisco, thinkin' you had no future. But now you've earned your dream position and you're in a relationship with a great man. You can't predict how things will work out."

"You're right. But I don't see myself holding out the olive branch."

"You don't need to. She does. But she's in no position right now to even think about that. Let things play out. That's all I'm sayin'."

Late that night, Heather was reading in bed, propped up on a small mountain of pillows, when Robert called, his voice drained and flat. "They've just moved Pop to the ICU. He's in a medically induced coma and they're artificially coolin' him. They said it helps recovery. But he made it through the procedure fine, and the doctor said his heart is doin' better after the stents were placed."

"Well, that sounds like good news. How are you holding up?"

"Ok. Eddie went home to get some sleep. He'll have to captain tomorrow, and I'll need to help too. The doctors said Pop's stomach symptoms were his heart, not indigestion. Mom won't leave the hospital." He paused, his breathing loud over the phone. "I haven't talked to her about this afternoon yet, but I will. I promise."

Heather drew her knees up and hooked her arm around them. "Don't add any more strain to the situation. I had a really good talk with Cindy this afternoon and she reminded me people do things they regret during stressful conditions. Something I have too much experience with. Right now, your dad needs to be the priority. Your mother and I can wait."

THE FOLLOWING MORNING WAS QUIET, with golden light shining across Heather's back patio. A chorus of birds hopped around the yard as she sipped her coffee, a reminder that even when terrible events happen, life goes on. Bennett's heart attack made her miss her own parents. Fortunately, both were younger than Robert's parents and in excellent health.

On the table, her phone vibrated, her mother's face lighting up the screen. "Do you have ESP or something? I was just thinking about how much I miss you."

"Well, that puts a smile on my face," Laura said. "I'm glad I called."

"You at home in Palo Alto?"

"No, I'm at the house in Aspen. I'm organizing a charity silent auction, which will take place this weekend. I'll go home after that, especially since your father should be back from Washington, DC, by then."

"Is he still having problems with the senate committee?"

"It's finally settled. He had to testify before them and prove the acquisition wouldn't create a monopoly. He managed to convince them that YouTube wasn't going anywhere, and they approved the merger."

"That's good news."

Laura laughed grimly. "Not if you're a Carrington. Their financial situation has taken a stark negative turn."

Heather smiled, unable to resist the satisfaction of knowing her father had outsmarted her ex-fiancé's family.

"How are things with you?" Laura asked. "Any particular reason you're missing us?"

The previous day came crashing down again as she filled her mother in. Robert had sent a text that morning saying Bennett was stable and they were keeping him in the coma for another day. But they were pleased with his progress. "And Robert is helping on the fishing boat, so his photography gigs got canceled for a while."

"What's the name of the hospital? I'll send a flower arrangement."

Heather hesitated. "I'm not sure that's such a good idea. Althea was pretty angry that I came with Robert."

There was a long pause on the phone. "All right. I won't lie and say I'm not disturbed by her reaction to you."

Heather absently watched a small brown bird hopping around her feet. "I'm pretty upset myself. But I don't want to put any more stress on Robert."

"You two do have very different backgrounds, Heather. Robert's mother is right about that much. He might need to decide about whether his family or you are more important."

The bird took flight, soaring out of sight. "I'm wondering the same thing. But Bennett is doing well, so we'll just wait for him to get better and go from there."

A FEW DAYS LATER, Heather was working at the restaurant bar washing wine glasses when Robert slumped onto a stool in front of her. His face was drawn, and a fringe of curly black hair lined his head. Her heart clutched hard.

His light-brown eyes were dull and full of pain. "God, I've missed you. I had to come by."

She put the glass down and gave his hand a quick squeeze, wishing she could do more. "Me too. It's great to see you. You want a beer?"

"Please. I just left the hospital and could use a drink."

While she poured him a Leatherback, he gave her an update. "They moved Pop out of ICU this afternoon. He's fully conscious, but very weak. The cardiologist said he was lucky, and that his progress has been excellent." He took a long pull before saying, "I just can't believe the thin old man in that bed is Pop."

"I'm sorry, but it sounds like good news overall... how's your mother doing?"

He rubbed a chapped hand over his face. "She finally went home tonight. My aunt is stayin' with her to keep an eye out. Mother's still not functionin' real well."

"Some sleep should help with that."

Robert turned his haunted gaze to her. "You haven't said a word against her, which is more than she deserves. I'm not sure I can completely forgive her for what she said. I tried to talk to her about it, but she just cut me off and walked out of the room."

After a quick glance that no one was looking their way, Heather gave him a quick kiss. "Now that the crisis is over, give her some time. She needs you, Robert—now more than ever."

His eyes were bleak. "And I need you."

She grasped his hand. It was warm, yet rough and dry. "You've got me. I'm not going anywhere. Your dad is on the mend, and I think the situation between your mother and me is a wound we need to let time work on. At least for a while longer."

Chapter Thirty-Five

NOVEMBER...

Robert stood on the deck of *Althea*, folding up a fishing net. Lifting his Davis Fishing baseball hat, he swiped an arm over his forehead to wipe away the sweat from the sweltering afternoon. He swept his gaze around the deserted dock. Robert was one of the few still working, and he smiled grimly at his hands, which were no longer raw and sore. Two solid weeks of fishing had seen to that. His photography clients had been understanding when he'd explained his circumstances, but most had no other choice but to use the referral he gave them.

Thank God I already got all the photos for the gallery openin'.

Since Bennett's emergency, he'd worked three times at Half Moon Bay, soaking in the tranquility of doing a job he loved and the peace that came with it. Those days also gave him the opportunity to see Heather, though that only reminded him further how much he missed being with her. Their nights together had been more exhaustion and stress on his part, rather than romance and seduction. And Heather stayed by his side for all of it.

As Robert tossed the net on top of the others on the deck, his phone rang, and he removed it from his pocket to find the screen flashing Unknown Caller. That wasn't unusual since many photography clients weren't in his contacts, and he didn't hesitate to answer it.

"Hello, Robert, this is Beatrice from the St. Croix Tourism Board. You're Althea's son, aren't you?"

He had no idea who Beatrice was, so he simply answered, "Yes, ma'am, I am."

A trill of laughter came over the phone. "Oh, don't call me that! Makes me feel a hundred years old, even if I'm not such a spring chicken anymore. Your mother and I have been in Bible study together for ages. I knew you when you were just a tiny thing."

Still baffled, Robert couldn't resist a small smile as he said, "Well, what can I do for you, Beatrice?"

"I've been workin' on a project for the Board, and havin' a mighty difficult time with it, I don't mind tellin' you. Then the perfect answer dropped right in my lap!"

"I'm glad to hear that..."

"We've been so busy around here the last few months. You just wouldn't believe it, Robert!"

He rubbed his eyes, then stared at the remaining nets he still had to put away. It wasn't getting any cooler. *How do I get her off the phone?*

Beatrice continued, "We got a big grant from the US government for tourism promotion, so we've been tryin' to divvy it up. Each of us got a handsome budget to work with—boy, is *that* a new experience for me! But, as I said, I just couldn't decide what to do with it. So I returned to one of my other projects that had stalled out when we got the grant."

"Sounds like quite the conundrum." Robert stared at the wooden wall of the console in front of him, debating whether to bash his head against it.

"Oh, don't you know it! But I was so glad I did. My project was a full update for the database listing for Half Moon Bay Resort. It's incredible what Hope has done with that place, isn't it?"

"Yes, Beatrice, you're right. She and Alex have been busy."

"I know! I had a wonderful time puttin' all that together and the resort looks amazin'! Every image Hope sent over was just stunnin'. And when I saw the watermark in the corner, I enlarged one and discovered they were taken by you! Isn't it a miracle what a small world we live in?"

Robert had turned away from the wall and stared at the deck, much more interested now. "And that's a fact, Beatrice."

"I didn't even know you were a photographer. Althea has never said a word about it—I can't imagine why."

"I've only been doin' it professionally for a short time. Mom probably didn't want to mention it in case I'm not successful with it."

Beatrice's laugh sounded over the phone again. "Don't think you need to worry about that, Robert! Especially now."

"Why now?" Robert was listening with acute intensity, though no less perplexed.

"As soon as I saw those images for Half Moon Bay, I had my answer! I ran to my boss's office and told him all about it. Would you believe he agreed with me one hundred percent? Well, of course you would."

He made certain to keep the consternation out of his voice. "Would what, Beatrice?"

"Why, Robert. We want you to be the photographer for the new advertising campaign we're designin' for St. Croix!"

Robert's legs gave out from under him, and he sat on the wooden deck with a loud thump.

"What was that?" Beatrice asked. "Is everythin' all right?"

"Fine. You want me to shoot a campaign for the *entire island?*"

"Oh, yes! It will be an international marketin' promotion, seen in the mainland US, as well as Europe and Canada. We're makin' a point to only use local talent on this campaign, so we'll showcase you as the photographer. We'll pay you a retainer of $30,000 up front and another $30,000 upon delivery of the images."

The boat appeared to be rocking wildly, but it was because of Robert's dizziness, not the waves. He clenched his eyes shut. "Sixty thousand dollars? Did I just hear you right?"

For one *gig?*

"Yes! I told you it was amazin' we got that grant money. Now, we need to get started by next month. I'm sure you need a couple of weeks to plan, and we'll have to discuss our concepts with you. When can you come into the office so we can meet?" Then she laughed again. "Oh, I haven't even officially asked—do you want the job?"

Do I want the job!

Then the vision of his father lying in his hospital bed popped into Robert's head. It was quickly followed by the memory of Bennett walking slowly in the corridors, supported by a physical therapist on each side. Robert flinched. "I absolutely want the job. But Beatrice, have you heard about Pop?"

There was a pause. "Come to think about it, the pastor did request prayers for Bennett. He's been ill?"

Robert caught her up on the situation, calming Beatrice that Bennett was recovering from his heart attack. "He's doin' great and will be discharged home in the next few days. But I've been workin' full time on the fishin' boat to help out. The timin' isn't exactly ideal."

"Oh, I'm so sorry! I must call Althea. But Robert, the Board needs to get movin' on this. I can stall my boss for a few days to give you time to work things out, but we'll have to go with another photographer if you can't do it."

"Thank you, Beatrice. I'll call you by early next week. I can't tell you how much this means to me."

After ending the call, Robert sat dazed on the deck as the boat creaked soothingly around him. The morning's catch was long gone, but there was plenty left to do. The same situation would exist tomorrow and the day after—his father was in no shape to work for a long time, if ever. "Now what am I goin' to do?"

THE DOORBELL RANG, and Heather, freshly changed into a tank top and leggings, rose from the couch. She barely had the front door open before Robert burst through. He grabbed her face with both hands and kissed her ardently, walking her backwards into the room. She giggled against his mouth before pulling away to say, "Wow, that was some hello! Good news?"

"Incredible news! This makes the Ember openin' look like spare change." Then he frowned at the carpet. "But come to think of it, I have Hope to thank for this too."

"What are you talking about?"

"You remember when I took all those photos of Half Moon Bay, and the original pictures from the grotto?"

"Yeah." She led him by the hand to the couch, where he perched, thrumming, on the edge. "Hope talked about that at our girls' night out. The Tourism Board took forever to process her listing because of some project they were working on."

He burst into laughter, bending over his knees, but finally quieted as she stared at him. This was such a change from the stressed, despondent Robert of the past few weeks she wanted to cross her fingers.

Robert took her hand. "Ok. Let me tell you the entire story." He did that in admirable fashion, not bursting into maniacal laughter once. "They want to pay me sixty grand and give me *international* exposure!"

"My God, Robert. What an incredible opportunity. When do you start?"

The smile fell from his face, and Heather's heart wrenched.

And... the other shoe drops.

"They want to meet next week. The woman who called me is a friend of my mother's, and I told her all about Pop. She gave me a little time to get things at home straightened out."

"Can you work your dad's boat and do this photo shoot?"

"I doubt it. For somethin' this important, I need to be prepared to move instantly to take the pictures I want. Especially for shots involvin' rainbows and storm clouds."

"Can't you get someone to take your place on the boat?"

"Yeah, that shouldn't be too hard. I feel so guilty about it, though. Pop has a heart attack, and I desert him for a photo gig."

"It's not just any photo gig. You need to make him understand that."

He laughed, but it was a mere shadow of his earlier giddiness. "Yeah, talkin' to him about photography has gone so well before."

Heather pulled him close, knowing how difficult this was. His family loyalty was one of the things she loved most about him. But loyalty would only take him so far with an opportunity like this. She was even more reluctant to bring up Althea now.

But I'm proud I stood up to her in the hospital and spoke my mind. I'm not terribly eager to see her again, so Robert can get this settled with his father before we cross that bridge.

Or burn it down completely.

Chapter Thirty-Six

ROBERT FOLLOWED HIS PARENTS' old sedan down the narrow road toward their house. The afternoon was lovely, punctuated by a soft breeze and fleeting clouds that kept the heat at bay.

The perfect day for a homecoming.

Althea parked in their gravel driveway, and both doors opened as Robert pulled up behind them. Eddie had been held up because of a boat repair that was more extensive than expected, so only one Davis son was on hand to welcome Bennett home.

Althea wrapped a protective arm around her husband's waist as they slowly climbed the three front steps onto the covered patio. "Do you want to sit in your chair in the livin' room?" she asked.

Bennett stopped, a thin sheen of sweat on his forehead. "No, I've been inside for weeks. I'd like to sit on the front porch and enjoy this fine day."

With a nod, she herded him to the long swing, where he flopped down with a grunt. "Can I get you anythin'? Iced tea?"

"No," Pop replied, giving her a tired smile. "I'm not thirsty."

Althea wrung her hands. "I promised I'd call people the moment you got home, so I'd better get to it. You sure you don't need anythin'?"

"No, Althea," he said softly, then turned to his son. "Robert will sit with me a while, won't you?"

"Absolutely, Pop."

Robert hurried over and took a seat on the swing next to him, taking care so it didn't rock. The door shut softly as his mother retreated inside to make her calls. Robert had said nothing in the three days since Beatrice's call, and wasn't sure this was the right time either as he made a note of Bennett's thin chest rising and falling with his rapid breaths. The brief journey from car to swing had wiped him out.

Robert had hardly slept since Beatrice's phone call, filled with exhilaration and guilt. Not only about the Tourism Board opportunity, but his mother too. He'd tried to talk about her reaction to Heather, but she'd pursed her lips together and looked at the floor, finally saying, "I'm prayin' hard on that, Robert. You just let me be." More and more, a choice was looming—one between his parents and the life *he* wanted to live.

But how can I bring any of that up when Pop just got out of the hospital?

Now Bennett sighed, a small smile playing at his lips as he slowly swiveled his head, taking in the vista before them. "I wasn't sure I'd see this view again, and I mean to enjoy it."

His parents' house didn't have the expansive view Robert's did, being located lower in elevation, but the sparkling ocean was still visible. "You gave us a pretty good scare, Pop."

"Yeah, I know. A heart attack is quite the wake-up call from above."

"We're grateful you're gonna be ok."

The two men sat in silence for several minutes, watching a flock of white pelicans circle the shore below. Robert tried to imagine how much more beautiful the view would be after an experience like his father's.

"How's your photography goin'?"

Robert was so startled by the question, he nearly jumped. After a pause, he answered honestly. "I've actually been given an opportunity. A big one." He explained about the Tourism Board campaign.

"I heard you've been helpin' out every day since I went into the hospital. Thank you for that—I know fishin' isn't your favorite thing."

Robert shook his head. "Don't thank me. I didn't even have to think about it." *But how can I tell you if I keep helpin', I'll lose the opportunity of a lifetime?*

Bennett leaned forward, clasping his hands together as he rested his gnarled elbows on his knees, still focused on the view. "Bein' face to face with death makes you see your life differently."

"I can imagine it does."

"I had an experience early on. I don't remember much from when I was in the ICU, but this was so clear. It was a dream, but not really. After I woke up and thought about it, I realized it was a memory. One I had completely forgotten about."

Robert turned to focus on his father. His wiry gray hair was longer than usual, and the top of his dark head was shiny, like it had been polished.

"I was only a boy, seven or eight years old, and we lived in Frederiksted proper. A fire station was down the road, with one big fire truck. What a racket that truck made barrelin' down the road! I used to tear out of the house and stand on the edge of the road as it roared by. And the firemen always waved at me."

Bennett smiled, the faraway look still in his eyes. "Well, to my young eyes, that was just about the most amazin' thing I'd ever seen. I wanted to be a fireman when I grew up. More than anythin' in the world."

Pop shook his head, the faint smile still there.

"One evenin', we were sittin' on the porch. The whole family—my folks, my two brothers and my sister. And that truck went screamin' by and I ran out to wave at the firemen, practically on fire myself. I strutted back to the porch, just as proud as a peacock, when my father said to me, 'Why you chasin' after trucks, boy?'

"I puffed out my chest and told him I was goin' to be a fireman when I grew up, so I needed them to know who I was. My daddy stared at me, then said, 'Look at your two older brothers, son. Look at me. What do you see?'

"'Fishermen. But I want to be a fireman!'

"'I understand, but the sad thing is it doesn't matter what we want, son. You're goin' to be a fisherman, just like the rest of us. Fishin' is what the Davises are made to do. So put this foolishness about fightin' fires out of your mind. It's time you started lendin' a hand on the boat, anyway. You'll come with me tomorrow.'"

Robert stared at his father. His face was more deeply lined than it had been a month ago. Robert had never heard of Bennett's hopes or dreams. Pop had only talked about what was in front of him at the moment.

Bennett finally turned and looked straight at him. "And startin' the next mornin', I officially became a fisherman. In time, I lost the desire to be a firefighter, especially after I realized how much I loved fishin'. Eventually, I forgot all about it. But the memory was so clear in that hospital room. I was *meant* to remember that—now. My father destroyed the dream of a young boy, though he ended up bein' right. But son, there is a world of difference between a seven-year-old and a grown man of thirty-three."

He heaved a deep sigh and looked down at his hands as Robert's heart pounded, sweat breaking out on his palms.

"I've got no right to tell you how to make your livin'. Especially when you're obviously talented at what you've chosen to do. God has blessed me with two strong, good sons. And one of them is perfect to take over Davis Fishin'. Only I've been too blind and set in my ways to understand. But I see it now. Eddie's ready to captain and has been for a long time. I just didn't want to admit I was gettin' older."

Bennett laid a wrinkled hand on Robert's knee and squeezed. "We can easily hire a hand to replace you on the boat. Follow your dream, son."

A single tear rolled down Robert's face. "Thanks, Pop. I can't even begin to tell you how much it means to have your blessin'."

"You do. Your mother and I have been hard on you, especially these last six months or so. I'm sorry about that." He paused, bringing his hands together again and twirling his thumbs around each other. "Eddie told me your mother said some unkind words to Heather when you arrived at the hospital."

Wiping his face, Robert swallowed hard. "She did. Unkind is puttin' it lightly. And I'm havin' a hard time gettin' over that, Pop."

"Your mother is the finest woman I've ever known, son. But sometimes her mouth has a way of runnin' away from her. Now that I'm out of the woods, she'll be reflectin' on how she spoke to Heather. If this experience has made me rethink things, I imagine it might do the same for her."

"I hope so. But you didn't see her face when she saw Heather at the hospital. I love this woman, Pop, and she didn't deserve what Mom threw at her. If Mother doesn't come around soon, I'm not sure what's goin' to happen."

Robert turned his gaze back to the glittering ocean, his heart lighter now. But the central issue of him and Heather remained. Would Althea give her blessing as easily as his father just had about Robert's career?

Chapter Thirty-Seven

HEATHER POURED a scoop of kibble into Lucky's bowl. He sat politely three feet away, his tail softly bumping the cement floor of his kennel. As soon as she took a step back, he padded over and began eating. "You're such a good boy. How can you still be here? Probably because I want the perfect home for you." The previous week, a couple had been interested in him, but they had young nephews who visited often, and Heather had been worried Lucky wouldn't be happy.

So here he was. Still.

Moving down the line, she fed the other dogs, who showed a variety of levels of food eagerness. But none were aggressive about it, which made placing them much easier. After Heather returned to the desk in the reception area, she started evaluating the photos Robert had taken two days prior, posting them on the shelter's website. Now that Bennett was home again and had given his blessing to pursue photography, there was a palpable relaxation in Robert. If only their other thorny issue could be solved as easily.

Pet Paradise had received a new litter of kittens, and Robert had repeated their idea of the bed with balls of yarn. Heather's smile widened as she cycled through them. These kittens were a mixture of smoke gray and black and white. She quickly determined the winner was the photo showing two youngsters having a tug of war with a ball of yarn.

As she was dragging the picture onto the website builder, the front door opened, and someone walked in. "One second, please," Heather said, then placed the image securely in its slot and looked up with a smile.

Althea stood before her.

Robert's mother, holding a white purse with both hands, was dressed in a light-green dress with cap sleeves and sensible shoes. Her straightened black hair was tied back in a neat bun at the nape of her neck and her face was carefully guarded, as if she were afraid to show what she was feeling.

Heather's smile froze on her face and her heart flopped to a stop before resuming at double time. "Good morning, Mrs. Davis. This is a surprise. Are you interested in a pet?"

Althea opened her mouth, but no sound came out. Then she licked her lips quickly and tried again. "I am. I've decided to get a companion to dote on a little. My sons are grown men and fully capable of runnin' their own lives."

Heather kept her face pleasant, even as she thought, *They are, but when has that stopped you before?* "You're lucky to have two such wonderful sons."

"Yes, I am." She darted a glance around the small room, still clutching her purse. "Would it be possible for you to step out for a moment? Maybe take a short walk in the sunshine?"

Heather rose, trying to ignore the feeling of dread spreading over her. She doubted Althea showed up just to look at a pet. *Might as well get it over with. She needs to understand Robert and I aren't going to stop seeing each other.* "Of course. We can walk around the meadow. If anyone drives up, I'll be able to see them."

They exited into the balmy afternoon. A light breeze tickled the leaves of the shade as they stepped onto the grass. "I'm very relieved Mr. Davis is doing so well."

"Thank you. So am I."

The two sentences were followed by a long pause, but Heather remained silent. Althea was obviously there for a reason, so she could lead the conversation. Heather wasn't looking for another argument, but she was done shrinking from this woman.

They were walking next to the chain-link fence enclosing the dog park when Althea cleared her throat. "I've always tried to live my life so I didn't have regrets—to be a good wife and a good mother, and set a proper example. There haven't been many occasions when I have felt true shame over my actions." She swallowed thickly. "But how I spoke to you in the hospital was one of those times. I came here to apologize."

Heather was so surprised, she paused mid-stride. She quickly recovered, rejoining Althea's side. "Thank you. You were under a lot of strain."

"Yes I was, but that's no excuse. If one of my boys had spoken to someone like that, I would have torn into him without even hesitatin'. The Good Book talks about not castin' stones unless you're without sin, and I'm certainly not. Heather, I'm askin' for your forgiveness."

The dread washed from Heather's body as a smile rose. Althea wasn't the only one who had rushed to a quick judgement. Heather had been so busy preparing for a fight that she hadn't even considered Robert's mother might be there to hold out an olive branch. "I can do that. Maybe we can start over."

"I'd like to try."

This visit took a lot of courage for her. Meet her halfway, Heather. "My roommate was born in St. Thomas and comes from a traditional family too. She's helped me understand why you might be hesitant about me in Robert's life."

Remorse and concern lined Althea's brow. "I'm afraid of losin' him and all we've tried to instill in him. But it's pretty obvious that I've only been pushin' him further away. It's hard to believe what I said at the hospital—I was in a complete panic over Bennett. And when I laid eyes on you, I saw the perfect outlet for my fear."

"I know better than most people what it's like to do something you regret during a traumatic event. My fiancé left me at the altar. Afterwards, I had too much to drink, then went to work and was quickly fired. I lost everything. That's why I left San Francisco and moved here. And on St. Croix, I've found exactly what I've been looking for."

Althea's light-brown eyes softened, now more similar to the eyes Robert possessed. Heather stared back and the first connection formed between the two women. Althea reached out and touched Heather's elbow. "I thought you were some spoiled rich girl who was tryin' to make her parents mad. I'm sorry that happened to you."

"Thank you. It hasn't been easy to move past it, but I mostly have." Heather gazed at the sunlight sparkling on the distant turquoise ocean. "I don't think you need to worry about Robert forgetting his roots. St. Croix is a part of him—it's why he's such a great photographer. He simply *sees* aspects of each image that others don't."

Althea smiled, showing only genuine warmth now. "I know. Bennett and I taught those two boys what matters, and it's time we let them prove that themselves."

"You're right about one thing, Mrs. Davis. Robert and I do come from different worlds. But maybe that's a positive. We can learn from each other."

Robert's mother heaved a deep sigh. "I think we could all stand to learn from each other. And please call me Althea."

They walked along the tree line in the dappled shade. "Thank you for coming by, Althea. This means the world to me."

"I'm glad I did too." She hesitated for a moment, glancing into the trees. "Robert's ex-wife was everythin' I'd ever wanted for him—the perfect local girl. I was so in love with the picture of who I wanted her to be that I was blind to who she actually was. And Robert paid the price. He hasn't been shy lettin' me know how much he loves you, Heather. I raised a good man—I understand why you'd love him right back."

Heather laughed, and Althea joined her. "Robert is an amazing man. Everyone loves him—I'm just lucky to be the woman he loves back. One of them," she said, and Althea nodded.

They were nearly back to the entry of the purple building. "Did you come here only to speak with me? Or do you really want to look at a pet?" Heather asked with a smile.

Althea's brows rose. "Both. I came to apologize, but I do want a dog. One I can take for walks, but who isn't too excitable. Do you have an older dog? One who wouldn't mind a home without a lot of hustle and bustle?"

Heather broke into a giant smile, her heart overflowing. "I certainly do. I know a dog who is exactly what you want, and I think you're the home he's been waiting for. His name is Lucky."

HALF AN HOUR LATER, the two women were back in the reception area. Lucky stood beside Althea, wagging his tail as she held his leash in one hand. Her other arm carried a canvas shopping bag with a starter supply of dog food, dishes, and toys. "Are you sure I don't need to fill out any paperwork?"

"I'll waive it. Lucky is a special dog, and I'd like him to go home with you right away. I think you and Bennett are the perfect home for him."

Althea smiled at the brown and black dog before raising her gaze to meet Heather's. She opened her mouth, quickly shutting it again. Once more, showing that same hesitancy and unsureness she had upon arriving. With a start, Heather recognized the emotion was fear of rejection, not dismissal. The older woman gave her a shaky smile. "I have one more thing I'd like to ask you. Thanksgivin' is next week. If you don't have plans already, I'd be honored if you and Robert would join us."

Heather swallowed over the sudden thickness in her throat. "I would love that. Thank you."

ROBERT SLID into a booth across from Alex and Jack in the bar section of Breakers. The bartender, Maurice, promptly brought over three Leatherbacks and Alex held his up in a toast. "Here's to having you back on the boat again. We missed you."

The three bottles clinked together. "Thanks," Robert said. "I loved bein' back. Beats the hell out of fishin', that's for sure. And when I haven't been on the boat, I've been workin' on the photos for Ember. They're all at the framer's shop now. Divin' today was the perfect escape."

"So, your dad is home and recovering?" Jack asked.

Robert nodded. "He and I had a really great talk last week, right after he got home. The heart attack finally made him realize Eddie is the one who should take over Davis Fishin'. He's over the moon about it—captain at last. And I can do what I want without feelin' guilty about it." He picked at the label on his bottle, reluctant to keep going.

"But..." Alex prompted.

Robert looked up and alternated his gaze between the two men. "Yeah. There's a big but. Mother and Heather."

Alex leaned back in the booth. "Families can be tough. Sometimes you just can't make everyone happy."

"If your dad came around about the fishing, your mom might with Heather," Jack said.

Robert briefly squeezed his eyes shut, trying to banish the image of Althea screaming at Heather. "I'm not sure. It's my mom more than Pop. And I'm *really* not sure what to do about it."

"Maybe she needs more time," Alex said. "At age seventeen, I told my parents that I wanted to enlist in the Navy. They weren't too happy about that. When I came home a year later, and said I was going to try out to be a SEAL, they *really* weren't happy, especially my mother. But after I made it all the way through, she changed her mind. She was still concerned for me, but proud too. Maybe your mom needs to get used to the idea and get to know Heather better."

"Perhaps. I just don't know—we've given her plenty of time. I feel like everythin's comin' together on one side and fallin' apart on the other."

Alex sighed and took another drink. "You might be headed toward a hard decision, Robert. Heather or your family. There's no right or wrong choice, but you'll have to live with the consequences, whichever way you go."

Robert looked him in the eye. "What would you do if you were in my shoes?"

Alex smiled crookedly at him. "If I had to pick between Hope and the status quo? My parents have been gone for a long time—which is also something you might think about, since you almost lost your father. They won't be around forever. Having said that, nothing in the world could keep me away from Hope. Nothing."

Jack shrugged. "Or me from Sara."

The thought of not having Heather in his life opened up a gaping void inside him. "I love her," Robert said bleakly.

"Is that enough?" Alex asked.

The void was filled as an iron resolve rose in him. He took a sip and slammed his bottle down on the table. "Yes—more than enough. I need to talk to Heather right now."

With a final nod, Robert stood and marched out of the bar.

Chapter Thirty-Eight

AS HEATHER DROVE to Robert's, she was brimming with energy from one of those perfect coincidences. Donna had arrived at Pet Paradise while Althea had been getting acquainted with her new dog, leaving Heather free to leave. And after Althea had left the shelter with Lucky, Heather had been aflame to share the incredible news. Immediately pulling out her phone to call Robert, Heather had just opened it when a text came through from him.

Robert: Can you come over to my place?

Heather: Yes! I was just going to call you. I'll be right there!

Robert: Can't wait. Hurry.

Still reeling from Althea's visit, she gripped the wheel tighter and let a smile rise to her face. Heather didn't ask, but she suspected Althea hadn't told Robert about her intentions ahead of time. Which meant he'd likely be as floored as Heather had been.

She parked behind his SUV and nearly ran up the stairs, entering his house after a quick knock. "Robert, honey! Where are you?"

"In the kitchen. Come on back."

Heather hurried through the hall and living room to find him retrieving two beers from his refrigerator and opening them. Trying to keep her grin from going overboard, she gripped his face in both hands and kissed him hard. Robert wrapped both arms around her and kissed her back with equal fervor. She pulled back with a grin. "You won't believe what just happened! I can't wait to tell you."

His face was completely serious. "I can tell you're excited, but I need to say somethin' first. Can we go out on the patio?"

Her smile fell. "Sure." A worried flutter tickled her stomach as they settled around the table. The last vestiges of daylight were hanging on, and the horizon showed a broad streak of orange. Robert leaned forward and grasped both her hands in his, brushing his thumbs over the back of them. "Is something wrong?" All thoughts of Althea and good news fled at his somber expression.

"Maybe. I'm not sure." He raised his head to stare into her eyes. "Heather, I love you, and I don't want to live without you. You've never made me feel like I wasn't enough. That was the wound that my marriage left, and you helped heal it."

Her heart twisted. "Of course you're good enough. I can't believe that your ex-wife felt differently. And my background has nothing to do with that. Robert, you're good enough for *anyone.*"

"Thank you." He raised her hand to press a soft kiss to it, then met her eyes again, intensity burning in his. "Pop has come around, and I don't think you'll have any issues with him. And God knows I've tried to give Mom her space and let her warm up to you on her own. But every time I've talked to her about what happened at the hospital, she brushes me off and changes the subject."

He dropped his shoulders and sighed. "I love my mother

very much, but you're my future. If she won't accept you, we'll have to live our lives without her. I won't stand by and let you be treated like that. If Mother won't welcome you, she can't be a part of my life."

His voice cracked on the last few words, and Heather's heart clutched hard even as a bright light soared within her.

Robert squeezed her hands. "I mean it. I know Mom—"

Heather silenced him by placing two fingers against his lips. "Stop. You don't need to choose between me and your family."

He clenched his eyes shut while shaking his head. "Heather, I know you've been sayin' that, but—"

She gripped his hand tightly, and he opened his eyes. "Robert, that's what I came over here to tell you—why I'm so excited. Your mother visited me at Pet Paradise today."

His face went blank with utter stupefaction.

Well, that answers whether he knew.

"She showed up at the *shelter*? And she knew you'd be there?"

Heather laughed. "Believe me, I was more surprised than you are. She came to apologize, and we had a really good conversation. I even told her about Grant and getting fired in San Francisco. She invited me to have Thanksgiving dinner with your family."

Robert slumped in the chair, as if all the tension had drained out of him. "Really? This is Althea Davis we're talkin' about, right?"

Another laugh tumbled out of Heather's mouth. "The one and only. I'd recognize her anywhere—you've got her eyes. You were willing to give up your family for me?"

"Yes. Though I was hopin' if it came to that, Mom would come to her senses." Then he paused, biting his bottom lip. "Heather, you went through a terrible experience in San Francisco, and I'm sure it's made you gun-shy about commitment. I won't pressure you, but you need to know I'm in this for the long haul—I'm not goin' anywhere."

"Neither am I. I'm in no rush to get married, but you're ten times the man Grant ever could be. I love you so much."

"I love you too." He leaned forward again and kissed her, brushing the side of her face with one hand. Then he pulled back, wrinkling his brow. "Why did Mother go to the shelter? She could have gotten hold of you at Half Moon Bay."

Heather's smile threatened to break her face in half. "She adopted a dog. She said she needed something to dote on besides you and Eddie."

Robert laughed long and hard. "Well, I'm sure not gonna argue with that."

"Best of all? The dog she took home was Lucky. I think your folks are the perfect home for him."

"You're probably right about that. I hope Donna realizes what a lucky day it was when you walked through the door."

"I'm the fortunate one. It was the shelter that really brought you and me together, you know."

"Half Moon Bay had a part in it too."

"A huge part. And now Ember is making our dreams come true." She paused, tilting her head as something occurred to her. "I wonder why Hope is just calling it Ember, and not Half Moon Ember?"

Robert reached forward and slid his fingers through her long, fiery hair. "She knows better. You're the only Half Moon Ember, you know."

"Is that right?"

"This is more right than anything I've ever known."

Robert slid to the edge of his chair and cupped the back of her head, drawing her into a long kiss. Their tongues brushed delicately over each other, and Heather moaned softly.

She broke the kiss and looked upward at the starry sky, the

last faint hint of orange to the west. "Do you still have the blanket we used that first time? It's too beautiful a night to be indoors."

Robert rose. "You pick the spot and I'll be right back with it."

HEATHER CHOSE a grassy area close to where they'd made love the first time. The view of Frederiksted was equally beautiful, but she was much more interested in the man before her. They lay on the quilt, facing each other, and she rose slightly to unbutton Robert's shirt. Sliding the two sides off his torso, she ran one hand over the smooth skin of his chest and its scattering of tightly curled black hair. "I love looking at the contrast of our skin." She raised her gaze to look into those liquid brown eyes. "We're so beautiful together."

"You're the beautiful one."

The night air around them was filled with the gentle chorus of crickets, and the quilt was smooth and cool underneath her. Robert sat up and pulled her shirt off in a single motion, quickly unhooking her bra and tossing it next to the blanket. His dark fingers traced a feathery touch across her breasts and goose-bumps rose, making him smile. He moved his head to her breast, taking it into his mouth as he pressed her onto her back.

They weren't new lovers anymore, and he knew exactly what she liked. He swirled his tongue in slow circles while he mirrored the motions with his hand on her other breast. Heather gasped and arched her chest harder against him, giving herself over fully. He moved lower, brushing his fingers across her abdomen and making the skin quiver and jump, then slid under her shorts and panties.

He moved his mouth to hers again as he began stroking her,

and she moved her hips in rhythm with him. She was breathing deeply, and he slowly kissed his way to her ear, brushing his tongue across it as she jolted. Every muscle in her body twitched.

"Don't get too excited, sweetness. We're not in any hurry."

"Don't blame me," she breathed in his ear. "You're the one doing that."

Smiling, Robert sat up. She raised her hips so he could get her shorts off before quickly removing his own. Heather lay on the blanket with her knees together and bent. After depositing their remaining clothing out of the way, Robert ran both hands in a caress from her feet up her shins. Then he held her with his eyes as he slid his fingers between her knees. He pressed them apart, moving in to kiss the tender skin on the inside of her knee. Every inch of skin he touched was aflame, and the intimacy of their locked gazes only intensified the sensations rolling up and down her body.

Opening his mouth, he traced his tongue up her inner thigh, a soft breath of wind cooling the wetness he left behind. Heather bunched both hands in the quilt, closing them tightly as he settled between her legs and swept his tongue in a long, deep taste.

This time, she didn't just arch her back. She bucked, gasping into the night. As he continued, she clutched his head with both hands, urging him on. He fanned both hands wide around her hips, grounding her to the earth as her climax swept her away. She threw a hand over her mouth and bit down to keep from screaming. With her heart roaring in her ears, Heather had hardly come down from her high when Robert climbed up her body and entered her with one hard, powerful thrust.

She met him, measure for measure. They slammed together, tenderness but a memory as bare need took over. He cupped both hands under her and drove into her, his breath exploding with every exhale. Heather tipped her head back, closing her eyes, and they rode a long wave together as the black, eternal sky watched over them from above.

A WEEK LATER, the small assemblage sat around the table, laughter and warmth filling the room. Heather scooped a portion of beans and rice, smiling at Althea. "I've never had rice and beans with Thanksgiving dinner. This is wonderful! Thank you for letting me help." The rice and beans were Althea's family recipe. She and Heather had spent several hours in the kitchen preparing the lavish meal. They were still tiptoeing around each other, but the mood was completely opposite of the first dinner Heather had attended.

Robert's mother smiled and pointed to the turkey, rolls, and green beans. "We like to add a little local touch, but everyone loves traditional Thanksgivin'. How are your parents spendin' the holiday?"

"I spoke with both this morning. Thanksgiving has always been a special holiday for my family. When my father first started Galendo, he made a point of inviting anyone at work who didn't have Thanksgiving plans to our house for dinner. The celebration has grown in size over the years, but my parents make sure no one is left out. When I was a girl, we had a dozen or so people over, but Mom said this morning that this year they're renting several ballrooms at The Drake Hotel."

"What a lovely tradition," Althea said, handing her a plate of fish fillets.

Eddie pointed at the platter with his fork. "That wahoo is fresh caught this mornin'. We did a quick session, but still made a good catch."

"Don't point with your fork, Edward," Althea said mildly, and Eddie immediately placed his fork on the plate as Robert grinned at him. He squeezed Heather's knee and winked at her, his happiness obvious.

Eddie returned to the small mountain of mashed potatoes on his plate that he was systematically destroying, and Heather tried not to grin too widely. "Are you enjoying being a captain, Eddie?"

He raised his head, sheer joy transforming his broad face, and it warmed Heather's heart. "Lovin' every minute. It's goin' great. Well, once we got the greenhorn off the boat who kept throwin' the net off the wrong side."

Robert picked at his turkey, muttering, "I only did that once."

Laughter erupted around the table, led by Bennett. "*Althea* and *Margaret* are both in good hands. Maybe I'll go out with you soon, and just sit on the deck with the wind in my face."

"You're always welcome, Pop," Eddie said, all traces of humor gone.

Bennett cast a warm eye over them all. He had been fairly quiet that afternoon, but when Heather and Robert had arrived, he welcomed her with a heartfelt embrace. This holiday was an extra blessing for him. He took another roll, and Robert grinned at him.

"Eat up, Pop. Got to get your strength back."

"I'm feelin' better every day. I've been takin' some slow walks with your mother and our new friend." He peered into the corner of the living room, where Lucky lay curled up on his bed, polite as always. Bennett grinned at Heather. "That dog sure was happy to see you."

She raised her napkin to her mouth and laughed. When she and Robert had walked in the front door, Lucky had run to her, jumping up and down and nearly bowling her over. "I was glad to see him too. He's settling in well here?"

"Yes," Althea said with a smile. "I've been takin' him on walks every day, and he likes his bed over there. He's a wonderful dog—quiet without too much energy."

After dinner, they ate a homemade apple pie Althea had baked, and Eddie helped himself to a second slice. "So how fancy is this gala openin' goin' to be?"

"You're goin' to have to dig out your suit, Eddie," Robert said, trying not to laugh. "Mom, you might need to get the mothball smell out of it."

"Whatever it takes, son. We'll do you proud." She and Robert shared a long smile. The day after Althea's visit to the pet shelter, Robert had sat down for a long talk with her and cleared the air between them. Now as they smiled at each other, the warmth between mother and son was clear on both faces.

"It's formal dress, but that's taking into account we live on a casual Caribbean island," Heather said. "Eddie, you'll fit in fine. I imagine we'll see everything from suits to tuxedos, and a variety of dresses for the women."

"Are your pictures ready?" Bennett asked Robert.

"Gettin' there. Vera, who owns the framin' shop, is workin' on them right now. She has promised to have everythin' ready a week before the openin'."

"At that point, you'll have to show them to me. Whether you like it or not," Heather said, giving Robert a playful punch on the arm.

"You haven't seen his photos?" Althea asked, her face blank.

"No! It's top secret, and I'm the subject in several. You better not make me look bad, Robert."

He smiled at her for a long moment, but finally said, "Sweetness, that isn't even a possibility."

Chapter Thirty-Nine

HEATHER WALKED across the spectacular floor, her dressy flats clicking softly as she moved toward her parents. It was 8 p.m., and the gala opening of Ember was in full swing, with a roomful of patrons strolling around, sipping champagne as they admired Robert's beautifully lit photos.

Heather snuck another delighted glance at the small card she held in one hand. Tim and Laura Galen stood before what was unquestionably the centerpiece of the exhibit, a photo Robert had taken while shooting from above. Heather's pale, outstretched form, contrasted against the black rock below her, nearly leaped from the picture as she reached toward the glass float. Her hair fanned about her in a crimson wave as she stared straight into the camera, and a tiny smile lifted her lips, as if she had some secret. The photograph was printed on a vast expanse of glass, three feet tall by five feet wide, and also held the largest price tag of the night: $10,000.

Heather had been astonished when Robert showed her the

finished pieces as they were preparing the exhibit. Each was magnetic, drawing the eye, and she couldn't believe she was the model in most. The prints captured a haunting, captivating beauty in both her and the scenery, sensual yet not at all risqué.

Laura, wearing a dark-green evening gown, saw her and burst into an enormous smile. Her diamond necklace glittered in the lights. "There you are! These are amazing. We were admiring this one."

Her father, wearing a tailored black tuxedo, gazed around the softly lit interior, filled with the buzz of conversation and soft jazz music. "Knowing you were in charge, my expectations were high, but this place is incredible." He glanced downward and his eyes became round. "I can't get over this floor. Wow."

Hope had kept the final, perfect element of Ember to herself, not unveiling it until just before they opened the doors. Hidden lights were installed under the blond wooden floor, and when she turned them on, the wide, crisscrossing veins of orange and red *glowed*.

"It all turned out pretty well, I have to admit," Heather said, trying to hide a smug grin. "The gallery design is Hope's and I arranged Robert's exhibit."

Tim pointed with his chin at the glass print before them. "We'll take this one. How do we arrange payment?"

Heather laughed and lifted the small *Sold* card she held, placing it in a slot over the price tag. "Sorry—you're too late! Someone else already bought it."

Her father scowled. "Like hell. You're my daughter. Whatever they offered, I'll double it."

Heather arched a brow at him. "It's not an auction, Dad. And there are plenty of others to choose from."

She waved an arm, gesturing to the large room around them. A dozen prints of her in the rock pool were placed prominently, and others showed Alex free diving at a much greater depth. He only wore board shorts, but the specialized long fins and his natural underwater grace lent the photos a surreal quality. St. Croix landscapes and underwater reef scenes complemented the Grotto pictures and were spaced throughout the venue.

Tim gave her a reluctant smile. "Ok, you talked me into it. We'll keep looking. You look incredible, by the way."

"Thank you." She smiled, gazing down at her floor-length black dress. It was tightly fitted and strapless, very classy.

"Your hair is just beautiful," Laura said, reaching out and running a section through her fingers.

"Well, it should be. I got it from you!" Heather laughed and shrugged one shoulder. "I had some help from a professional."

Robert had made one request—that she wear her hair down tonight. Earlier in the evening, Sara had herded Heather and Hope into the still unfinished Aqua, and sat them in two stylist stations that were mostly functional. An hour later, Heather's hair lay in a flat, glossy copper sheet down her back. It had never looked better. After arranging Hope's hair into a fancy updo, Sara had styled her own into long, dark-brown ringlets.

"Well, we'd better keep looking," Tim said, gazing narrowly at the other patrons. "Before anyone else steals one of these out from under us." Then he grinned and offered his elbow to Laura.

As they strolled off arm-in-arm, Heather swept her gaze around Ember. A small section near the front of the gallery was sectioned off with high walls. After tonight, it would house works from local artists who weren't prolific enough to warrant a full exhibit. But now, black cloth draped over the three partitions, and eight by ten photos hung of the pets currently available for adoption at Pet Paradise. Donna sat at a nearby desk, wearing a voluminous lavender dress and a bewildered expression. The slightly stunned expression was due to a succession of people who brought her a picture of the animal they had chosen so they could fill out an adoption application.

Hope stood in a small cluster with Sara and Cindy, and Heather headed their way. She passed Alex and Jack, who were on the other side of the room. Alex, looking ridiculously handsome in a black tuxedo, accepted a glass of champagne from Clark while he stared intensely at his wife, as if he wanted to devour her on the spot. Heather continued toward the women, trying to determine what was slightly off about Alex's appearance.

"Hello, ladies," she said, then the answer came to her. The former SEAL was wearing a fitted white shirt with black buttons and black coat, but something was missing. "Hope—Alex forgot his tie."

Hope closed her eyes and heaved a long-suffering sigh. "No, he didn't. Earlier, I was informed that if he had to choose between being shot or wearing a tie, he'd take the bullet. Some battles are unwinnable, and no one can out-stubborn Alex Monroe." She tilted her head, appraising her husband as a small smile rose. "But he still looks pretty delicious, so I call it a win."

They were all laughing when Heather caught sight of the man of the hour, walking straight toward her. Robert had dispensed with the tuxedo, wearing a new tailored black shirt and suit instead. It was modern and very dashing, with silk lapels, and a royal-blue necktie only added to the effect. He joined her side, lifting her hand to brush a kiss over it before sweeping an admiring look over the four women. "You ladies are all so beautiful—I'm nearly blinded."

They all groaned, and Robert burst into laughter, but Heather had to admit they looked pretty good. Hope was gorgeous, dressed in a tight, shimmering silver gown with a slit up one leg and spaghetti straps that crossed in back. Wearing matching four-inch stilettos, she was still shorter than Heather.

Sara, like Heather, wore black, but her dress featured an empire waist which emphasized her décolletage before falling loosely.

The next thing she knew, Alex and Jack were there. Alex nudged Sara aside so he could stand beside his wife. "Move over, Sara."

She mock-punched him in the arm, then shook out her hand, grimacing. "Ow. You are so bossy. I don't know how Hope puts up with you."

Alex positively smoldered as he slid an arm around Hope's shoulder, his smile widening at her wide-eyed expression. "She'll remember later tonight."

Sara rolled her eyes. Jack laughed, pulling her close, and she turned to him, a delighted smile forming as she smoothed her hand over his tie. "At least my man is willing to sacrifice to make me happy. You look amazing." Jack wore a navy-blue suit, but it was livened up with a dark-red and orange diagonal striped tie which complemented their surroundings perfectly. There was no doubt Sara had picked it out.

He inclined his head. "Thank you. I'm just trying to keep the hurricanes at bay tonight."

Sara narrowed her eyes at him as Hope, Alex, and Robert laughed, and he quickly forestalled her with a kiss. At first, Heather didn't get the joke, then she remembered Sara's nickname.

Cindy was dressed in a vivid red dress that was stunning against her dark skin, and several braids around her face were dyed to match. She turned to Robert, saying, "Did you get all the shots for your Tourism Board project?"

"I got most of them last week and I'll finish up the rest in a few days," Robert replied, tracing his hand up and down Heather's bare back. "Jack and I went divin' and I took a bunch of underwater shots, usin' him as a model."

"Couldn't get your first choice, huh?" Alex asked, grinning.

"I do occasionally have to work, and this last week of preparations has been pretty hectic," Heather said. "And I have to admit, Jack was likely a better dive model than I would be, given his experience."

Jack burst into warm laughter. "Judging from all the photos hanging around this place, I seriously doubt that."

Clark appeared with a tray of filled champagne flutes, and Heather took one. "Sorry, Clark. Looks like you're going to have to train a new bartender."

He shrugged, effortlessly balancing the flutes. "That's no problem, as long as you promise not to give away my secrets."

"Scout's honor. And Eli is fully recovered?"

His eyes became wide. "Oh, wow. Yeah—crawlin' everywhere now. We can hardly keep up with him." He glanced at Hope. "You might need to hire more than one bartender. The other day, I had a guest ask me if we were puttin' in a bar at the Grotto."

Hope closed her eyes and laughed. "Over my dead body. But I'm very glad it's been such a hit with guests. And I'm even more glad no one has mentioned a bar to me. Everyone I've talked to likes its pure, unimproved state."

Clark turned to Robert. "Congratulations, man. This is incredible, and well deserved."

"Thanks." Then Robert looked around the small circle. "This group is a perfect example of what people can accomplish when they work together and support each other."

"I'll drink to that," Heather said and held up her glass.

After they all drank, Robert looked at Hope and Alex. "You two have any big Christmas plans?"

"No," Hope said, resting her head briefly on Alex's shoulder. "We'll have a quiet day at home, I imagine."

Sara frowned at her. "Well, I hope you plan to include us."

"Aren't you going to Texas to visit Jack's family?"

"Not until early January."

Jack stepped forward and faced her. "Sara, what are you talking about? We leave in a week."

Sara's face went blank before filling with panic. "We talked about Christmas, but I thought we decided to go after the holidays. You want me to meet your gigantic family for the first time at *Christmas*?"

"Yes, I do." He said the words softly and kindly, trying to calm Sara's skittish expression.

She stood there, opening and closing her mouth, but no sound came out.

Alex was grinning broadly. "Look at this way. You've got an entire week to figure out the details and arrange gifts for Jack's five thousand siblings."

Clark swapped out Sara's empty flute for a full one as she continued to gape at Jack. "Here. You look like you need this." He nodded and left to serve the next group of people. Cindy saw a co-worker and moved off as well.

Jack wrapped an arm around Sara's shoulders and steered her away from the circle. "Excuse us. We need to have a little chat."

As they walked away to a deserted corner, Hope grinned. "Never a dull moment with her around." Then she assessed the crowd and patted Alex on the chest. "Let's go for a stroll—we should mingle. As owners of the resort, we need to talk with everyone."

His smile became wolfish as he slid his hand behind her. "Better do your strolling now, baby. Because you're not gonna be able to walk tomorrow."

Heather and Robert burst into laughter as Hope blushed crimson. "*Alex!*" She darted a glance around, making sure no one overheard, even though Alex had spoken quietly.

His expression instantly changed to one of wide-eyed innocence, and he held his elbow out to her.

Hope slowly slid her arm through his, slitting her eyes as though he might be dangerous, and the two ambled away. Alex was still much taller, even with Hope's four-inch heels. Heather's and Robert's smiles lingered.

"I don't think we need to ask if married life agrees with them," Robert said.

Heather entwined her fingers in his. "They might even be as happy as us. Maybe." Charlotte, the main server at the restaurant, walked by, carrying a credit card reader. She was handling sales tonight and hurrying around the gallery, adding *Sold* cards to the photographs, which were beginning to outnumber those still for sale. "We're making a lot of money for Pet Paradise—and for you. I'm really pleased."

"I'm goin' to donate half my earnings from tonight to them."

She squeezed his hand. "You don't need to do that. There will be plenty of money."

"You're right. I don't need to—I want to."

Heather let her gaze wander over the assembled crowd, a sense of accomplishment filling her.

Then she froze at what she saw in one corner.

Her parents and Robert's parents stood in a small cluster, and all four were smiling. Althea wore a light-pink dress and Bennett an ironed brown suit, sharp creases down the front of both legs. "Do you see what I'm seeing?"

"Yeah," Robert nearly whispered. "I'm almost scared to go over there and break the spell."

Eddie, dressed in a gray suit and light-blue tie, left the assemblage to follow a server carrying canapes. His suit wasn't as neatly ironed, and Althea stared narrowly at him.

"Come on," Heather said. "Fortune favors the brave, and all that."

As they walked across the floor, they passed Sara and Jack, standing to one side. He stroked her upper arms with both hands, wearing a calm, reassuring expression. Robert snorted. "Someone's gonna have an excitin' Christmas, I think."

"She looks pretty nervous about meeting his family. I can sympathize. Though if we were able to work things out with all our trials, I'm sure Christmas will be wonderful for Sara and Jack."

When they joined their parents, Laura gave Robert a quick hug. "We were just telling Althea and Bennett how incredibly talented you are."

Robert placed his hand on the small of Heather's back, and she leaned into him, enjoying his warm solidness. "It's not so hard when she's the subject."

"You must be very proud of him," Tim said, and Bennett looked straight at Robert.

"Incredibly proud." He gave a creaky laugh and shook his head. "We had no idea he had this kind of talent. And I'm sorry about that, son."

"Don't mention it, Pop. That doesn't matter now."

Althea looked at Heather. "This gallery is absolutely beautiful—like a dream. And the party is obviously a big hit. Robert's not the only one with talent."

Heather inclined her head, accepting the compliment.

"We're still trying to figure out which piece to buy," Tim said. "And we need to hurry, Laura. Before they're all gone."

"Did you see that framed photo of Heather in the corner? It's gorgeous!" Althea pointed to the far reaches of the gallery.

Robert nodded at Tim. "That picture is my favorite, even more than the big one. Heather's look of wide-eyed wonder is incredible. Only someone who really knows her would understand her expression, which is why I didn't place it as prominently. You guys should check it out."

"That sounds perfect!" Laura peered over several heads in front of them. "Which one?"

"Come on," Althea said, beckoning. "We'll show you."

As their parents hurried to the far corner, crossing the veins of glowing glass in the floor, Heather and Robert slid their arms around each other.

"Well, who would have thought that would happen?" Heather asked.

"Sometimes folks need a little nudge. My parents are good people—they just have a hard time lettin' go."

She gazed into his clear brown eyes. "Of course they're good people. They made you, didn't they?"

He stared back at her, and the gallery fell away around them. They were just a man and a woman in love, apart from the rest of the world. "You mean the world to me, Heather Galen. I hope you know that. We won't rush into anything, I promise. But I want you to know I might ask you a question someday. An important question."

She beamed at him, and a radiant warmth filled her body, fear completely vanquished. "And when that time comes, I'll have an answer for you."

THANK you for reading *Half Moon Ember*! I hope you enjoyed Heather and Robert's story as much as I did. I loved the depth and richness of these two characters, and thought they were perfect for each other.

And how about that Ember opening in the final chapter? That was *wonderful* to write! Are you curious how Sara and Jack's Christmas is going to play out? I hope so, because we are returning to them for Book 7, *Half Moon Aqua*! Grab your copy now...

· · ·

HALF MOON AQUA: HALF MOON BAY BOOK 7

When dreams clash with realities, will they be brought closer together or flung apart forever?

Sara Collins has been patient, enduring endless setbacks with her dream spa at Half Moon Bay Resort in St. Croix. Just when things are coming together, life throws her a major league curve ball.

Jack Powell has finally cemented his dream job when their relationship faces its first real test—his family at Christmas. Then the resort dive manager makes him an offer too good to refuse. Except it comes with complications.

When the couple believes they've surmounted all obstacles, they are faced with their biggest challenge—one that might actually be the greatest opportunity of all.

If they face it together.

Can Sara and Jack learn to chase individual dreams while remaining a couple? Or will their personal desires tear them completely apart?

***Half Moon Aqua* is Book 7 of the Half Moon Bay beach romance series. It features the vivid tropical setting, enthralling characters, and spicy romance readers have come to love.**

Order Half Moon Aqua today!

***

WANT to keep up with all the goings-on at Half Moon Bay? Would you like another glimpse into Heather and Robert's life together? Sign up now for my Beach Read Update, and I'll send you a **free bonus chapter featuring Heather and Robert**!

It takes place a few weeks after *Half Moon Ember* ends, providing a little Christmas cheer when Heather and Robert spend the holiday with the Galens at their home in Telluride.

My Beach Read Update subscribers hear about all my free content, plus exclusive offers and sales. I'd love to have you along!

Sign up to download this exclusive bonus today.
(www.erinbrockus.com/ember)

If you're already on my list, I've got you covered! At the bottom of each newsletter is a link to all my free content for subscribers. Just find your last email from me to read this bonus, as well as any others you might have missed. Or you can simply sign up again—you'll have your bonus in a flash.

KEEP READING for my Author's Note and a preview of *Half Moon Aqua*, Book 7 of the Half Moon Bay series...

Author's Note

Robert has been one of my favorite side characters since he made his debut in the first book of this series, *Finding Hope*, where he plays a small, but vital, role. Heather is newer to the series, but I loved her back story, and how she wanted to carve out her own life separate from her famous last name.

Both he and Heather personify my theme in this series that Half Moon Bay is a place for second chances, and a place where people can become what they were meant to be.

Throughout the series, I've fictionalized the dive sites, though most are based off real site located elsewhere in the world. But Cane Bay Wall is real, located on the north side of St. Croix. It's a dizzying feeling to be diving on a wall where you can't see anything below but blue, and you know the bottom is hundreds (or thousands!) of feet below.

I've been wanting to feature a pet shelter for a while now, and I love how it came together for this book. I'd love to meet Igor the Iguana in person!

With the Davises, I tried very hard to portray a traditional Caribbean family without falling into stereotypes or caricatures.

In this series, I wanted to explore an interracial relationship and the challenges faced, and *Half Moon Ember* is the result.

Hopefully, you enjoyed the glimpse of traditional island life offered by the Davis family. I loved both the families in this story, and the fact that no matter what people's backgrounds are, many struggles families face are universal.

For the next book, the Half Moon Bay series is returning to Sara and Jack. They are a happy, committed couple now, but that doesn't mean there aren't still hurdles to overcome! And I believe there's the small matter of a spa that's still under construction...

Keep reading for a sneak peek at *Half Moon Aqua.*

Erin Brockus
December, 2022

Half Moon Aqua Excerpt

DECEMBER ...

Sara Collins crossed her arms as she stood on the beach, staring at her dream. Correction—her dream in progress. She drew her brows together, indicating the mixture of anticipation and dread roiling her stomach. The long rectangular building stretched out in front of her, even whiter than the sandy beach of Half Moon Bay Resort in St. Croix. The far-left portion of the enormous structure was complete, and its dark, smoked-glass exterior mocked her, its success evident. The art gallery—Ember —had opened recently with few delays or complications.

The same could not be said of her project, Aqua, which encompassed three quarters of the building. Designed to be one of the premier spas on the island, Aqua's lack of progress had been a trial for Sara since construction began.

That would change today.

With a determined sigh, Sara strode toward the spa's double entry doors, contained within a smoked-glass wall. The entry complemented Ember next door, giving the building a harmonious look. Behind her, the late-afternoon sun cast the white walls on either side of the dark glass into blinding brightness.

"I'm calling it Aqua for a reason," she muttered. "And this time I'd better hear water when I enter."

The glass was only tinted on the exterior, and after opening the door, a modern, bright lobby greeted Sara. The air conditioning wasn't operational yet, making her grateful for the breezy, rose-colored sundress she wore. After gathering her long brown hair and arranging it over one shoulder, she swiped a hand over the back of her neck, wiping away the sweat.

On the far side of the room, a floor-to-ceiling reinforced wall ran nearly the width of the large lobby. The main entrance door from the parking lot, a smaller version of the glass doors she had just passed through, stood to the left of it. The towering wall would eventually become the undeniable focal point of the lobby.

If the stacked stone that was to cover it ever arrived.

Several burly men in construction vests clustered around a broad, two-feet-deep rectangular basin in front of the expansive wall, their hands parked on their hips. But the floor occupied Sara's attention. More specifically, she focused with laser intensity on a four-feet-wide channel meandering through the lobby.

An empty channel.

As her gaze followed the bare, white-painted concrete trench to its source, the rectangular basin at the base of the wall, her stomach twisted. The winding canal originated from the basin, then split in two directions. One offshoot channel wandered to the salon on her left. The other curved to her right toward the treatment and massage rooms.

The shallow pool at the base of the wall was filled with water, which set Sara's heart racing. But that was the only water in evidence. She approached the foreman, a tall, lanky man named George. Sara's professional eye noted his light-brown hair was overdue for a cut and curling at the neck. He carried a clipboard and had a walkie-talkie clipped to his belt.

She pasted a smile on her face and kept her voice pleasant. "I thought we'd have water in the canals today. What's up, George?"

The foreman turned around and gave her a tight smile. "Afternoon, Sara. We're just about to open the valves."

Hallelujah! About goddamn time. "Sounds like my timing is perfect. I can't wait."

George nodded to another man, who held his thumb over a button in a nearly hidden recessed panel next to the wall. All eyes focused on the base of the channel leading from the pool. When the worker pushed the button, a white panel slid open, and water poured into the two-feet-deep canal. It trickled by Sara before splitting to run in the two directions.

She broke into a broad smile and couldn't resist clapping. "There it goes! This is so exciting."

George grinned back. "Hopefully not too exciting. We'll fill it an inch deep and keep a close watch to see if the water holds."

Sara's smile disappeared. "Holds? What do you mean?"

George shrugged but eyed her evenly. "It's water. Flowing in a brand-new channel for the first time. Don't be surprised if there's a leak or two."

"Oh, don't tell me that!"

"Just being honest. I've got guys stationed throughout the building so we can shut off the water if anything dramatic happens."

Sara ambled toward the salon. Halfway across the room, the meandering river took a turn and a shallow bamboo bridge rose over it. She stopped on the bridge, delighting in the serene sound of the water trickling below. Eventually, the entire canal —floor and sides—would be covered in gray, flattened river rock.

But that would come after they were confident the channel would hold water.

Continuing, she stopped at the broad open entry of the salon. Eight hair stations would line up on one wall, with mani-pedi stations along the other. She was even considering a fish pedicure area. Her station, at the far end, was the only one in semi-operational order.

The water-filled channel continued its lazy path through the salon, two more bamboo bridges providing crossings. A large man with chocolate skin and heavy work boots paced back and forth at the far end of the salon, his thick brows drawn as he studied the small river. He raised a walkie-talkie to his mouth. "George, we gotta problem here. Turn off the water."

"Roger that, Harry. Turning off now."

The man hunkered down on his knees and bent over the channel. Sara rushed across the room, crossing two more bridges. This time, she was too worried to enjoy them as she hurried toward Harry. Opening her mouth to ask what the problem was, it became obvious when she neared. Water was draining at the seam where the channel ended at the far side of the room, the water level noticeably decreasing.

Harry vaulted to his feet and grabbed a nearby sandbag, throwing it into the channel. Then he followed with two more. The small dam held most of the water back, but the section near the end of the little river drained steadily. He looked up at the sound of Sara's rushing footsteps. "I'm sorry, Miss Sara. There's a leak here for sure."

His walkie-talkie squawked with a new voice. "We have a leak on the other end by the treatment rooms too. Maybe two of them."

"Dammit!" Sara said, panic clawing its way up her ribcage.

George and another man arrived and stopped next to Harry, staring at the channel. "Good thing we had the sandbags ready."

"What's underneath there?" Sara asked. "Is something under the floor getting flooded?"

"Yeah, no doubt." George said. "Plumbing, electrical, and all kinds of stuff run under the floor. We'll tear out the area around the leak and mop up the water." Sighing, he shook his head as he kneeled and ran a hand over the canal's wall. "Our usual sealant was on back order, so we used a new kind. Can't say I'm real impressed with it."

Sara snapped her head up. Panic turned to fury as she closed the distance to stand directly in front of the project manager. He towered over her, and she bent her neck back to glare at him. "A *new sealant*? You tried something completely untested on this project? We aren't paying a single extra penny for this, George!"

He held up a hand, taking a step back. "I'm not asking you to. This was the best solution we could come up with, but it obviously isn't going to work. Getting supplies to an island in the middle of the Caribbean is always a challenge. We all agreed on the bid amount, so any cost overruns are ours to eat, not yours."

"Damn right they are!" She swept her gaze around the room, wanting to explode but looking for a more productive outlet. "Maybe we can install the stations and get things running without the water feature. Could we open, then get the river inspected later?"

George's shoulders sagged as he shook his head. "There's no way they'd give you the final permits with something that major still unfinished. I know setbacks are frustrating, but hang in there. It will be worth it in the end. I promise."

"If the end ever gets here!" She sighed, stepping forward as she looked down at the water-filled channel on the far side of the sandbags. The water was almost gone, and her anger bubbled up again. "Why isn't the channel made of waterproof material?"

"We thought the sealant would work just as well. We could put in a complete liner, but that will increase the cost."

Sara whirled around. "What? You just said—"

Harry took a large step back. George stood his ground this time, though he held out a placating hand. "I said we agreed on a specified bid. Sara, a full waterproof liner isn't in the contract. Look, I know you're mad. I'm not real happy about this myself. Let me make some calls and see if I can find the sealant we usually use, and we'll go from there. Everything will work out, ok?"

All the energy drained out of Sara. Her shoulders could have weighed a thousand pounds. "Fine. I need to discuss this with Hope anyway."

Sara pushed through the back door and stepped onto the beach. She raised a hand to her forehead, shielding her eyes as the sun neared the horizon. The turquoise water of Half Moon Bay lapped softly on the beach, and she took a deep breath of salty air, making an effort to shake off her frustration.

She turned left, passing by seven wooden bungalows. Four were on the beach with direct ocean views, and three more sat behind, at the edge of the thick tropical vegetation. Next was the main resort complex, with a rectangular infinity pool and attached bar. The restaurant sat on the far side of the pool. The lobby was a separate building near the restaurant. Four more bungalows were on the south side of the complex and construction had begun on the three Rainforest bungalows which would sit behind them. But this late in the day, the sounds of hammering and sawing had quieted.

Voices coming from the long pier to the right drew her attention. Two men walked toward the resort, and her bad mood faded as a smile rose on her face. One man rose over six feet tall and was light-haired, while the other was of average height with neat, dark-brown hair. Sara's heart soared at the sight of the shorter man. Then she saw the bulbous-headed three-feet-long fish he carried.

Huh? A fish?

Jack Powell saw her and returned her broad smile as he scratched his trimmed, dark-brown beard. The other man, Alex Monroe, was married to her sister Hope. The Monroes owned Half Moon Bay Resort and lived in a house distantly visible at the south end of the beach. Alex and Jack were integral members of the resort dive team.

The men descended a short staircase onto the sand, and Jack reached out an arm, pulling Sara close for a hello kiss. She leaned into him, avoiding the fish but melting into the softness of his lips. "Thanks. I really needed that."

He backed away, wrinkling his brow. "Bad day?"

"Just another problem with Aqua. Again." She turned to Alex. "I was on my way to give Hope an update."

Alex pointed to the iridescent blue-green fish, and Jack held it up triumphantly.

"You can tell her later when we come over to your house," the tall man said. He was in his early forties, but you'd never know it from his muscular build. "We threw out a couple fishing lines coming back from the afternoon dive and landed this mahi-mahi."

"I invited Alex and Hope over for dinner," Jack said. "This fish is too big for just us. I'll fillet it up and grill it."

Sara's frustration slipped off her shoulders and disappeared into the sand, replaced by excitement. She turned to Alex. "Oh, that sounds perfect! Jack just built a fire pit, so we can officially christen it." And it had been too long since she and Hope had relaxed together.

Alex waved goodbye. "We'll be over in an hour or so."

Sara's gaze returned to the pier. Halfway down, a building stretched across it, creating a tunnel for people to walk through. Her current spa, Hibiscus, took up the entire second floor.

Looks like we'll be staying there for a bit longer...

As they walked along the sand, Sara gave Jack a quick update on the water fiasco at the new spa. Then she asked about the other major item on her mind, considering it was December 20th. "Is everything ready for our trip?"

Jack nodded, a smile lighting up his face. "I confirmed the hotel reservation in Galveston. Stop worrying, darlin'. My family will love you."

She put on a brave smile, knowing how important this visit was to him. "I hope so. This is a lot of pressure, you know. Meeting your parents and your ten thousand siblings for the first time. At Christmas, no less."

Order Half Moon Aqua today!

CALYPSO KEY SERIES:

Main Novels:

Visions of You: A Small Town Single Dad Romance

Because of You: A Small Town Fake Relationship Romance

Memories of You: A Small Town Second Chance Romance

Shades of You: A Small Town Forbidden Romance (Coming Oct, 2024)

Associated Short Stories and Novellas:

Traces of You: A Small Town Rivals to Lovers Romance*

* Subscriber exclusive

Standalone Books:

In Too Deep: A Second Chance Romance

Beached in Bali: A Friends to Lovers Romance

Dive into steamy small-town romance, where passion meets paradise!

Erin Brockus writes steamy small town romances that transport readers to exotic, tropical destinations, and provide a perfect beachy getaway from everyday life. Her mature, relatable characters are impossible not to root for, and she weaves breezy romantic adventure into her stories, emphasizing scuba diving and the ocean.

Drawing on her twin passions for diving and travel, Erin infuses her characters and narratives with a sense of excitement and passion. Her idea of the perfect day involves sipping a cocktail on the beach after exploring the ocean depths.

Erin lives in Washington wine country with her husband, who is also a scuba instructor. She is currently hard at work on her next island adventure. When she's not writing, you might find her out for a run or cycling through the countryside on the next quest for adventure.